KIMCHEE DAYS,
OR, STONED-COLD WARRIORS

TIMOTHY V. GATTO

KIMCHEE DAYS, OR, STONED-COLD WARRIORS

A Novel

The Oliver Arts & Open Press
http://www.oliveropenpress.com

Library of Congress Cataloguing-in-Publication Data
Gatto, Timothy V. 1950
KIMCHEE DAYS, OR, STONED-COLD WARRIORS
A Novel by Timothy V. Gatto

ISBN: 978-0-9819891-4-3

The Oliver Arts & Open Press
2578 Broadway, Suite #102
New York, NY 10025

DEDICATION

I dedicate this book to all of the Air Defenders who saw service during the "Cold War." We gave everything, working 24 on and 24 off, 365 days of the year. I dedicate this book also to my daughter Melissa, who read every page that came out of the printer as I wrote it, and cheered me on to the finish.

And I dedicate it, as well, to Miss Im.

ACKNOWLEDGEMENT

This work of fiction is based on my own three tours in Korea in the early 1970s. Kimchee is a food that is the mainstay of the Korean diet. "Winter kimchee" is a fermented cabbage that has qualities that–for a newcomer–can only be likened to a backed-up septic tank. This was one of the first things that an American was subjected to when he arrived in Korea. Now, forty years later, I've become a pretty good kimchee chef myself and like it almost as much as my wife does. – *TVG*

KIMCHEE DAYS, OR, STONED-COLD WARRIORS

— Prologue —

Patrick Fallica was on KP. He wasn't scheduled for KP, but he was broke again, and the detail was good for a couple of bucks from somebody who wanted out of it. He was on KP so much that the cooks in the mess hall kind of accepted him as one of their own.

Enlisting in the army had seemed a good idea at the time. His father had wanted him out of the house after he quit high school. Joining the army was seen as a way to see the world and get some valuable training he could use to make a career out of. So the army put him in Nike Hercules surface-to-air missiles and stationed him in New Jersey.

Everyone knew that missiles were a great avenue to future employment. He was sure that when he got out, hundreds of companies would compete for his missile-system talents. As far as travel went, he could tell his friends on Long Island that he knew what lay over the Goethals Bridge.

Cleaning the dining-room floor in the mess hall wasn't exactly the fun and adventure he was promised when he enlisted, although it was a lot better than pots and pans. Today he was dining-room orderly, DRO. He was attacking a patch of yellow, built-up wax with a putty knife when Lieutenant Tuck came in. "Hey, Fallica, they finally found something you're capable of. You missed a spot, though." The lieutenant pointed with the toe of his boot toward a small area of yellow.

"Thank you for pointing that out, sir. I can understand now why you're an officer. It takes a leader such as yourself to keep us Neanderthal enlisted people straight. Someday sir, I'm going to go to college and take ROTC so I can become just like you."

The lieutenant's eyes turned to slits. He didn't like this New York wop. It seemed like every time he offered a suggestion or made a remark, a wise answer followed. But this time he had something up his sleeve, something that would take the wind out of this wise-ass.

"Like rice, Fallica?"

"Sure, sir, love it. Eat it all the time. Have it with spaghetti sauce. It's better than spaghetti; I don't have to wrap it around my fork."

"Good, Fallica; I'm glad you like it, really glad. In fact, it really makes my day."

Now it was Fallica's turn to burn. What the hell was he talking about? Why this rice bit? Something was up. The warning bells rang in his ears. This lieutenant wasn't the brightest guy in the world.

"Yeah, Fallica, you like rice, but in a couple of months, you're going to like rice a lot. Every day. Lots of it. You can have all the rice you want–rice and zips." The lieutenant turned and walked toward the mess sergeant's office.

Rice, rice and zips. Zips and rice. What the hell was he talking about? It just didn't make sense. But Fallica was sure that something was wrong. The lieutenant seemed too cocky and pleased. Something was wrong, and he was sure it wouldn't be long before he knew what it was. Meanwhile, the lieutenant had left his coffee cup on the serving line. Fallica had a little trick for him. It might cost him a few bucks, but what the hell. Fallica reached into his fatigue pocket and groped around.

What he came up with was a small piece of tinfoil. Inside the foil were two small pink dots. Two small psychedelic pink dots, one of which found its way into Lieutenant Tuck's coffee cup. Have a nice trip.

After Lieutenant Tuck left the mess hall with his coffee cup, Fallica went to see the mess sergeant. "What did he say?" he asked.

"About what?" asked the red-nosed, burly mess sergeant.

"About rice and zips."

"He didn't say a thing about rice and zips. What the fuck are you talking about, anyway?"

"The prick was asking me if I liked rice and zips. He's up to something; I can tell. What did he say?"

The mess sergeant, who was named Cooley, laughed. He looked at Fallica and smiled an almost-benevolent smile. "Well," he replied slowly, "this is a mystery: only one word comes to mind when you mix two words like rice and zips."

"What is that word, Mr. Knowledge?" Fallica asked sarcastically.

"How much is it worth to you?" Cooley asked.

"How much is it worth to you for me to shut my mouth about you and Lieutenant Tuck's wife?" Fallica shot back.

"Okay, okay, relax, don't get your balls in an uproar. I'll tell you. It's not so bad. In fact, it's probably the army's best-kept secret," he said.

"What? What the hell are you talking about?" Fallica was

losing his patience. "What the hell are we talking about?"

"Korea," Cooley answered finally.

— Chapter 1 —

After a thirty-day leave, Patrick J. Fallica found himself sitting in a 747 headed toward Seattle, looking out the rain-flecked window at his mother and father. His younger brother was waving at the airplane with one hand and holding his mom's hand in the other.

Everyone seemed more excited than he was. He wasn't excited at all. In fact, he felt nothing at all. When he was first handed his orders, it had been exciting. It had been exciting to tell his family and friends that he was going overseas. It had even been exciting to not be going to Vietnam, but he hadn't gotten a farewell piece of ass from his girlfriend, nor had anyone thrown a going-away party for him. The only thing he felt, now, was kind of sad.

He supposed that he would miss everybody. Korea was thirteen thousand miles away. His older brother told him that the army was sending him as far away as it could. If it sent him any farther away around the world, he would soon just be coming back. The whole family got a good laugh out of that one.

His girlfriend was a slut. He knew that. She wouldn't let him bang her before he left, but that didn't mean she was a virgin. Everybody else had gotten a little. It was a classic case of "I want you to respect me." He guessed she really didn't care if anyone else did. He was kind of happy to be away from her. She was like an addiction. He knew she wouldn't be waiting for him when he came home.

Looking back out of the window, he could see the building start to slide by as the plane began its journey to the runway. His little brother was still waving furiously. He felt like crying. He swallowed hard and made a gulping noise. The old lady next to him glanced over and smiled sympathetically. It was the uniform. She had probably seen too many World War Two movies–or maybe, considering her age, she'd experienced something similar.

Anyway, he wasn't going to break down. He was Regular Army, goddamn it, and crying in uniform was just unbecoming to the military. He imagined Genghis Khan riding at the head of Mongol warriors blubbering like a baby. It made him chuckle to think of it.

The plane was airborne now, and the stewardess came over and asked him if he would like something to drink. Patrick ordered a bourbon and coke. She mixed it up and handed it to him. Great, he thought. No age limits in the sky. Patrick Fallica was only seventeen years old.

After Patrick had had three drinks, the old lady became middle aged. After five drinks, she became a fox. Patrick was cut off, and succeeded in embarrassing everyone he talked to. The stewardess asked him how old he was. He was too drunk to lie.

She apologized for serving him. Patrick accepted; in fact, he said he didn't mind being drunk at all. The old lady clucked her tongue.

The stew's name was Mandy. She was cute, but a little on the wrong side of thirty. She worried about her job, and she worried a little bit about Patrick. He was slobbering drunk.

He didn't look seventeen years old. Maybe it was the uniform. It really didn't matter. He was her responsibility now. She knew what she had to do. She had to take him home.

And, after they landed at the Seattle-Tacoma airport, that's what she did.

Patty got sober. It was a great way to get sober, too. Mandy lived in an apartment not too far from the airport. She served him breakfast in bed and even helped him to get dressed.

Patty thought that this was great. She told him that he was great in bed. He took her word for it. He had to: he didn't remember anything. (In reality, nothing had happened.) The only thing Patty worried about now was that he was AWOL. AWOL Big-Time. He wanted to stay a little longer, but he was afraid of what would happen if he got to Fort Lewis later than he already was. He thought about it in the taxi on the way. What the hell were they going to do to him, send him to Korea?

— **Chapter 2** —

He arrived at the Fort Lewis Reception Station one day late. They called it "A Day of Grace." He hadn't known about that. If someone had only told him, he could have stayed at Mandy's and knocked off another piece (or so he thought). Leave it to the army to fuck things up. He hadn't even asked for her address. The least he could have done was send her a postcard. She was a great girl, and he could tell she really liked him. Maybe, when he got back, he'd look her up.

They put Patty in an old World War Two barracks. The tiles were coming off the floor and the latrine had green slime growing on the shower walls. It was really depressing. He was made "Barracks Chief." The sergeant told him that he wanted these barracks as squared away when he left as when he got there. In Fallica's mind, that wouldn't be hard to do. The only thing that could make this place look any worse was a wrecking ball.

It rained all the time in Seattle. The roofing on the houses said so. The shingles were loose and faded. Patty thought the whole place was just miserable. Besides this, he was lonely. They told him that it would be at least five days until he shipped out.

Patty started to drift off to sleep when he felt the bunk shake. Looking up toward the top bunk, he saw a huge body. Fallica had to pop his head out to the side and stretch his neck to see what the face looked like. What he saw wasn't pretty.

The guy had to be at least six-ten. He had flaming red hair, a scar running from his ear to his chin, and bright green eyes that were definitely bloodshot. He had a handlebar mustache that was positively against regulation. All he needed was a beard and Patty would swear that Paul Bunyan had moved into his room. The guy looked down at him. "What the fuck you lookin' at?" he said with a crooked grin.

Fallica realized that he was staring. He pulled himself over the side of the bunk and stood face-to-chest with the man. "Sorry," he said, "I didn't mean to stare; name's Fallica." And he stuck out his hand.

The red-haired man grabbed his hand and pumped it. "I'm Shawnessy, but my friends call me Smokey Joe. Glad to meet you. Been here long?" he asked.

"Got here yesterday," Fallica replied. "Seems like I been here all my life. There was nobody in the barracks except me. I thought that they'd made a mistake and sent me to the wrong place and then forgot about me."

"Yeah, they do that. The army don't give a fuck about nobody. You'd think that they would have someplace for guys going overseas to relax in. Like a USO or something like that. This place sucks," Shawnessy said, looking around the barracks with obvious disgust.

"No shit. Wait till you been here awhile," Fallica said. "Gets on your nerves."

"Got bad nerves, huh? Well, I got somethin' for that." And

he proceeded to reach into his travel bag and pull out a plastic baggie. His other hand reached into his pocket and came out with a pack of Zig-Zag rolling papers. "Let's get high."

Fallica looked around. He couldn't believe that this guy was going to smoke a joint in the barracks with a guy he didn't even know. Anyone could walk in and bust them. "What the fuck you doin'? You want to get us busted? Put that shit away," he said excitedly.

"Don't you want to get high?" the new man asked.

"Sure, I'd love to get high; but you can't tell who's going to walk in. Let's get out of here and find a place where we won't get caught."

Smokey Joe smiled sheepishly and agreed. Fallica liked the guy almost immediately.

They left the barracks and found themselves on the company street. Both of them had no idea where anything was. They found a sergeant with an armband that said "Courtesy Patrol," and asked him where the snack bar was. He told them, and he also told Smokey to trim his mustache. Smokey told him to go fuck himself. The sergeant was kind of taken aback, but he didn't press the issue.

Fallica asked Joe if he were crazy or what. Joe replied that he didn't think the sergeant would write him up because he probably just wanted to get out of Fort Lewis and get overseas as bad as they did. Fallica asked him how he knew that the guy wasn't permanent party. Smokey told him he had a First Army patch and that there were no First Army guys west of the Mississippi.

They passed an abandoned warehouse. Fallica and Smokey walked around to the back and sat on the loading dock, hidden from view of the main road. Smokey brought out his stash and proceeded to roll a joint. After a few minutes, they caught a buzz. They started talking about themselves.

Smokey was from Oregon. He had joined the army to escape his drunken father. This was his second tour overseas. He had spent a tour in Thailand in 1966. He said he liked it in Asia. The women were friendly and the dope was plentiful, and the army didn't play chickenshit games. He got busted when he got back to the States for insubordination to some chickenshit little second looey. He'd been a Spec Five; now he was a Spec Four, the same rank as Fallica.

Fallica himself had been busted three times. It was a miracle that he'd left his unit as an E-4. The reason Fallica got busted so much wasn't that he was such a bad soldier; in fact, he was a great soldier—but every time they let him go home, he would forget to come back.

They talked about Korea. Smokey had heard that it was pretty good duty. Fallica had heard the same. Most of the married men said it sucked. A lot of the single guys said it did, too. But the guys that liked to screw around, drink, and get high loved it. Married or single. Fallica really didn't know if he wanted to go or not. He wanted to see Asia, but he wasn't particularly interested in oriental women. Besides, he was only a month away from being eighteen and would have just as well preferred staying home.

They were really getting high. Smokey had rolled another joint and it was pretty good stuff. They started getting hungry and decided they would try to find a snack bar. They walked about a half mile and saw a branch PX with a huge snack bar attached.

There must have been a hundred guys inside. Some were playing cards, and others were just talking. The garbage piled up at the tables they sat at showed that almost all of them had been there a long time. The place was loud. The sound of the jukebox could hardly be heard above the voices.

Fallica noticed pitchers of beer on the tables. He nodded toward one on the table closest to them. Smokey picked right up on it and, with a wink, headed for the tap. They bought two pitchers and some burgers, and settled down to spend the afternoon.

They had a great time. Most of the guys there were on their way to Vietnam. A few were going to Korea, some to Japan and Okinawa. Patrick was glad he wasn't going to 'Nam. He had volunteered for it to impress his girlfriend and to show his first sergeant how much he hated him, but you had to be eighteen to go to a combat zone. They played cards and drank three two beer all day. It wasn't too bad. At about six in the evening they staggered out, smoked another joint on the way back, and fell into their bunks.

— Chapter 3 —

The next morning they had a formation. The barracks had filled up and the place was a disaster area. The first sergeant read off the rules and regulations and made threats. He told them that every morning he would read names. This was the manifest for that day's flights. The men would also be picked for details such as KP and courtesy patrol, and a police call would be held after every morning formation. If you were AWOL, well, then, you would get an Article 15. Just because you were going overseas didn't mean you weren't still subject to the uniform code of military justice, by God–and you would be busted, fined, and restricted when you got to your next duty station, all arranged before you left the States. They claimed efficiency at Fort Lewis.

Smokey said "balls" to that. He said he wasn't about to stand formation and get details thrown at him. Nobody was taking roll call anyway. All they'd have to do was find somebody to listen for their names. After the formation, all they'd have to do was find out if they were on the manifest. No sweat.

That's what happened. For the next two days, they smoked dope and played cards at the snack bar. Winning at cards was like taking candy from a baby. Fallica stood behind the players, and if they had more than three of a kind, he would cough. Smokey, facing him, would fold. Sometimes, though, he would have a full house or a flush and yet wouldn't fold. Most of the time he won. Once or twice he lost.

It got boring after awhile, though. Nobody caught on; Fallica couldn't believe how stupid they were (even though he admitted to himself that if he caught Smokey cheating, he wouldn't say anything, either).

Finally, their lookout, Casey, told them that both their names had been called. They packed up their things and reported to the orderly room for their boarding pass.

The first sergeant was working at his desk. They stood by his desk, and Fallica cleared his throat. The First Shirt looked up. "It's nice of you to show up, boys. We've missed you around here for the last couple of days."

Smokey and Fallica looked at each other. Their expressions said, "What the fuck?"

The first sergeant smiled. He stood up and rubbed his hands together. He looked like he was having a lot of fun. "Well, I suppose that you two expect to be flying out of here soon; am I correct in that assumption?"

Fallica gulped. They were caught.

"Yes, Top," said Smokey.

"A top spins around in circles; do I look like a fucking top, soldier?"

"No, First Sergeant." Smokey looked irritated. Fallica was afraid he was going to start mouthing off like he did with that first lieutenant. He nudged him with his foot.

"Can I ask you something, First Sergeant?"

"What, Fallica?"

"How the hell did you know we didn't make formation? You never called roll."

"No, I didn't; but I inspected the barracks, and they were a mess. So I went to find the barracks chief. When I couldn't find the barracks chief, I went looking for the assistant barracks chief. You see, boys, when we assign the troops to the barracks, we make the first two men assigned to the barracks the 'barracks chief' and the 'assistant barracks chief.' Understand?" He was grinning like hell.

"So what happens now, Top—I mean First Sergeant," Smokey said.

"What happens now is that you two assholes are going to live up to your responsibilities and get that barracks ready for inspection. I don't care how you do it, but it better be ready by ten hundred hours, or you don't go nowhere. Am I making myself clear?"

"Yes, First Sergeant!" They both said in unison. They left the orderly room.

"What the fuck are we going to do now?" Smokey screamed. "That barracks is a disaster area. It'll take a week for us to clean it."

"Leave it to me; I got it all figured out." Fallica was smiling. "But first, let's get stoned." That's what they did.

Twenty minutes later, they were walking into the barracks. Most of the guys were already packed, and either playing cards or just bullshitting around. Fallica walked into the center of the squad bay. "Formation!" he screamed.

Instinctively, the men began falling in, kicking trash out of their way as they did so. The place really was a mess, and it smelt like shit. Some of the commodes were stopped up, and the water from the latrine floor had seeped into the bay.

Fallica took a place directly in front of the formation. "Stand at ease!" he shouted. The men stood at ease. So far, so good.

Smokey stood behind him, incredulous. He whispered in Fallica's ear. "You can't get away with this, Fallica; some of these guys outrank both of us put together."

Fallica shot him a dirty look that said shut up. He continued: "We're all in a lot of trouble. We just got back from the orderly room, and heard the first sergeant talking to some full-bird colonel. The colonel told the First Shirt he wanted to inspect the barracks." Fallica was pleased with himself. He had their attention. "Now, I don't know what to do, because I'm only a lowly Spec Four, but I felt that we're all in this together, so I figured I'd let you guys know. I think that we should all..." He was cut off in mid-sentence by a skinny sergeant first class.

"We don't give a rat's ass what you think, troopie. Who the hell do you think you are, giving orders to your superiors?" A few other sergeants started muttering their agreements.

"I'm sorry, Sarge," said Fallica. "You're right; the senior-ranking man should take care of this, but since nobody's showed much interest or leadership [he emphasized the word "leadership"], I figured that as a responsible soldier I should take responsibility for getting this place squared away."

The skinny SFC walked up to the front of the formation. "Thank you, Specialist, but you're relieved of this responsibility. Let NCO's do NCO work." And he began to hand out details to the other men.

By ten hundred hours, the barracks was standing tall. The first sergeant came in and was amazed. As he walked out, he glanced at Smokey and Fallica. Smokey thought that they had blown his mind, but Fallica wasn't quite sure. He remembered him saying "I don't care how you do it." He wondered how many times the same thing had happened in the past.

By early afternoon, Fallica was airborne and headed toward Korea. He felt bad that he and Smokey had been split up, but they promised to find each other at the replacement station that the old-timers called the "repo depo." Fallica looked out the window and felt a tug in his chest. See ya later, America; Patty Fallica's leaving for awhile–but stay just the way you are, 'cause I like you that way.

— **Chapter 4** —

Eight hours later, Patty's feet were itchy and swollen. The pilot came on the intercom and informed the passengers that if they looked out toward their left, they would see Mount Fuji. Patty peered out the window expecting to see just another mountain, but what he saw took him completely by surprise. Below, he saw the biggest mountain he had ever seen. Snow-capped, just like in the pictures he had seen. He thought of how beautiful it was. It looked as if the whole island of Japan was made of Mount Fuji.

Soon they were landing at Yokota Air Force Base. Patty saw the rice paddies throughout the countryside and was mesmerized. This was exciting stuff. At that moment, he was glad that he had joined the army. He knew that he would never get here any other way. This was an adventure, and he was going to treat it as such.

He imagined that he was Bond, James Bond, on a mission disguised as an American soldier. He didn't exactly know what the mission was, but he'd figure it out soon enough.

The passengers were made to wait in the lobby until the plane was refueled. World Airways, the armed-services charter airline. He looked out at the tarmac and saw how many aircraft there were with that big red tail. He guessed (correctly) that most were going to Vietnam, and he was glad that his plane was going to Korea.

Soon, he was airborne again and heading toward his destination. Korea, The Land of The Morning Calm. (He'd learned that little tidbit from the booklet the army had supplied him. It also had a few Korean words in it that he hadn't bothered to learn.) The pilot came on again, and informed the passengers that it was only an hour and a half to Kimpo Airport in Seoul.

Soon, the plane was over land again. It didn't look good to Patty. The land below looked foreboding. Lots of mountains and hills, and a lot of browns and grays. They were too far up to make out specific details, but it just didn't look good. In fact, it looked like the kind of territory that might still contain dinosaurs. He chuckled. He cracked himself up.

The seat belt sign went on, followed by the No Smoking sign. They were going to land. Looking out of the window, he could start to make out details. The first thing he noticed were the rice paddies—lots of them.

The second thing he saw were roads, all of them dirt. There were houses coming into view, if you could call them that. They looked like huts with mud walls and grass roofs. Holy shit—what kind of place were they sending him to? Other GI's were peering out of the windows, all chattering away excitedly. The land rose up toward the aircraft. They were making their approach to the runway. The chattering abruptly stopped. Surrounding the airport were sandbagged bunkers with anti-aircraft guns in each one of them. Hey, he thought, this shit looks real! All of a sudden he didn't want to be here anymore.

— Chapter 5 —

The passengers were herded into a large hangar. They were told to fall into a formation. Once they were properly assembled, an order was given to count off by threes. Patty was a number two. After everyone had counted off, the men with the number three were told to fall out and to reassemble to the right of the formation. After they fell back in, they were marched off and out of the hangar.

Patty was jealous. He wanted to be with them: they were probably going to get their assignments right away. After they were gone, an old, gnarled NCO addressed the formation. "Does anyone here want to go with them?" he asked.

Patty almost raised his hand, but the thought of volunteering scared him. His father had taught him never to volunteer for anything.

"Good–because those men are being diverted to Vietnam. Now put all your gear to your right and drop your drawers."

Patty looked around and saw two teams of medics with pushcarts. They started from the front and the rear. "What are they doing?" he asked the man next to him.

The man looked at him. He was a wiry old platoon sergeant. He just looked at Patty like he was a leper, and grunted. "GG shots," he replied.

"What are GG shots?" Patty asked.

"Gamma globulin. Stops you from getting hepatitis."

"Are they painful?"

"Only for punks," he said.

The medics were getting closer. They were administering the shots to the line of men directly in front of Patty. The man in front of Patty bent over to get his shot. Patty was amazed at the size of the needle. "HOLY CRAP!" the man grunted.

Now Patty was really nervous. The platoon sergeant next to him laughed, and turned to another NCO on the other side of him. "What a faggot," he said. "Fuckin' punk. That's all we got in the army now—punks, faggots, and hippies." The other NCO laughed.

The medic heard this and looked over toward him. "Who said that?" he asked angrily.

"I did," said the platoon sergeant.

"With all respect to your rank, sergeant, I'll have to ask you to please be quiet in this formation," the medic said sternly.

"Okay, Boy," said the platoon sergeant.

The medic scowled. He was black.

As the medical team went down the line, other men moaned and screamed as the GG shots were administered. Each time it happened, it prompted the platoon sergeant to utter another mindless epithet such as pussy, queer, asshole and such. Patty decided that the man had a hard-on for the whole human race.

Now the medics were starting up the line Patty was on. Sooner than he wanted, they were next to him, getting ready to do the old platoon sergeant. "Bend over and try to relax your cheeks, Sarge," said the medic. "It'll be worse if you tense up."

"Just shut up and do it, Boy. I ain't scared of no goddamn shot."

The medic just shrugged his shoulders and stuck the needle in. Patty couldn't tear his eyes away. The medic was pushing on the plunger like he was trying to shoot molasses out the end. The platoon sergeant started to perspire. His eyes were screwed shut. The medic was steadily pushing at the plunger; it seemed like a full minute had gone by, and the platoon sergeant dropped to one knee.

"Oh sweet Jesus!" he screamed. (His scream had definitely been the loudest so far.) Patty almost pissed himself. It seemed like another sixty seconds went by before the medic removed the needle. Guys were snickering up and down the line.

"Okay, Sarge, it's all over; you can pull up your pants now."

Patty looked at the old platoon sergeant, who by this time had tears streaming out of his eyes. Patty was horrified. Now they were standing behind him.

"Relax your cheeks, Specialist," said the medic.

Patty willed his cheeks to relax, and waited. A sharp pinch was all he felt.

After a minute or so the needle was removed. He hardly felt a thing. In fact, all he felt was the pinch of the needle entering his skin.

"Okay, man, you can pull 'em up," the medic said.

"That's it?" he asked.

"That's it."

"That wasn't so bad."

The medic put his mouth up to Patty's ear. "That's because the old cocksucker next to you got your shot and his. That'll teach the asshole. But don't worry; the shit don't work anyway."

Patty broke out laughing. The platoon sergeant next to him rubbing his ass shot him a dirty look. "Welcome to Korea," the medic said.

— Chapter 6 —

Walking out of the hangar toward the bus, Patty smelled it. It was indescribable. It kind of smelled like he imagined Paris would smell at the height of the bubonic plague. It just smelled rotten, like dead bodies and diesel fuel. "What the hell stinks so bad?" he asked the man walking next to him.

"Beats me," replied the man with a shrug.

"Smells like shit," someone behind him said.

"Smells worse'n shit," said another.

"It always smells like this; but don't worry, after a couple of hours your nose kind of dies and you don't smell it anymore. You kinda get used to it," said the driver, who was leading them to the bus. "It's the kimchee; the whole country smells like fuckin' kimchee."

"What the fuck is kimchee?" someone asked.

"Shit the zips eat. Cabbage and fish heads they bury in the ground. After about six months they dig it up and eat it. If you think it stinks hanging in the air, wait until you smell their breath. It's enough to gag a maggot," he said.

"Goddamn," said one of the men, "I ain't lettin' none of 'em around me. This smell is makin' me sick."

"You'll let 'em near you, newbie; that is, if you want to get laid. After a few drinks, you won't care what they smell like. Some of these babes can look pretty good, and believe me, all of 'em can be had," the driver said knowingly.

They boarded the bus and headed out for the repo depo. The bus turned out onto a highway that reminded Patty of the Long Island Expressway. He was surprised to see a highway so big here. "At least they have nice roads," he said to the driver.

The driver laughed. "Shit," he said, "this is the only paved road they got in this country. It's called the Seoul-Pusan Highway. Stretches from north to south. They built it for the military. See how wide it is in places?"

Patty looked. Every so often the road would widen from four lanes to six, with extra lanes at the shoulders. "Yeah, how come it does that?"

"Because if they have a war, this road can become an airport. The places where it gets wide become landing strips. They got concrete bunkers for anti-aircraft guns all around 'em."

Patty saw that the driver was right. He could see three bunkers just ahead. "Kinda scary," he said.

"You'll get used to it," said the driver.

Patty didn't think that he would ever get used to it.

The bus was extremely quiet as they traveled the highway. Most of the men were staring out of the windows, getting their first real impression of the land they would call home for the next thirteen months.

Patty was mesmerized. It was October. The rice paddies on both sides of the road were, for the most part, cut. A few were being harvested. He was amazed at the rough wood carts attached to oxen. To Patty, who was not one of the world's great travelers, it looked like a scene straight out of National Geographic.

The small villages they passed amazed him. The huts seemed made out of mud, and the roofs were grass. They seemed out of place here. He'd expected the tile roofing he had seen in pictures. These seemed to be made of rice stalks. He figured this out because the farmers were cutting down the rice and tying them off in bundles. To him, it looked more like what he'd imagined Africa would look like.

He could see no telephone poles, no TV antennas. He poked the driver on the shoulder. "How do they get electricity to the villages?" he asked.

"Lightning," the driver replied. Some of the guys in the bus snickered.

"You can be a real wise-ass," said Fallica.

"You're all ass," said the driver. More snickering.

The bus pulled off the main highway and headed down a dirt road. The men inside cursed as the bus lurched and rolled. Luggage fell from the overhead racks.

They pulled up to a gate. Over the entrance was a sign: AS-COM–GATEWAY TO KOREA. Underneath, in smaller letters: DRIVE SAFELY AND ROTATE. Patty wondered what the hell that meant.

Some GI's near the entrance started whistling and shouting to the bus. Patty couldn't make out what they were saying except for a few words. Some were making a gesture with their thumb and index finger. Patty knew what that stood for. It meant "short." That was one of the words Patty could make out.

Once inside the gates, Patty could get a good look at the

guys inside. He could tell which men had been here for awhile, and which were new like himself. The new guys were wearing dark green wrinkled fatigues and had short hair. The others had longer shaggier hair and fatigues that were almost gray. They were creased and starched, though. In fact, they looked better than the ones he himself had.

Patty knew he looked bad. "Sorry" was the word most GI's used. He had his khaki uniform on. It had been starched and pressed when he put it on at Fort Lewis, but after the ten-hour flight to Japan, and another two hours to Korea, it looked like hell. It was wrinkled, and it had large sweat rings under the arms. He couldn't wait to get out of it.

The bus lurched to a stop in front of a building with a sign out in front that read: 121st Replacement Station. The driver told everyone to get out and make a formation in front of the sign. They got out and did what they were told.

It wasn't too long before a small staff sergeant came out with a clipboard. He told them that they were there to be processed and assigned units. Some of the men had direct assignments, and they would be the first to be processed. The stay at AS-COM would be anywhere from one to three days, except for the guys going to the Second Infantry Division up north. This division only came once a week, on Monday, to pick up their replacements. He said that the staff at the replacement station would try to make their stay as pleasant as possible, as long as the men obeyed THE RULES. He then told them what THE RULES were:

1. Between the hours of 0800 to 1800, they were restricted to the company area.

2. They were to listen for their names being called on the loudspeaker.

3. They were restricted to the confines of the compound at all other times.

4. They were not allowed to use any American currency. All currency would be exchanged for military payment certificates known as MPC's.

5. No Korean nationals were allowed in the company area, especially females.

The staff sergeant then proceeded to tell them where the mess hall was, and its hours of operation. He wished them a pleasant tour in Korea, and dismissed them to the barracks for the evening.

Patty thought that the formation was pleasant enough. He was glad to have a direct assignment. He didn't want to stay in this place for three days. He also noticed that threats weren't made like they were at Fort Lewis. In fact, the sergeant had a real laid-back attitude. Grabbing his duffel bag, Patty made toward the barracks with the others.

— Chapter 7 —

Patty walked into a carnival. He couldn't believe he was in an army barracks. In the right corner was a traveling tailor shop. At the rear of the barracks were paintings done on black velour similar to the ones sold in Juarez, Mexico. There were Korean salesmen going from bunk to bunk selling everything from Bibles to pornography. GI's were either in bunks or standing around the displays. Patty saw a beer in almost every hand.

The new men looked at each other. Almost immediately, they were descended on by beseeching salesmen. "Hey, newbie, you buy Bible for you Mommy? You Mommy like. Gold leaf trim. Numbah-one Bible, okay?" one said.

"You need kimchee jacket. Numbah-one kimchee jacket. Hometown printed on jacket. Nice. You buy girlfriend. You pick dragon on sleeve, okay?" another wailed. Patty almost gagged as the man blew his breath in his face. This was his first up-close exposure to the dreaded kimchee breath. It was worse than he expected. Patty thought for sure that if this guy was examined by a doctor, he would be told he was rotting from the inside out. He felt lightheaded and faint; then he realized he was holding his breath. He broke from the guy's imploring pitch and headed to an empty bunk against the wall.

The level of activity was unreal. Patty was tired from the travel, and now with the noise coming from the barracks, he had a pounding headache. He wished that he could just get out into some fresh air. The whole Quonset hut reeked of kimchee breath. A space heater that looked like a garbage can burned cherry red in the center. Between the oppressive heat, the noise, and the smell, he thought he was dying. At that particular moment he was also homesick. He crawled up onto the bunk and buried his face in the pillow. Before he lapsed into oblivion, his mind kept repeating one thought: "A zoo! I got sent to a fuckin' zoo! Help me, God, they sent me to a fucking zoo."

A few hours later, Patty was awakened by a hand shaking his shoulder. He looked up to see a familiar face peering down at him. It was Smokey Joe from Fort Lewis. "You know, Fallica, I been thinking," he said. "I been thinkin' that they sent us to a fuckin' zoo."

Patty cracked up. He was really glad to see Joe's ugly face. He glanced around the barracks and saw that it was empty. Empty and quiet. He looked back again at Joe. "When did you get here?" he asked; and before Joe could reply, he asked again, "What time is it?"

"It's six o'clock; mess hall's closed. I got here this morning. Already got my orders. I'm going to a place called Camp Humphreys, but they call it K-6. All these places got two names."

Patty raised himself on his elbow and tried to shake the drowsiness out of his head. He rubbed his eyes. "Mess hall's closed? Did you eat?"

"No, not yet. They got a club here. We can get something

there. You got any civvies?" Joe asked.

"Yeah; let me go take a leak. Where's the latrine?"

"It's about four or five barracks down. You got to piss?"

"Yeah," Patty said. "What do you care?"

"The only reason I asked was because, around here, they all just piss out the back door. The whole place smells like piss."

Patty's eyes widened. "Jeez," he said. "That's disgusting."

"Whole place is disgusting. These guys act like animals. One guy told me they got three thousand whores in the village here."

Patty's eyes lit up. "That's disgusting!" he said again.

"You know what's more disgusting than that?" Joe asked.

"No," Patty said with a grin. "What?"

"They'll take you home and fuck you for five dollars. Can you handle that?"

"I guess I'll have to," Patty laughed.

"Yeah, I guess I can, too," Joe laughed.

Patty went out the back door and took a leak. Joe was right: the place smelled like piss. He went back in and opened his duffel, rummaged around, and came up with a pair of jeans and a shirt. He put them on. He had no civilian shoes, so he put on his low-quarters. He realized he had no jacket.

The weather in Korea in early October was the same as in New York. Both areas shared the 32nd parallel. Joe said that Patty could borrow a sweatshirt he had. They walked over to Joe's barracks and Joe handed him an old gray sweatshirt. In no time, they were on the company street heading for the main post. "Too bad you couldn't bring that pot," Patty said.

"Who said I couldn't bring that pot?" Joe asked.

"I don't believe it. You don't give a shit, do you?" Patty meant it.

"Hell, no, but thanks for askin.' " Joe proceeded to pull out the baggie. "You roll it; you do it better than me."

Finding a place to smoke was easy. This side of the post was deserted. A few minutes later they both had a good buzz on. They walked on a little while in silence. Patty was thinking about how, just last night, he and Smokey had been doing the very same thing in Fort Lewis, USA. It seemed like weeks ago. So much had happened in the twenty-four hours since. It seemed that Fort Lewis, in fact the whole United States, was almost unreal. It was weird. Reality, for Patty, was Korea. This was the here and now. "Hey, Smokey," Patty broke their silent thoughts.

"What?"

"You know what the guys here call home?"

"Yeah–the World," Joe said.

"I kinda think I know why."

"Yeah, me too; but tell me what you think."

Patty took a deep breath. Being tired and stoned, it was hard for him to put his feelings into words, but he felt it was important to do so. "I think it's because this place is so weird. I mean, it's so different. The guys who have been here awhile are kind of strange, like they don't give a shit about nothin'. You know?"

Smokey grunted in acknowledgment. Patty went on. "And there's no regular cars; just army trucks and taxi cabs. And there's no American women, no American kids, just zips. This country has dirt roads and shacks. All the writing on the buildings is in Korean. I mean, even their letters are different; you can't even guess what they say." Patty was on a roll. Smokey agreed again with a grunt.

"I mean, even the army is different here. They don't seem to care what we do. Usually they threaten you and give you a big list of rules and stuff. Here, they don't seem to care much. Have you thought about it?" Patty asked.

"Yeah, I guess I have. But you see, I been through it before. I was in Thailand, remember? It's different in Asia. Nobody brings the Old Lady and kids with 'em. It's a hardship tour, like 'Nam, except you don't have people shooting at you every day–but still there is this possibility that maybe, just maybe, somebody will. Did you know that the guys in the second division north of the Imjin River get combat pay? Did you know that there are a million zillion North Koreans fifty miles from here who would like nothin' better than to blow Mrs. Fallica's little boy Patty to smithereens? Ever think about it?" Joe asked.

"No," Patty answered, "I never did." He looked down as he walked.

"Maybe that's why the army is a little different here. Maybe that's one reason nobody sweats the small shit like pissin' out the back door. Most of these guys aren't like me and you. A lot of 'em are married with kids and stuff. A lot of 'em are drafted and don't want to be in the army in the first place, and they're more than just a little pissed off to be here. Can you dig it?"

"Yeah," Patty said. "I can dig it."

"Well, consider it dug," said Smokey.

They passed the PX and movie theater. Next to the theater was a small white building with a sign reading "Army and AirForce Exchange Service (ACIFES) Bath House." Under the heading, it provided a list of services. One of them caught Fallica's eye: "Massage $5.50." He jabbed Smokey and jerked his head in the direction of the sign. "Do you see what I see?" he asked.

"Yeah, so what?"

"Wanna get a massage?"

"Do you?"

"I want to get more than a massage," Fallica said. "Think they give anything else?"

"Depends on the girl. The PX doesn't run a whorehouse, but maybe you can get a little extra stuff that isn't on the price sheet if you play your cards right. These slope girls will do almost anything for a buck," Smokey said.

"You got any money?" Fallica asked. He had forgotten to exchange his money for MPG.

"Yeah, I got some. I'll lend you ten, but you gotta pay me back," Joe said.

Fallica looked hurt. "Do I look like a thief?"

"Yeah, Fallica; you look like a thief," Smokey laughed, and they walked inside.

— Chapter 8 —

Patrick Fallica had a hangover. The first full day in Korea started out with a hangover. He could hardly remember getting back to the barracks. The noise in the barracks was making his head feel like a bass drum. He was thirsty. Drinking always made him thirsty the next day.

He slowly raised his head from the pillow. It was still early. Guys were walking around in towels and underwear. It smelled funny. It still smelled like that kimchee stuff. God, he thought; I'll never get used to that puke-smelling shit.

He slowly swung his legs over the bunk and stood up. The lights hurt his eyes and made him squint. He ran his hand through his hair and tried to get his thoughts together.

"God, you look terrible in the morning." Smokey was standing in front of him looking like he had just had his best night's sleep.

"I feel terrible," Fallica said.

"Get yourself a shower and meet me in the mess hall. You'll feel better in a while."

Fallica nodded and turned toward his locker to get his shower things. He scratched his head again and turned back to Smokey. "By the way, what happened last night?"

Smokey laughed. "I'll tell you all about it over breakfast. Hurry up and get dressed; we got a long day."

Half an hour later, Patrick was sitting down over eggs he didn't want to eat. He was remembering what had happened in the massage parlor. The girl he'd gotten had been about thirty-five years old and not the prettiest thing he had ever seen.

The first thing he'd done was take a shower. He'd been embarrassed, because the girl had just stood there while he was naked. Then she'd made him get into a steam box. It had felt nice at first, but after awhile it had gotten so hot in there that he'd thought he was going to die. The next part had been the best part, but even just thinking about it now made him flush with embarrassment.

The girl had put him on a padded table with just a small towel over his ass. She had proceeded to beat the living shit out of his back with her hands. It had hurt like hell at first, but after awhile it was relaxing and he almost fell asleep to her rhythmic ministrations.

He'd woken up when she'd started down his legs. She'd seemed to get into every muscle he had. God, it had felt good. Patrick had thought about her hands as they worked up his legs toward his ass. He hadn't really thought that she would massage that, too, but he was wrong. That was when the hard-on had started. He hadn't thought too much about it until she'd asked him to turn over. God—he'd felt like he was back in ninth grade and the teacher had asked him to stand up in class.

She'd been so straightforward about it. She'd smacked it lightly and giggled. She'd said it looked as if his "Little Man" was angry, or some stupid shit like that. Then she'd forgotten it was there, and had started on his chest and shoulders. That had felt great, and even Patty had forgotten about the hard-on.

He'd forgotten about the hard-on until she'd started on his upper thighs. She had hands that made Patty think she was the most desirable girl this side of Yokohama. God, how he'd wanted that girl! Lust had seized his heart like a steel vise. He'd been totally in its grip. She'd worked her way up higher toward his crotch, her flying fingers occasionally brushing the straining pecker that had made the towel look like a pup tent. He'd just been ready to grab her hand and put it inside the tent when it had happened. He just hadn't been able to help it. God–the embarrassment! She couldn't have helped seeing his body go into spasms. She'd just stopped and stared.

When Patty was normal again, he'd wanted to crawl under the table. He couldn't believe that it had happened. He'd wanted to kill his "Little Man" that was now retreating under a wet towel.

She'd laughed so hard he'd felt like killing her. She'd seen his look and had stopped. She'd gotten a Kleenex and had given it to him. "Cherry Boy" was what she'd called him after that. All he'd wanted to do was get the hell out of there. The worst part had been sitting in the lobby waiting for Smokey to get done. She'd kept talking in Korean to her co-workers, who'd kept giggling and looking over at him.

"Why are you so quiet this morning? This is the first time I've ever seen you shut up for any length of time. Anything wrong?" Smokey asked.

"No; I just got a bad hangover, that's all," Fallica replied dejectedly.

"Well, I hope that's all that's the matter. I'm glad you're not thinking about how you fucked up with that girl."

"What are you talking about?" Fallica asked, startled out of his reverie. "Just what the hell do you mean by that!"

"Don't get your balls in an uproar," Smokey said. "You know, the girl in the massage parlor."

Fallica looked around to see if anyone was listening. "How the hell did you find out about that?" he said softly so no one could hear. He was looking down at his plate.

"The guys were talking about it in the barracks this morning. The girl's boyfriend is the first sergeant," Smokey said.

"Oh, God!" Fallica said. "I'm not in this country a whole day and I'm already the fucking asshole. Oh, shit, I'm ruined." His head was very close to the plate.

"You're an asshole if you believe that, kid." Smokey was looking at him with a small smile at the corners of his mouth. "I heard all about it after you got drunk. I told you then and I'll tell you now, it's nothing to be ashamed of. You're thirteen thousand miles away from home. Halfway around the world. Nobody cares what you do over here. Anyway, it could of happened to anybody."

"Yeah, but it happened to me," said Fallica dejectedly.

"Well, you'll learn that nobody gives a shit around here, except when you're late for a formation, which we are. Let's go."

A short time later, they found themselves in formation. The company clerk read out their names. Patrick was scheduled for his processing at 10:20. Smokey was down for 09:00. It didn't take long. Patrick didn't even have time to be bored when his time rolled around. He walked into the Quonset hut, and was directed to a desk where a young buck sergeant was shuffling through records. "You Fallica?" he asked.

"Yes, Sergeant," Patty answered.

"You're a 16C?"

"Yep."

"We're short 16C's. Those missile sites are critical assignments. Don't even think of trying to get anyplace else. We got two batteries that are really under strength–Charlie Battery and Foxtrot. Charlie's in the boondocks. Even the Koreans don't like it there. It's near a place called Sosan. The pits. Foxtrot is next to Inchon, about 20 clicks south of Seoul. About 10 clicks from here. Nice place, Foxtrot. They got a good bunch of guys there. Bet you twenty dollars you go to Foxtrot."

"I don't gamble," Fallica stated.

"Too bad," said the clerk. "Since I don't have a bet to win, I guess there's no point in fixing things up. God, but Charlie's a miserable place."

A light bulb went on in Fallica's head. "You know, Sarge," he said, "like I was saying, I don't gamble–but only a fool would turn down a chance to bet on a sure thing. I just know I'm going to Charlie Battery, because I have such rotten luck. I'm gonna take my chances on that rotten luck and bet you twenty dollars that I go to Charlie Battery."

The clerk stopped typing, and looked up and smiled. He scratched his head and squinted at the papers in front of him. "Too bad," he said flatly. "You do have rotten luck."

Patty Fallica squirmed in his seat.

"Listen, son, no matter where you think you're going, the United States Army puts you where it needs you. Sorry."

Patty's heart sank. He thought that this guy was an ass for playing around with him. Clerk'n son of a bitch, he thought. Clerks were weird, anyway.

"You lose, kid. The army says Foxtrot. Pay me." And with that, the clerk smiled and held out his hand.

Patty put two ten-dollar greenbacks in his hand.

"That was the best bet you ever lost," the clerk said, as he quickly shoved the money into his fatigue pocket. "You got to report to K-6 first. That's battalion headquarters. If they try to divert you to another battery, tell them you got a direct assignment. The bus for K-6 leaves at 13:30 in front of the barracks. Be on it." He shoved a set of orders at Fallica and turned back to his typewriter.

Patty didn't move. The clerk turned around and looked at him. "Any questions?"

"Yeah, I got a million of them, but I don't think you have the time to answer them all."

"Got that right. Just remember, you got a good assignment."

"I got a good assignment."

— Chapter 9 —

The bus ride to K-6 was almost uneventful. They traveled down the Seoul-Pusan Highway for about an hour. They got off at the exit marked PYEONGTAEK. The road turned to dirt immediately, and Patty and the others lurched from side to side as they headed through town.

The guys on the bus exchanged conversation and seemed pretty excited, but Patty felt a little out of place. Smokey wasn't around, and for the first time since leaving home, he felt a little apprehensive. "Nervous in the service," as his drill sergeant used to say. He felt suddenly alone and depressed. He didn't want to be here anymore. He wanted to be in New York with his slut of a girlfriend.

In his mind's eye, she was no longer a slut. Traveling thirteen thousand miles had transformed her into a sweet, innocent girl who waited for him to return home. He just knew that she spent hours staring at his picture and missing him. (In reality, she picked up a guy at a party the night he left. The guy's name was Jocko, and he was a swarthy Italian fellow whose idea of a good time was amphetamines and oral sex, with him on the receiving end. Patty had no idea that his sweet thing thought that Jocko was the greatest thing since the pill.)

The bus was now traveling through a large town. Every other place of business along the road was a bar. He saw that the signs were in English. He saw the 7-Club, the Top-Hat, Players Club, and of course the famous Kit-Kat. He saw lots of GI's in civilian clothes on the street, heading in and out of the bars. He saw women dressed in miniskirts and boots. Patty started to cheer up immediately. This place didn't look too bad.

The Gate to K-6 was the standard archway with CAMP HUMPHREYS lettered across it, with the slogan "Drive Safely and Rotate" underneath. Rotate on this, thought Patty.

The base was clean and American-looking. They traveled for perhaps two miles and came to a stop in front of a dilapidated Quonset hut. The sign in front said "4th Battalion (HERC) 44th Air Defense Artillery." Patty got up, grabbed his duffel bag, and got off the bus. The bus took off down the road with the other guys, and he was left alone in front of the building. He went in.

A fat sergeant sat behind a desk reading Penthouse. He briefly looked up when Patty came in, then went back to the magazine. Patty waited, uncomfortable, shifting back and forth on his feet. Eventually the fat sergeant put down the Penthouse and asked him what he wanted. Patty told him he was new to the battalion. The sergeant told him that they didn't process after 14:00, and that he should go to the transient barracks around the corner and to report back in the morning. Patty thanked him and went to the transient barracks.

This Quonset hut was worse than the others he had seen. There were no blankets on the bunks, and it was filthy. The stove was in the center, burning cherry red. The only person other than himself was a chubby Korean fellow in a business suit, sitting on a bunk. He looked up at Patty and smiled. "Hello, newbie," he said.

"Hi," said Patty. "Where is everyone?"

"You only newbie today. Other newbies go to units. Just you now. My name is Mr. Kim. You name?"

"My name is Patty Fallica. I'm from New York."

"Oh, New Yowk numbah hanna. We be good friends, you know. Koreans say chingo. Chingo mean friend. You and me be numbah-one chingos and you take me to see New Yowk, okay?" Mr. Kim had a twinkle in his eye.

Patty was flustered. He didn't really know how to react to this. Mr. Kim saw this and proceeded to lay it on.

"Yee, that is best idea Mr.Kim have in long time. You take me to America with you. Okay, chingo? We have numbah hanna good time."

Patty played along. "Okay, Mr. Kim, I'll take you to America with me. I'll show you around, get you a good job, and we'll have a grand old time. But first you have to show me your country."

"No sweat, Farrica. You come my house. I have numbah hanna house in all town. My wife make you Korean food and we go to club. I find you nice Korean girl. We get tacson stinko."

"Stinko?" asked Patty.

"Drink whiskey, get stinko. Oddaso?"

Patty guessed that "oddaso" meant "understand," so he nodded his head Yes.

Mr. Kim seemed pleased. "You got clothes, Farrica?"

"Yeah, Mr. Kim, but I got no pass." Patty realized that even if he wanted to go with this half-baked Korean fellow, he didn't have a gate pass.

"No sweat. Mr. Kim make you choagie pass," he said matter-of-factly.

"Choagie pass?" Another new word.

"Neh, 'choagie' mean 'go' in Korean. We make you pass and you can go, oddaso?" And with that, he reached into his pocket and pulled out a stack of blank passes.

"You need SOFA card, too." Mr. Kim took out a card and handed it to Patty. "You write name on paper. I go make pass." He reached into his shirt pocket and handed Patty a pen and a small note pad. Patty wrote his name.

Mr. Kim left the barracks, saying he would come back "mos skoshe," which Patty gathered meant "pretty quick." After he left, Patty looked at the SOFA card. "SOFA" meant "Status of Forces Agreement." It stated that Americans fell under both American and Korean law. It further stated that, if he were arrested, he had the right to contact the American military police.

Patty had changed into his civilian clothes by the time Mr. Kim returned. He handed Patty the pass, and he looked at it. It looked authentic. It was typed out with his name and his unit. It even had a captain's signature on it. "Is this a real captain's signature?" he asked Mr. Kim.

"No. You want real captain to sign? You wait. You wait long time. Pass good, you want pass you take. No want pass, you wait."

"I'll take the pass," Patty said.

"Good, Farrica. We have numbah-one good time. Get plenty stinko. Boom-boom plenty pretty Korean girl. We go now."

Patty shook his head, and out the door they went.

— Chapter 10 —

Fred stood watch on his domain. The soldiers moved off to their sections, and everything seemed well. Fred had not had anything to drink the night before and felt in top form. It felt good to be here at the top of the mountain looking down upon his charges. He stretched and yawned. Fred had it made and he knew it. He never wanted to leave this place.

Meanwhile, as Fred lulled in silent contemplation, the battery commander was looking over the morning report. It seemed that they had picked up a new man. He was still at K-6 processing in. He would have to send someone to get him. The last time they left a new man there, he got into a bar fight and had his head split open.

He didn't want to lose this new guy. He was an experienced radar operator, and right now he was short. In fact, he was always short–short of everything. One good thing, though: he was also "short" in Korea. Thirty-two days and a wake-up. Then he could go home and see his wife and kids. A year was a long time to be away.

Captain Green often wished he was an enlisted man. They seemed to have it made. They just took things as they came. They seemed to adapt better. In fact, some of them adapted so well they went "native." They took Korean girlfriends, and as often as not married them. They had their own hootches in the village and, in a pinch, even drank the local rotgut. But in spite of all the hardships put upon them by cultural change, they seemed happy. They even seemed to thrive. The funny thing about it was that the soldiers who went native were always the most dependable.

He would miss this place, in a way. The camaraderie and enthusiasm the men had were unlike any place in the world he had ever been to. He wondered if it was the isolation of being a detached unit of two hundred fifty in a city of five million—or was it the women, booze and

drugs?

That last thought reminded him of the surprise health-and-welfare inspection that they had lined up for today. The MP detachment at ASCOM was supposed to be bringing the dogs to sniff out marijuana. He hoped that nobody would be caught. He couldn't afford to have another security clearance pulled. He really did need every man he could get. He had let the supply sergeant overhear him talking with the First Shirt about it yesterday. He knew that word would be all over the battery. He just hoped that the guys would take it seriously.

Tomorrow he had to go to Seoul and attend a staff meeting on site security. He didn't like to miss these meetings. The number of infiltrator incidents was up. Last week, a boatload of North Korean sappers was intercepted within five clicks of B Battery further south down the coast.

He hoped that General Emerson would skip this briefing.

The good general was the commander of the Second Infantry Division that guarded Korea's border with the North. Life was hard up there in the DMZ, and General Emerson didn't make life any easier for his men.

You see, he liked football. He liked to see his men play football. The only problem with that was that his sense of fair play was a little extreme. To accomplish his training goal, every man in the division who didn't pull duty the night before ran five miles every morning before breakfast. The football rules were a little different here than in the States.

The contestants played with boots, fatigues, helmets and full field gear. The sizes of the teams were only limited to the sizes of the companies or battalions they had on hand that particular day. As for the rules–there weren't any rules: just get the ball over the opposing team's goal line. That was it.

Broken bones were badges of honor. That was the whole ball game, so to speak. General Emerson even had a nifty little name for it. He called it Combat Football, and in the second division it was the only game in town. The rumor mill had it that he wanted General Blake, the Eighth Army Commander, to require all units in Korea to play at least once a week. Bad news travels fast, and every idea General Emerson articulated traveled at the speed of light. Captain Green grabbed his cap and walked out the door. Another day at Foxtrot had begun.

— Chapter 11 —

Patty was awake. He knew he was alive, but he didn't know for how long. His head was killing him. He tried to remember what had happened. Slowly, the cobwebs lifted, and he recalled leaving the base with Mr. Kim. They'd gone over to his house, and he'd watched him fight with his wife. She was screaming in Korean, and he and Mr. Kim had left the house for town.

Mr. Kim was a pisser. He was just like most of the guys in the States. As soon as they'd left the house, Patty had tried to apologize for being the cause of the argument between Mr. Kim and his wife. Mr. Kim just waved the apology away, smiled, and said "Fuck her!"

Patty still didn't know where he was. He remembered going into a club and being amazed. The glitter was unbelievable. There were mirrors all around the place, with colored lights and strobes blinking to the beat of rock music. It was crowded as hell. The best part was that most of the people in the club were women. There were hundreds of women, all wearing sheer tops, miniskirts and high heels. They were all friendly, too.

Everyone he came in contact with wanted him to buy her a drink. Except they said "drinkee." He finally ended up with a tall girl dressed entirely in black. The last thing he remembered was that she was on his lap, and Mr. Kim had a girl dressed in red on his. He remembered that both he and Mr. Kim were very drunk.

Patty very slowly raised one eye. He looked at the ceiling: it was covered with wallpaper. He slowly turned his throbbing head to see who was lying next to him. He was surprised to see that he was alone. He sat up and looked around the room. A clock next to the bed said seven-fifteen. Holy shit, he thought, he had to be back to process in this morning. He started to panic. Where the hell was he? He didn't have the slightest notion about how to get back to the base.

He had to piss. He pulled the covers off and put his feet on the floor. He reached for his shirt lying on the chair next to the bed and put it on. He looked down for his pants. There were no pants. He took a better look around the room. There were no clothes, no personal things that suggested that anyone lived there. Patty heard a rooster crowing outside. Bending down, he looked under the bed. Still no pants.

Now panic was completely clouding his brain. What the hell was he going to do? The only things in the room were the sheets on the bed. That would have to do. He was in trouble. He had no wallet, no pass, no IU card. He was almost AWOL. Deep shit, Fallica; deep shit, he thought.

He pulled the blanket off the bed (it was more like a comforter) and walked out the sliding paper doors. Two small children were playing near an old red-handled pump in the center of a courtyard. They looked at him and went hysterical. An old woman came out of one of the rooms and, when seeing him, burst out in laughter. He walked over to her. "Where is the woman who has that hootch?" He pointed to the room he had spent the night in.

"Moolah," she said between fits of laughter.

"Do you speak English?" he asked.

"Moolah," she said again.

He looked at the kids who had by now stopped laughing. He approached the boy who seemed about seven or eight. "Do you speak English?" he asked.

"Moolah," he replied.

"Moolah, moolah, moolah!" Patty screamed. He was pissed.

This caused the three Koreans to erupt in screams of laughter. The more they laughed, the madder Patty got. He walked toward the gate. He figured that these people were all mentally ill. As he approached the gate, the old woman yelled to him. "Where you go with my blankee?"

Patty turned back toward her. "Now you talk English," he said.

"I talkee," she said.

"You understand my speakee?" he said.

"Sure , GI, you think I stoopid?" she asked.

"Then where the hell are my pants?" Patty screamed.

"Moolah," she said.

"Moolah my ass. Where the hell are my pants? Where the hell are my shoes? Where the hell is my wallet? Where the hell am I?" He felt like crying.

She hobbled over to the entrance of the hootch. Bending over, she reached under a low porch and pulled out Patty's low-quarters. "You shoes!" she said.

Patty felt a small ray of hope stir inside of him. "What about my pants and wallet?"

"Slickie girl takee. Sorry 'bout that, GI. Numbah-ten slickie girl," she said simply.

Patty had already figured that out. He was dumb, but not stupid.

The old woman raised a finger and told him to wait. She returned in minutes with a sheet. A dirty sheet with holes. "You takee this. Kajawa blankee." And she reached out for her blanket.

Patty considered this. He had no underwear on. He was about to explain to her that he had to go inside to change, when she reached out and grabbed the blanket.

Patty couldn't react in time, and he stood naked with just his shirt on in the morning breeze. The kids by the pump were beside themselves. It must have been great entertainment. The boy started strutting around, holding an imagined giant penis. Even Patty smirked. He grabbed the sheet from the old woman and wrapped it around himself.

Armed with the sheet, he walked out the gate. He was determined to get back come hell or high water. Fuck that asshole Mr. Kim. He knew damn well he was new in country. Shit, he didn't even know if he got laid.

He walked down the alley until he heard street sounds, and turned in that direction. Soon he saw a main street. He was hesitant about stepping into it, but he really had no choice; he just had to get back. He figured the MP's at the gate would have a field day with him.

Patty no sooner got onto the street when a deuce and a half almost ran him down doing a good forty miles an hour on the congested roadway. He gave the driver the finger, almost dropping the sheet he had bunched at his waist. The truck skidded to a halt. The guy in the passenger side stepped out and motioned him to come over. Patty didn't know whether to run over or run away. The guy put his hands on his hips and cocked his head. "You comin' or what?" he screamed.

Patty ran as best as the loose sheet allowed. He reached the truck and looked at the soldier who'd motioned to him. The other GI looked back, shaking his head. "What the fuck happened to you?" he asked.

At that moment, the cars that were being blocked by the truck started to blow their horns, and the drivers were swearing in Korean. The truck driver reached out and gave them the finger. "Neemie sheemie peck peck poji da!" he screamed.

The GI shoved Patty toward the truck. "We gotta truck on out of here," he said.

Patty climbed into the cab. Both men in the truck were snickering. Patty started to explain. They told him to shut the fuck up and get down on the floorboards, because they were coming to the main gate. The driver put a lit bowl that reeked of pot under the seat. The truck soon rolled to a stop at the side of the guard shack.

A swaggering MP came up to the driver's side. "Got a trip ticket?" he asked.

"Yeah, but I left it under your momma's bed," said the driver.

"Don't be a dick, wise guy, or I'll lock your funky ass up," the scowling MP replied.

The driver reached under the seat and pulled out an olive-drab logbook. The MP made a cursory glance and handed it back. "Get the fuck away from my gate asshole," he said, and walked away.

The truck took off with a lunge, throwing Patty against the shift. "Get up, man," said the driver. "Somebody's going to think you're doing something unnatural under there." They both laughed.

"Where you going, newbie?" said the other.

"Fourth of the 44th," Patty replied meekly.

"You sure are one sorry asshole," the driver said in a southern accent. "Some slickie girl run off with your wallet and pants?"

"Yeah, how did you know?"

They both started laughing. "It doesn't take a fuckin' genius to figure it out," said the man on Patty's right.

"Got to watch these heathen scum," said the driver. "Steal your fuckin' DEROS if they get a chance. "

"What's a DEROS?" Patty asked.

Both men looked at each other and shook their heads as if they were dealing with a hopeless retard. Patty flushed. " 'DE-ROS,' " said the driver, "means 'Date Estimated Return from Overseas.' In other words, that's the day you get to go home. You really must be new. How long you been in country?"

"Three days," Patty replied.

"Three days and he's already fuckin' up. Better take care, newbie. At this rate, you'll be half dead by the time you're ready to go home."

The truck pulled to a stop. "Ride's over, man. Better sneak through a back door." And the man on the right opened the door and jumped to the ground.

"Hey, thanks a lot, guys, you really helped me out a lot," Patty stammered.

"No sweat, kid. Don't want to see nothing' happen to our replacements," the man said as he climbed back into the truck.

Patty watched the truck move off down the road. Nice guys, he thought, not noticing the sergeant major walking up behind him.

"What the fuck you doing, soldier? Where do you think you

are, Rome? Where the hell are your pants?" he screamed.

Patty turned around and saw the red-faced sergeant major. He thought he was going to piss. "I guess I lost them, Sergeant Major." Patty didn't know what else to say.

"Well, I suggest you find them. And when you find them, I'd like you to put them on. Now move!" he bellowed.

Patty moved. He ran tripping over the sheet all the way to the transient barracks, stopping by the latrine to empty the bladder he thought would burst.

— **Chapter 12** —

The guys at Foxtrot took the scuttlebutt they heard from the supply sergeant seriously. Nobody wanted to get busted. Almost nobody. There was always the one that could fuck up a wet dream. His name was Murphy.

Every unit has a Murphy. Murph was a true-blue fuck-up. He didn't try to fuck up, it just happened. He wasn't stupid; in fact, he was really smart. The trouble was that his brain moved so fast it didn't have time to settle on one thing.

Murphy didn't have any close friends. Everyone liked him, but they could only take him in small doses. He moved so fast and tried to do so many things that whoever was with him would become exhausted.

He always seemed to be any place that trouble happened. Usually he had nothing to do with starting it; trouble just seemed to find him. Murphy would go into a bar to have a quiet drink and the guy down the end of the bar who had a death wish would seem to zero in on him. He just seemed to have had the type of face you wanted to change.

Murphy wasn't big. He wasn't small, either. He wasn't ugly, wasn't good-looking. He was five feet ten with dirty-blond hair and weighed in at about one sixty-five.

The only thing he had to brag about was his dick. Murphy had a pecker that was at least ten inches long. In the morning he would make a ritual in the shower.

Every morning, he would soap his member up and talk to it. Sooner or later somebody would tell him to cool it. That was when he would go into his act. He would walk over to the offended bather and ask him if his talking to his dick bothered him. Then he would proceed to tell the fellow that, if he had a dick like his own, he would talk to it, too. Then he would try to show it to him.

Petting it while talking to it in the same way a guy would talk to his girlfriend. The scene would always end up with the other guy admitting that Yes, you have a big dick, Murphy, just to get rid of him. This made Murphy happy.

Today Murphy was in trouble again. Everyone had gotten rid of their drugs and other assorted illegal objects. Everybody but Murphy. The battery commander shook his head from side to side as the big German shepherd from ASCOM alerted on his locker. The MP's sent for him, and he opened it up. Right on the top shelf was his stash. The MP reached in and pulled a bag of pot out that must have weighed three or four ounces.

The BC was pissed. Murphy was the best missile-tracking radar operator in the unit. The first sergeant was beside himself. He was a law-and-order freak. His time in service went back to the good old days where, if somebody stepped out of line, everyone beat the shit out of him.

His name was First Sergeant Norman Marshal. Everyone at the unit called him Marshal Marshal, or just The Marshal. He was happy. He went off singing "They'll be a "Court Marshal" in the old town tonight." The captain was disgusted with Murphy and told him so.

Murphy was disgusted with Murphy. He really felt miserable. You could tell that Murph didn't like to get into any trouble. He always got real quiet and didn't want to talk about it. After the MP's and everyone left the barracks, the guys ripped into him. He didn't even respond. Even though he was tremendously stupid and the trouble he was in was his own fault, all the rest felt sorry for him.

The worst part about getting busted for any type of drugs was that it meant you had your security clearance lifted and you couldn't work on the hill anymore. The "hill" was the integrated fire-control area. It had nothing to do with integration or fires. That was where the radars that guided the missiles were: the IFC area.

The launching area was five miles down the road. That was where the BIFFI's worked. "BIFFI" stood for "Brute Force and Fucking Ignorance." The launching area had three crews. They worked eight hours on, then were off twelve. The next day they worked twenty-four hours. The next day they were off.

It wasn't great work pushing missiles around, but the hours weren't bad. The guys on the hill worked twenty-four off, twenty-four on. Three hundred sixty-five days a year. There were only two crews. Most of the time the two crews hardly knew each other. The only contact they really had was when they would either relieve the other crew in the morning, or get relieved. Once in a blue moon, they would get a deep maintenance status that would allow them to turn off the power to the equipment and work a regular week of eight-hour days. That hadn't happened at Foxtrot in over a year.

The rivalries between the two crews were intense. It took a certain amount of proficiency to run a crew drill and pass a combat evaluation. The way it worked was that an inspection team, from battalion level or higher, would walk into the communication corridor unannounced and blow the siren. The crew would have fifteen minutes to run all their pre-firing checks, track a target, and fire a missile. One major screw-up from any of the ten men manning the positions and the unit would get an unsatisfactory rating. This would mean that the entire unit would be called out of action until they were revaluated again. Sometimes that could take weeks, but usually the combat evaluation team would be back the next day. The US Army only had five Nike Hercules surface-to-air missile sites in the country.

The battery commander was the one who suffered the most if the crews failed to pass a Combat Readiness Evaluation. He would be relieved from command if the battery was continually called out of action for not passing CRE's. This did not look good on his Officer Evaluation Report. It could cost him his career.

The crews knew this. The launching area crews didn't have that much to do, so if they screwed up, it was unusual. The guys on the hill had to do and remember a lot. It took a lot of concentration to pass a crew drill. If anything, it was the most important job in the entire battery, and they knew it. This is why only the most intelligent soldiers became 16C's. This is also the reason they became prima donnas. Usually, if they were good operators, they could get away with anything, but not with getting caught with drugs. Murphy had gotten caught.

— **Chapter 13** —

The driver let Fallica out in front of the orderly room. Patty was amazed at how small the place was. He hadn't expected the Taj Mahal, but damn this place was small.

The battery seemed to be built on the side of a mountain. Everywhere you looked, you saw steps leading to one building or another. The orderly room was the building closest to the guard shack. Patty didn't see anyone waiting to greet him, so he slung his duffel bag over his shoulder and walked in.

Nobody was home in the orderly room, either. Patty dropped his duffel and walked to the rear. The arms room was empty also. He shrugged his shoulders and walked to the front again. There were three desks. The one closest to the door said First Sergeant. A door behind the desk had the words Battery Commander. He knocked on that door. Nobody answered. He was mildly surprised. It was two o'clock in the afternoon and the place was deserted. He sat down at one of the desks and waited for somebody to show.

Sitting with his feet propped up on the desk, Patty noticed

something on the desk closest to him. He got off the chair and went over to it. Sitting on the top of the desk in plain sight was a bag of dope. He picked it up and peeked at it. There must have been five or six ounces of pot inside. As he was looking at the weed, he heard somebody walking up to the door. Getting paranoid, he stuffed the bag into his shirt.

The door opened up, and a Korean with a shotgun looked at him. Patty was taken aback.

"Who you?" asked the Korean.

"I'm Spec-Four Fallica," said Patty.

"You newbie?"

"Yes," Patty answered.

"You looking for first sergeant? First sergeant in mess hall with MP," the Korean said. "You come I show you."

Patty picked up his duffel bag and followed the Korean out of the door. They walked around the building, past a sign that said BARBER SHOP, to a walkway that led to a set of stairs that went straight up. Patty moaned to himself.

"You go up to mess hall, top of stairs." And the Korean pointed toward the top of the stairs with his shotgun.

Patty thanked the man and began climbing up to the top. Halfway there, he remembered the bag of pot stashed in his shirt. He stopped and stuffed it into his duffel bag. Lifting one foot after the other, he reached the top.

The top of the stairs emptied into a road. On the other side of the road, the mess hall stood at the top of a smaller set of stairs. Patty proceeded to climb these. When he finally stood at the mess hall door he was completely winded. He took a deep breath, opened the door and entered the mess hall.

It was a typical mess hall, not much different from the ones they had at his old unit. He had walked through the doorway that led to the serving line. Looking toward the rear of the mess hall, he saw a group of people sitting at one of the tables. He walked over.

As Patty approached the table, he heard the one with the bald head laughing above the conversation. He noticed the first-sergeant pins in his lapel. Patty didn't like the looks of him. He had a scarred, mean-looking face. His lips, even while laughing, seemed to be curled in a perpetual scowl. He had big bushy eyebrows and a body that was running to fat. Fallica decided that he didn't like him very much.

"So this asshole Murphy is finally going to get his. Serves him right. That's the kind of scumbag that's fucking up my army," The first sergeant said to the group.

"Excuse me; I'd like to see somebody about processing in?" Patty said.

The first sergeant turned and stared at him. The table fell silent. Patty didn't know it, but he had just made an intractable mistake. Nobody interrupted the first sergeant; at least nobody interrupted him in Korea. Back in the States, he answered to his wife. She was a beast. Here in Korea, he was safe from her grasp. Now a little newbie pipsqueak was in front of him trying to steal his thunder.

"What's your MOS, Specialist?" The battery commander spoke from the head of the table. He sensed that the first sergeant was going to rip into this new guy, and he didn't want to see that happen during his first day at the unit.

"16C, sir," Patty said.

"Good; a 16 Charlie. Great. You can take that asshole Murphy's place. I hope you are not a hippie dope smoker like he was," the first sergeant said.

"Is, First Sergeant, not was. We didn't execute Murphy; in

fact, we haven't even charged him yet. Let us not put a poor impression on this new soldier. Granny, show this specialist to the IFC barracks, and have him report to the orderly room tomorrow morning." The commander rose from his chair and extended his hand to Fallica. "Welcome to Foxtrot," he said.

"Thank you, sir. Glad to be here." And with that, Patty turned to follow the man the commander had called "Granny." As Patty walked away from the table, he heard somebody say mockingly "Thank you, sir, just fuckin' wonderful to be here." Patty was sure it was the first sergeant.

Patty followed the man up another set of steps. This one was worse than the others. It seemed to go straight up the mountain. Granny had no trouble, and was fairly bounding up the steps. Patty was huffing and puffing as he reached the top.

"This here's the headquarter barracks," Granny said. "The one just below us is the security barracks. The site MP's stay in that one."

"Where is the IFC barracks?" Patty asked between breaths.

"We still got another set of steps. Tired?" Granny asked with a smile.

"Yeah. I'm tired. Don't you ever get tired of playing mountain goat?"

"I did when I first got here. Sometimes when I'm hung over it gets to me, but I guess I got used to it. You will, too," he replied.

"I'll never get used to this," Fallica said.

— Chapter 14 —

Patty opened the door and stepped inside. He was glad to see that the building was made of cinder blocks and was not a tin Quonset hut. The floor was a crappy blue and the walls were painted green. On the sides of the walls were cubicles with bunks and wall-lockers. Some had cabinets, some had stereos. A few were wide open, although most had blankets or sheets used for makeshift walls. Patty guessed that this was for privacy.

Granny had left him here with no instructions. The barracks seemed empty. He dropped his bag and walked down the hall. Patty looked into each cubicle as he walked, trying to glean some insight into the people he would be bunking with for the next thirteen months. Most of the cubbyholes had walls covered with pictures of cars or girls in various states of undress. Some were barren and Spartan-looking.

Fallica was disappointed that the barracks was devoid of people. He hadn't expected a welcoming committee, but he did have a million questions to ask. One question he had was, where the hell was he going to sleep? All the bunks were taken.

Fallica walked to the end of the barracks. A screen door was slightly ajar. He opened it and walked out onto a porch set on top of a cliff. At the bottom of the cliff was a good-sized stream. It was really pretty, Fallica thought. He glanced down at his watch, and noticed that it was almost four PM. He wondered what time they served dinner. He stood gazing at the stream when the door opened behind him. He turned and saw five or six men come out to the porch. "Hi!" Patty said, stretching out his hand to the guy closest to him. "Name's Fallica. Just got in from New York."

"Hi, Fallica-who-just-got-in-from-New-Yawk," said the man, ignoring his handshake. "I'm Murphy, and I just got in from being busted." And with this, Murphy turned and looked dejectedly toward the stream, putting his chin in his hands.

"Don't mind him," said another, walking up to Patty with his hand outstretched. "I'm Wagner, but they call me Kool McKool. You can just call me Kool."

Patty took his hand while sizing Wagner out. He was short, about five-seven. He wasn't fat, but he was kind of round. He had creases around his eyes that his mother used to call laugh lines. Fallica decided that he would like him. "Got busted? For what?" Patty asked.

"Pot, grass, hootch, weed. What business is it of yours?" Murphy said irritably. "Anyway, it doesn't concern you."

Patty saw the misery in Murphy's eyes. He wished he could help him. Fallica was a soft touch for hard-luck stories. His own life had had its ups and downs. "When did this happen?" he asked.

"This morning," answered Wagner.

A light bulb went on in Patty's head. "How much pot did they get you for?" he asked.

"Enough, asshole. About a quarter of a pound." Murphy was irritated at this intrusion on his misery.

"Anybody want to get stoned?" Fallica asked brightly.

"Sure, newbie, we'll just go down to the orderly room and ask for Murphy's pot back because we got nothing to smoke. I'm sure that the marshal would hand it right over," quipped a tall lanky boy behind Wagner.

"You guys got no pot?" Fallica was enjoying himself.

"You are brain-dead," said Murphy.

"Didn't we tell you that they pulled a bust today? We got rid of everything," Wagner said with exasperation.

"This boy needs a checkup from the neck-up," said the tall skinny guy. Everyone laughed.

"Hey Murphy, if they bust you, are they going to ship you out of the unit?" Patty asked.

"No, maybe not. Probably stick me in the mess hall or the motor pool," Murphy replied.

"Hey, no more twenty-four on and twenty-four off. Shit, no more hot status!" said Wagner.

"Yeah, no more shitty hour checks and crew drills!" said the skinny one.

"No more shifty chow in mermite cans!" said a fat guy from the rear of the group.

"Great, you guys, just great," Murphy said. "No more hangin' out on the hill for midnight meetings in the guard shack. No more days off running with you guys in town. Just great."

Everyone shut up as Murphy's head went down again. In a low voice, he continued: "Who's gonna take care of my MTR? Who's gonna get you guys to go boulder rolling? Who's gonna take care of Fred?"

"Fuck the MTR, fuck rolling boulders, and especially fuck

Fred!" said Wagner. Everybody except Murphy laughed.

Patty knew the MTR was the missile tracking radar. He didn't really know about boulder rolling. "Who the fuck is Fred?" he asked.

"You'll find out," said the fat one. "Better hope he likes you."

"Fred's a dog," Wagner said. "A big, mean fuckin' dog that chews up boots and wallets and leaves pecker tracks on everybody's blankets. I hate Fred."

"Yeah, well, everyone else likes him. Fred's great. He's the only one that can keep up," said Murphy defensively. "He's the only one who will stand up to the lifers. Fred's just like us. He can't help it if he gets the clap all the time. He only leaves pecker tracks on your bed, Kool. He only sleeps on your bed 'cause he loves you. And you hate his guts. Fred's just like a lot of women. If you treat him like shit, which you do, he loves you. If you treat him good, he doesn't give two shits about you."

"Fred only likes me 'cause I get him high," Wagner replied simply.

"The dog gets high?" Patty was amazed.

"Yeah, Fred gets high. He also fucks all the girl dogs in the vill. When you go down there, see how many dogs look like Fred," the fat one said.

"He bites lifers, too," said the skinny one. "Anybody E-6 or above who he doesn't know. Fred don't like strangers, and if you happen to be a lifer-stranger, you're a goner."

"I've been here more than an hour and nobody has offered me anything for my head," Patty said.

"We got beer in the fridge. You can help yourself," Wagner replied.

Patty walked back into the barracks, and located the refrigerator. He then walked back to his duffel bag and removed a small package and stuffed it in his shirt. He walked back out to the porch. "Hey, this is a great place to get high. You can see if anyone is coming up the steps."

"Yeah, genius, this is a great place to get high if you have anything to get high on," said Murphy. "What did you say your name was, Einstein?"

"Hey Murphy, if you lose your clearance, does that mean you'll go to another barracks?" Patty inquired.

"Yeah, why? Want my bunk?" Murphy had his back up.

"Well, I wouldn't mind a small place of my own," said Fallica.

"You'll have to share one with a guy from the other crew until you been here awhile. That's the rules," said Wagner.

"If I could get Murphy off the hook, I'd bet he'd give me his bunk," Patty said.

"Listen, asshole, if you could get me off the hook I'd give you a blow job in front of the whole battery. But you can't get me off. Nobody can. I'm just an asshole that got caught dead to rights."

"That's because you don't listen," Wagner said.

"I know, I know," Murphy said tiredly.

"Got any papers?" asked Patty.

"Got any smoke?" asked the fat boy.

"I got smoke if you got papers."

"We got papers if you got smoke," Wagner said, pulling out a pack of top cigarette papers.

"I never want to see any more pot for the rest of my life!" said Murphy as he started to walk away.

"Wait a minute, Murphy. I think you might like this. I think this might be your brand." Patty was all smiles.

"You really know how to get on someone's nerves, don't you. Why don't you just leave me the fuck alone," Murphy said.

"Wait a minute. I'm your friend. You don't realize it, but I am. Just wait a minute until I get this out of my shirt."

Everyone waited with their eyes glued to Fallica as he wrestled with the package in his shirt. Looking Murphy in the eyes, he pulled it out. Murphy looked at the bag and back to Patty and back to the bag again. A brief smile crossed his face. "Where did you get that?" he asked.

"Who cares!" said the fat boy. "Let's get stoned!"

"Where did you get that?" Murphy asked again.

"I just kind of found it," Fallica said, shrugging his shoulders.

"Where did you 'just happen to find it'?" Wagner chimed in.

"On the first sergeant's desk!"

Patty was an instant hero. Murphy was instantly Murphy again. "I'll take my pot back, if you don't mind," he said, putting out his hand.

Patty was a little surprised at his attitude. Murphy's manner suggested that Patty had stolen something from him. The others must have thought the same, for all eyes were turned on Murphy. All the faces seemed to have the same expression. Everyone waited for two words. Wagner said them: "Fuck you!"

"Fuck me?" Murphy said, pointing toward himself with the most innocent face he could muster.

"Fuck you!" they all shouted.

Murphy laughed. The rest laughed. Patty surmised that he had just witnessed a ritual of sorts. What an odd bunch of guys, he thought. The rest of the afternoon was spent talking and getting stoned.

Every guy on the porch had a tale to tell about Foxtrot. Every tale was different, yet every story had the same thread of absurdity that made it seem that they were all taken from a madman's journal. Each story would begin with a witness. The storyteller would ask one of the guys if he remembered the time that so-and-so did so-and-so. They both would laugh, and both would tell the same story together. After a short time, only the original speaker who brought up the incident would continue. It was entertainment. It was the history of the place.

Fallica listened intently. He started to realize that life was going to be a little different here than he had imagined. He couldn't believe the things they were telling him. But he couldn't disbelieve them, either. Everything was an adventure here. These guys were excited. This was the first time he had ever heard GI's talking about where they were stationed and leaving out little details such as work, sergeants, and officers, and the chow in the mess hall. Everything Patty heard about was centered around a place called the Seaman's Club, a place called the Yellow House, and a bar named Whiskey Mary's.

Patty learned everyone's names. There were Murphy and Wagner. The tall skinny one was named Larson, but everyone called him "Rope" because of his build. The short guy with the big hands and the hillbilly accent was called "Big O." His real name was Reeger, but everyone called him "Big O" or just "O." His name came about because he had dentures that he never wore. He also had a big mouth, and when he laughed, his mouth formed somewhat of a circle.

The little fat guy was Phillips. He was the youngest of the group besides Patty. He was from California. He did not fit the surfer type, however. Patty liked Phillips. He had a good sense of humor and a lot of energy.

Like Patty, the big quiet guy in the back was from New York. His name was Tim Purvis.

Everyone referred to him as "Vitaman Tim" or just the "Vi-taman." This was his third tour in Korea, and he was getting short.

The small black guy was named Toomer. He didn't say much. He just kept laughing at the stories that everyone told, and finished can after can of Old Milwaukee. Patty wondered where he put it all. He was only five foot one. He was a rip. Every time he took a sip of beer, he would wipe his mouth with the back of his arm and smack his lips.

Patty was doing a little lip-smacking of his own. It kind of crept up on him, but pretty soon he was more than just a little drunk. Between the dope smoking and the beer, the world looked a bit foggy.

Somebody suggested that they go have dinner at the club. Patty wondered what club they were talking about. He went with them, down the steps, past the mess hall, toward the gate. The club was next to the guard shack across the street from the orderly room. They went inside, and Patty saw a long bar with a small stage and about ten tables. To the side was a small dining area with four small tables. A huge Rock-Ola jukebox stood next to the stage.

Patty sat down with the rest at the table closest to the jukebox. He remembered little of the next few hours except that he drank more than his share of Falstaff, and that he ate a hamburger. He remembered climbing up the steps to the barracks and plopping into the nearest empty bunk he could find.

Chapter 15

Patty felt someone nudging his shoulder. He thought it was his mother. He remembered thinking that he didn't want to get up and go to school. He slowly opened his eyes to see a pock-marked oriental face staring down at him. "You go chop," the man said.

Patty sat up in bed and rubbed his eyes. The guys were all in various states of dress. Some had fatigues on and some were in their underwear. All around the barracks you could hear the sound of flip-flops sucking at the tiled floor and slapping against heels. Patty swung his legs down to the floor and looked around for his duffel bag. It was nowhere to be seen. The Korean was still by the side of his bed with a broad smile on his face.

"Have you seen my duffel bag?" Patty asked him.

"You no need duffle bag. I fix wall locker. Foot locker, too," the man replied.

"Where?" Patty asked.

"Here," replied the Korean, pointing to the wall locker closest to the bed.

Patty rose to his feet. His head was pounding. He was expecting it. This was his fourth hangover since arriving in the country four days ago. He had better lay off, he thought. He could become an alcoholic at this rate. He opened the locker.

His clothes were all on hangers, and his fatigues had all been pressed. He turned to look for the foot locker. The Korean pointed to one of two at the foot of the bed. He bent down and opened it. His underwear had all been folded and his shaving gear was laid out as if waiting for inspection. He noticed that his boots under the bunk were spit-shined. He had never seen them look so good.

The Korean was standing next to his bunk with a look of genuine pride on his face. Patty was astounded. "When did you do this?" he asked.

"Today. I numbah-one houseboy. You likee?"

"I like," Patty said. "What's your name?"

"My name is Mr. Co. You call me Co. You name?"

"Fallica, Patty Fallica."

"Fallica." It sounded like "Farrica." "I call you Patty," he said.

The Korean walked away and Patty grabbed a set of underwear. He threw a towel over his shoulder and walked toward the latrine. As he stepped out the door he was greeted by a blast of cold air. He sprinted toward the building.

Inside, he saw other soldiers in the showers and at the sinks, shaving. He recognized some. He took off his underwear and entered the shower. The water smelled like chlorine. He turned on a nozzle and soaped himself, feeling the hot water warm his muscles. He heard a commode flush. Everyone jumped out of the spray. Too late, Patty screamed and jumped out of the water. Steam filled the shower stall. He looked at his shoulders to see if any blisters appeared. He swore. Murphy laughed. The others did too.

"You have to be fast. When you hear the toilets flush, you got a half second to jump, or you'll get cooked," Murphy said.

"Yeah, I noticed," Fallica said.

Patty showered, shaved and returned to the barracks. Donning his uniform, he went to the mess hall. The breakfast was excellent. The powdered eggs he ate were okay if he drenched them in butter. He was just finishing when a small skinny staff sergeant sat next to him. "Are you the new 16C?" the man asked Patty.

"Yep. Just got here yesterday."

"Well, you got to process in at the orderly room. After chow, go down there and get it done. After that, call the hill and we'll send the truck down for you. What position do you run?"

"TTR and MTR. Azimuth, Elevation, and Range," Patty said proudly.

"Good," said the sergeant, "we can use you. Don't count on coming back down until tomorrow. You're working tonight." He got up and walked away.

Patty gulped down the rest of his coffee and started down the hill toward the orderly room. He walked to the front of the building and walked in.

The first sergeant was already there. He looked up from the papers in front of him and glared at Patty. "What the hell do you want?" he almost shouted.

"I want to process in," Patty said.

"Go to the arms room, get a weapons card and a meal card, and you are done. Can you understand that, Mr. Noo Yawk?" he said menacingly.

"Yes, Top," Patty turned to walk away.

"Look at me, asshole!" the first sergeant barked.

Patty turned and looked at him. His eyes were turning to slits, and his top lip turned into a sneer. It was all Patty could do not to give him the finger.

"Do I look like a fuckin' top? A top is something kids play with! Do I look like the type of person a kid would want to play with?" he screamed.

Patty said nothing, not trusting himself to reply.

"I said, do I look like a top, dickhead?" he screamed again.

"No, First Sergeant, you do not look like a top," Patty said between gritted teeth.

"Good. From now on you will refer to me as First Sergeant, not Top. Not The First Shirt, just First Sergeant. Got that?"

"Yes, First Sergeant."

"Good. Now get the fuck out of my sight. But before you go, asshole, I want you to know two things. First of all, I don't like you. In fact, I hate your fucking guts. Second of all, I know what you did yesterday, and if I could prove it I would have your ass in Leavenworth for fucking with U.S. Government evidence."

He paused and allowed the statement to sink into Patty's mind. "You have gotten off to a bad start with me. I better not hear your goddamn pussy name again for the rest of the time that I'm in-country. And remember this: I'm not set to rotate until next August! Now get the fuck out of here!"

Patty turned and walked away. Rotate on this, he thought.

The armorer was nice. He issued Patty an M-16 that looked brand new. He also issued him a meal ticket he told Patty he would never use unless he ate in a mess hall in another unit.

Patty asked to use the field phone and rang the switchboard. The armorer told him to ask for "Yellow;" that would put him up to the hill. He talked to somebody who promised that the duty driver would be right down. He was instructed to wait in front of the mess hall.

By the time Patty arrived at the mess hall, the truck was just pulling up. The driver told him to go inside and get a cup of coffee. He did that. The driver disappeared. It was an hour later when he showed up again. They left the mess hall and got on the truck.

The ride up the mountain took about ten minutes. It was steep all the way. The driver, a VHF man named Morrison, told him that it only takes three minutes to get down. Patty made a mental note not to drive down with him.

The top of the hill was ringed with barbed wire. Bunkers stood out around the perimeter. Some were inside the fence line, and some were outside of it. The guard shack at the entrance was a little larger than the ones in the States.

Once inside, Patty saw that the radars didn't look much different than the ones he had worked on in the States. The vans on both sides of the corridor building were lined with sandbags, as were the tops. It didn't take Patty long to notice that everything was covered with sandbags.

The truck stopped between the corridor and the generator building. The ready room was directly in front of the corridor. Patty got out and started toward the corridor. He walked toward the stairs and couldn't help but notice a fairly large-sized dog sleeping in front of the door. This must be Fred, Patty thought.

He reached over the dog to push the door open. Fred looked up at him, made a deep menacing growl, and bared his teeth. Patty stopped in his tracks. Fred stared at him for a couple more seconds, then put his head back down, sighed and closed his eyes. Patty slowly pushed the door open and gingerly stepped over the sleeping dog. The dog didn't stir.

The interior of the corridor was bursting with activity. Everyone seemed to be talking at once. One person was talking on the FM radio, another was talking on the field phone, and everyone was talking to everyone else. Patty brushed past the bodies, looking for the staff sergeant who had told him to report there. He found him in the tracking van.

The staff sergeant, a headset held to his ear, looked up when Patty entered. "Fallica! Glad to see you made it. Welcome aboard. Get yourself a cup of coffee, and I'll be right with you after I command-cal these missiles."

Patty made his way back into the corridor. He saw Wagner inside the battery control van, also with a headset on, bending over the acquisition radar. Patty guessed that he was sending designated targets to the tracking station. There, the target-tracking radar would seek out an airplane in the designated quadrant and track it with a pencil-beam of RF energy.

Working in the tracking station was Patty's job. He was pretty good at it. Sometimes he felt as if the radar was an extension of his eyes. He could somehow find targets when nobody else could. Other operators would sometimes be awed by it. When they would ask him how he did it, he would tell them that he had "second sight." At times, he really believed that he did.

One of his goals was to become Tracking Supervisor. That was the job with the glory. A good "track sup" was paramount to passing a crew drill, or to running a successful mission. He stood behind the target-tracking crew with a box in his hand called the "remote." The target-tracking crew was seated in front of him. There were three men–the elevation operator on the left, the azimuth operator in the middle, and the range operator on the right.

A target would be designated from the battery control van using a broad-beamed acquisition radar similar to the ones used at airports. The acq operator, as he was called, would place a circle over the target, tap a switch, and the target-tracking radar in the tracking station would automatically slave to the area designated.

After that, it was up to the tracking crew to find that target. The radar would be pointed on approximately the right azimuth and range. As soon as the controls stopped slewing to the designated location, the elevation operator would bring the radar up and down to find the altitude. When the radar had the right elevation and azimuth, the target would appear on the scope as a line. The range operator would then slew the range until the line dropped into a small notch on the baseline of the scope called the range gate. Once that was accomplished, the target would be tracked.

With the target tracked, the information would be relayed to a computer in the battery-control van. The computer would, at the FIRE command, launch a missile and direct the missile-tracking radar to the coordinates it was receiving from the target-tracking radar, causing the missile to burst when it reached those coordinates. It was a good system, provided the equipment worked properly.

The tracking supervisor was responsible for insuring that the three tracking operators did what they were supposed to. He had to be qualified in each position—azimuth, elevation and range. The track sup was also responsible for electronic countermeasures in case the enemy aircraft used electronic warfare to jam the scopes. This was what the remote box was used for. During simulations, it was not uncommon for a tracking he ervisor to lose control of not only the radar, but of himself. A bad track sup could be responsible for allowing the radars to be saturated with enemy jamming, thereby losing the target and dropping the engagement.

The tracking supervisor also transmitted reports to the battery control officer, or BCO. That was the part that Patty liked the best. The whole fire-control area and the launching area heard him. The engagement effectively ended with the words "Burst in the gate, target destroyed." It was a responsible position, and one that Patty hoped someday to have.

Patty was close to qualifying for it. He was an azimuth operator. That meant he was also qualified in elevation. The azimuth operator was senior to elevation, and they both worked on the target tracking radar (TTR). The range operator was junior to the missile-tracking radar operator. During the crew drill, the range operator and the MTR operator worked together doing checks on the MTR. Patty knew the range position and had qualified in the States. The only thing he didn't know were checks on the target ranging radar (TRR). The tracking supervisor performed checks on this during the crew drill. Patty knew a little, and could just about do it with a manual, but he didn't have the expertise to handle a fifteen-minute crew drill without the book.

That was the whole point, of course. A manning crew had to be able to check out the equipment and fire a missile within twenty minutes. Fifteen minutes to check out the radars, and five minutes for the engagement. If the crew failed to do this, the battery was declared out of action for either equipment malfunctions or crew performance. The battery could not again be declared in-action or combat-ready until a new evaluation was performed. This could take anywhere from twenty-four hours to a week. Commanders were relieved for too many lost crew drills.

Every day the equipment was checked out. These were called dailies. The crew started on these every morning, and usually finished around ten-thirty. Nobody liked dailies all that much, but they were a fact of life. The crew was just finishing dailies when Patty arrived.

The staff sergeant walked over to where Patty was finishing his coffee. He motioned for him to follow. Patty followed him out the rear door of the corridor and through the back door of the ready room. Patty noticed that the ready room was clean and warm. He was surprised to see a TV over in the corner. At the far side, he saw a pool table. At the rear, near the door they had entered through, was a small room with a bed. Patty guessed correctly that it must be the duty officer's room.

The staff sergeant indicated for him to take a seat and then he walked over to a coffee pot and poured himself a cup. He asked Patty if he wanted one. Patty declined: his kidneys were floating already. The sergeant walked over to the table and sat down directly across from Patty.

"I read your two-oh-one file, Fallica, and I saw your last three enlisted evaluation reports. Your job proficiency is rated as excellent. Your last section chief said he has never seen anyone progress as quickly as you have in so short a time. I'm impressed," he said.

"Thank you," Patty replied.

"The other things in your file didn't look so good, though," the sergeant said with a grave tone. "You got three Article 15's in one year. How the fuck did you manage to keep SP-4?"

"I guess I'm just lucky," Patty said with a shrug of his shoulders.

"I think it was because you're a good operator. Fallica, I need good operators. This isn't New Jersey; it's Korea. We're only three minutes flying time from the DMZ. I don't care what the fuck you do on your off time. All I care about is whether you are here in the morning, and that you do what you are paid to do when you are up here. Do you understand?"

"Yes, Sergeant."

"My name is Brown. Harold Brown. You can call me Brown, Sarge, dickhead–anything you want to as long as you don't do it in front of the officers. From now on I am your section chief, and you are my responsibility. I am your father, mother, and your protector. If you have a problem, I want to know about it. I want to know about it before the orderly room knows about it. Have you met the first sergeant?"

"Yes. He doesn't like me," Patty said.

"He doesn't like himself. In fact, he is the biggest asshole we have. Try to stay clear of him. Got that?" Brown asked.

Patty nodded his head.

"Do you know why we went out the back door?"

Patty said he didn't know.

"Because of Fred. Have you met Fred?"

Patty told him that he had met Fred.

"Fred doesn't like me. I don't like Fred. I am afraid of Fred. Fred is not afraid of me. The only reason he doesn't tear me to pieces is because he knows that I run things up here, and that I take care of him. That applies to you, too. You can be just like Fred. Do you understand?"

Patty nodded his head and said that he understood. Brown said that they should get along splendidly. Now he should go over and tell Larson to take him through a set of dailies. Patty got up and walked back into the corridor. As he approached the door, Fred looked up at him. Patty stopped. "Do you know that I can be just like you?" he said to Fred.

Fred growled. Patty growled back. Fred licked Patty's hand. They were friends.

— Chapter 16 —

Evenings on the hill belonged to the crew. The platoon sergeant and the officers were gone. The only people in authority left at night were the duty officer and the section chief. Tonight, it was Lieutenant Hicks and SSG Brown. Both minded their own business. Most did. The duty officers usually stayed in the corridor or the ready building reading or watching TV.

After chow, eaten from mermite cans, the crew would finish six-hour checks. When these were done, usually about eight o'clock, they would either start a game of spades, play Risk, or just hang out. TV was usually ignored. In Korea, the only English channel was AFKN–the Armed Forces Korean Network. They played old reruns and sports shows that were days old. What fun was watching a baseball game when you already knew who won?

The news was a joke. The military only told what they wanted everyone to hear. Things like how we were winning in Vietnam, how good the folks back home were doing, and how much fun you could have in Korea courtesy of the Eighth

Army Command.

Patty was sitting in front of the TV. It was just starting to be apparent to him that the whole experience was meaningless. A public service announcement came on, and told him that did he know there were ten million alcoholics in the United States? "Ten million and one," Patty muttered under his breath. SSG Brown caught that and chuckled. Patty got up, stretched and looked around. SSG Brown told him he had guard duty in a little while. Maybe he should go out to the guard shack and get acquainted with the procedures. Why not, thought Patty.

Walking out of the ready room, Patty noticed that nobody else was around. Where the hell did they disappear to? He walked out and into the corridor and saw that only the commo guard was there. This shift it was Vitaman Tim. He tried to make a little conversation, but Tim was absorbed in his comic book. God, thought Patty, what a burn-out. I'll never get like that, he vowed.

He checked out his weapon, and walked toward the guard shack. The hill was dark; the perimeter lights along the fence line were shining outwards. The area outside the fence was lit, but inside the fence was dark. Patty tripped over some cables, but righted himself before he fell. It was spooky. He didn't like being out there alone. He guessed he would get used to it in time.

The guard shack was ahead. He could see the cherry-colored light that was the space heater inside. He turned the doorknob and stepped inside. Murphy was leaning against the wall with his rifle against the door. It fell as Patty closed it behind him. Murphy woke up with a start. "I wasn't sleeping," he said defensively.

"I didn't say you were." But Patty knew he was.

"You can't sleep on guard duty. It's important to stay awake," Murphy said. "This is Korea. Shit happens."

"What kind of shit?" Patty asked.

"All kinds of shit," Murphy replied, staring out the window looking at nothingness.

"What kind of shit?" Patty asked again.

Murphy looked at him with a strange, knowing grin. "I'll tell you what kind of shit. Shit like guys going out on patrol up north and never coming back. Or if they are found, they have been shot up or fragged, clothing missing, boots taken every time. They always take the boots," Murphy said.

"Who takes the boots?"

"The North Koreans. They like American boots. You can always tell it's them. They always take the boots."

Patty felt a chill start up his spine. Murphy had said it so slowly, so mysteriously. The words echoed in his head. They always take the boots.

Patty stared at Murphy and saw that his eyes were beet red. That was when he realized that Murphy was high. He started laughing. Murphy looked up at him, and a smile started at the corner of his mouth. He snickered, Patty snickered, and the snicker turned into a chuckle. Soon both were laughing hysterically until Patty thought he would puke.

Murphy got up and sprinkled something on top of the space heater. It started to smolder because of the intense heat. The guard shack filled with smoke, and Patty realized that it was pot. "Just take deep breaths," Murphy said. "This is the lazy man's way of getting high."

They sat and talked. Murphy said he really wasn't kidding about some of the shit that happened over here. It paid to be careful. Every once in a while, guys would get shot at. The inter-area cable between the launching area and the IFC area was constantly being cut, and sections of it taken. The commander and army intelligence said that slickie boys were doing it to get the copper from the cable, but the guys in the unit knew that that was a bullshit story.

The cable was only being cut during "hot" status, when their unit was the one on the highest state of alert. Also, it was only being cut in about two-foot sections, in two or three different places. If it was slickie boys, they would take more than that, and they would cut it when they were in a maintenance status and the power was shut down. That way, they could take more of it, and nobody would know it was cut for days. The BC was calling in a special-forces company anyway. He just wanted it stopped.

Other things happened. Last month, thirteen men were hanged in the square in Yoju, the town outside Delta Battery. They had wandered into town, and one of them had made the mistake of asking how much a pack of cigarettes cost. Everyone in Korea knew that cigarettes were sold by the government of Korea, and that they were all the same price. The townspeople had tried them and hanged them the same day. They hadn't wasted time.

Patty listened intently. Murphy told him that the village outside the gate had a whore who was a witch. She held séances to summon up the devil. Murphy wanted Patty to check that out. Patty was game. They agreed that it should be done as soon as possible.

Murphy looked at his watch and scowled. It was time to do a perimeter check. At least once an hour they were required to walk around the fence line. One person was supposed to remain at the gate, and the other would walk. Murphy told Patty that after 9 PM they did it together. If a truck came up, tough. They zipped their field jackets and left the guard shack. They walked to the left. They passed the VHF building and went behind the generator building. Patty saw something scurry into the cable run. He thought it might be a squirrel. Murphy told him it was a rat.

Past the generator building, the path took them downward. It looped around a cluster of boulders and down to level ground again. This was called the "Lower Forty," Murphy explained. Nobody liked to come down here alone because it dipped out of sight from the rest of the hill, and because it was just plain spooky.

Sometimes they would find that the fence line was cut. Almost every time that they did find the fence line cut, it was in the "Lower Forty."

Patty noticed that here and there the fence had indeed been repaired. He wanted to know why somebody would try to get in. Murphy told him that nine out of ten times it was slickie boys. Patty wondered about the one out of ten when it wasn't.

Murphy told him that Fred usually scared most intruders off. He was a great watchdog when he was up here. Once, when Fred wasn't around, a slickie boy came up and stole everybody's wallets while they slept. Since then, they took guard duty a little more seriously. This had happened last month.

An antenna with a box attached to the bottom greeted the two at the far end of the fence. This was the test set. It sent out a beacon that they used to calibrate the radars. It was part of dailies and six-hour checks to come down here and run some checks on it. The MTR operator usually did it. During the winter it was a bitch, because the wind blew like hell down here; and if there was a lot of snow, it was hard to get up and down the hill. Almost every year somebody broke a leg.

They traveled back up the hill on the opposite side of the one they had come down. Patty saw a huge building on steel girders about seventy feet high. An acquisition antenna revolved slowly at the top. Murphy explained that it was the A Bar. It usually didn't work. When it was in action, though, somebody had to be in there twenty-four hours a day. The little black guy, Toomer, was the A-bar operator. Murphy suggested that that was why he was so crazy. Pulling duty up there was like being in solitary confinement.

They moved along the side of the fence behind the radars. They passed the TRR and the MTR. Murphy stopped and gave it a pat. The MTR was his radar. The operator on the other crew, Murphy's opposite, was an asshole, Murphy explained. Murphy told Patty that it took hours to get it right after the other guy had it.

Patty laughed. This aspect of the job was no different than in the States. The other crew were always assholes.

Murphy pointed outside the fence. Patty looked. He didn't see anything but the lights from the village. Beyond that was only blackness. "What?" Patty asked. "I don't see anything."

"That's because past the village is the yellow sea," Murphy explained. "Sometimes you can see ROK troops searching the coastline for infiltrators. I've seen two firefights in the four months that I've been here."

Patty asked what they were like.

Murphy told him how the ROK's would break up and search the ground in huge boxes. You could see how they moved because they carried flashlights. If they found something, they would start shooting.

Patty asked why they didn't wait to see what they were

shooting at. That was when he learned about curfew. After midnight, nobody was supposed to be out. If somebody was out after midnight, especially someplace like on the beach, they were asking to have their ass shot off.

It was chilly, and Patty was glad to return to the guard shack. Murphy looked at his watch and told Patty that it was time for his shift to be up. Before he left, he rolled a joint and gave it to Patty. Patty appreciated the gesture. Murphy left the guard shack and walked toward the corridor.

Being in the guard shack alone unnerved Patty a bit. It was really quiet. He heard the wind whistling through the fence, and for the first time since being in-country, he felt really alone. He peered out of the window at the lights down below. He wondered what it was like outside the gates. He'd heard all the stories, but he really didn't know what was bullshit and what was fact.

He wondered if anyone missed him at home. Tomorrow he would write his mother a letter, he thought. He thought about his mother. He felt bad about the last full day he was home. His mother had made him lasagna, his favorite. They had planned a small party for him, too. Patty thought that it was a nice thing for them to do, but it didn't fit in with his plans.

The only thing Patty wanted to do was hang out with his friends and see Gayle. Bruce had sent him two black beauties in the mail, and Patty ate both around 11:00. By the time dinner was served that night, Patty was speeding his ass off and didn't want any part of the meal. That really upset his mother. He couldn't stay home, either. As soon as he could, he left the house and was off to the bar.

He had called Gayle that evening and she gave him a couple of hours, but she didn't seem overly concerned that he was going away. Well, she was like that. He always knew she didn't feel the same way about him that he did about her.

A wave of sadness came over Patty like a hard blanket. He felt like a tragic figure. In his mind's eye, he could see himself as a lone figure in a strange and foreign land. A poor, deserted, lonely GI doing his duty the best way he could.

The song that always crept up on him when he felt alone crept up on him again.

He heard himself sing:

"Well I ride on that train, babe,
can't buy a thrill.
Well I been up all night,
leaning on the windowsill.
And if I die on top of that hill,
well if I don't make it
I know my baby will."

Patty could get lost in song. He liked the sound of his own voice. By now he was totally relaxed, with his head tilted upward against the wall, eyes closed. He got ready to sing the next verse when the guard shack door opened. It made him jump, and his face burned with embarrassment at the thought that maybe somebody had heard him. He looked up and saw Vitaman Tim looking down at him.

Tim cleared a place in the corner of the shack and sat down. Patty noticed that Tim's eyes were different than before. They kind of were alive. He had a small crinkle at the corner of his mouth that suggested a smile. He looked at Patty and nodded his head. Patty had no idea of what to figure until he heard the next verse come from Tim's lips:

"Don't the moon look good, Mama,
shinin' through the trees.

Don't the brakeman look good, Mama,

flaggin' down the double E.

Don't the sun look good, goin' down over the trees.

Don't my gal look fine when she's comin' after me."

Patty couldn't believe it. A huge smile crossed his face, and an instant bond seemed created between himself and Vitaman Tim. This was the first time he had heard anybody but Bob Dylan or himself sing this particular song. In fact, he didn't know of anyone who had even heard of it. Tim smiled at Patty, and motioned with a back-and-forth wave of his hand that meant he wanted both of them to do the next verse. Patty hesitated, but eventually lost his inhibition, and they churned out the next verse:

"Well the wintertime is comin, Mama,

the windows are filled with frost.

I tried to tell everybody, but I could not get across.

Well I want to be your lover, Mama,

I don't want to be your boy.

Don't say I never wanted you,

when your train gets lost."

There was silence after the last verse. Patty had thought they sounded pretty good. They both just looked at each other. Soon, Tim and Patty were laughing and congratulating each other.

"Where in New York do you come from?" asked Patty.

"Long Island," Tim replied.

"Me, too. Where on Long Island?"

Tim told Patty that he didn't call anywhere his home town because he'd moved so much. His father and mother were split up since he was a kid, and he had been shuffled back and forth. They found out that they were both born in Huntington.

Patty's family had moved east towards Port Jeff, but Tim's family had stayed in the Huntington-Northport area.

Patty asked Tim what this place was really like without the bullshit. Tim answered that the place couldn't be described without the bullshit. It was different than any other place he had ever been in. It was good, but it could be bad. "What do you mean by good and bad?" Patty asked him.

"Well, it's good when you have a good buzz on and you're lying next to a pretty girl in a warm hootch with a full belly," he said. "It's bad when all hell breaks loose and you're not ready for it. That's what I mean."

"What kind of hell?" Patty was intrigued.

"You don't want to hear a bunch of war stories. Get me started and I'll go on all night," Tim said.

"So what?" Patty countered. "We got all night."

"What do you want to hear, the good parts or the bad parts?" Tim quipped.

"The parts that will help me understand this place; the parts that will stop me from fucking myself up," Patty answered seriously.

"That sounds logical. Okay. Stop me when you've heard enough." He handed Patty a small baggie and some rolling papers. "You roll and I'll talk." And then Vitaman Tim told Patty his story.

He went on for hours. He told Patty why he had joined the army. How he had volunteered for Korea to get out of going to Vietnam. Tim explained that he was only seventeen years old when he got to Korea. "Full of piss and vinegar" was how he described himself.

Tim was first stationed in Yoju. The only thing they had there was a small village. Everyone in the unit had a yobo. A yobo was a girl you rented by the month. Back in 1969, a yobo cost about sixty dollars. If she was ugly, a little less.

His yobo had been about forty-five years old. She took good care of him, though. He could get drunk and sick, and she would clean him up and put him to bed. The first couple of months he was there, nothing much happened. He drank too much, but he didn't drug. He went to work and did his job. Everything was fine for awhile.

"What happened to change things?" Patty interrupted.

"Garter changed things. At least for me."

"How?"

Tim took a deep drag off the joint and stared out of the window. He seemed lost for a couple of minutes. Patty started to think that maybe he had sort of shut down. Maybe the re-counting of this particular part of his life was a little too much for him. Patty was about to say something when Tim started again.

"Garter was a little weird. He was real smart. He was always reading some sort of book. But that was his problem. He was book-smart, but didn't know squat about the real world. He had no common sense." Tim looked at Patty to see if he understood. Patty was nodding his head. Tim went on.

Tim proceeded to tell Patty how things had gotten a little hairy with the communists. The Pueblo had been taken by the North, and nobody knew what was going to come down. The spy ship was just the beginning. It was Christmastime, and just about every night the siren would ring. It was always at about three AM. The guys would rush into the vans and fire up the radars. The worst feeling in the world was turning on the B scope and seeing hundreds of aircraft heading toward the south. Everyone would sweat bullets.

"What happened?" Patty asked.

"Well, they would get within a couple of miles of the border. Our planes would be heading north trying to intercept them. Just when it looked like they would engage, the commie planes would do a U-turn and head back up north."

He explained to Patty that the planes were only a part of it. The villagers would get real nervous. The fuel depot was constantly being refilled, and new equipment they had been asking for since he got there was being sent in every day. They enforced the policy of only having twenty percent of the personnel on pass at any one time. If you went to the village, you had to go in fatigues. If you were on post, you had to have your M-14 and 156 rounds of ammunition. On guard duty, your weapon had to be round-chambered. You slept with your weapon next to you. Yes, he explained; things were hairy.

Everyone was really uptight. Especially the guys down in the launching area. They were put on double shifts of guard duty, and they also doubled the number of guards they had out. This meant that other sections had to provide some men to take up some of the slack. That was why Tim had driver duty for the guard force that night.

It was snowing like hell. It was cold, too. It had snowed so much that week that the roads almost looked like tunnels without out a roof. The snow had built up steeply on both sides. Tim had dropped off most of the evening guard force, and only had one more stop to make. That was when he heard the bullet.

Tim stopped the truck. He was sure that he had heard someone shooting at him. He was taking no chances. He rolled out of the driver's seat and fell out of the truck to the ground, clutching his M-14 in his hands. He listened, but didn't hear any more shots being fired. He remembered that Garter was in back of the truck and started to low-crawl toward the rear. From a crouch, he banged on the tailgate. He received no answer. He banged again and yelled Garter's name. He still didn't get a reply.

At this point Tim's face went almost blank, but his eyes kind of half closed, almost as if he were in pain.

"What the fuck happened?" Patty said, caught up in the story.

Tim slowly turned his head and looked at Patty. "I climbed up into the deuce and a half. It was dark in there. I knew what'd happened, though, because I could smell the gunpowder. Garter was over in the corner behind the cab. His rifle was lying across his lap, and his helmet was on the floor. Half of his head was still in it. The other half was still sitting on his neck, but I couldn't recognize it."

"God, that's terrible. Jesus Christ!" Patty exclaimed. "What the fuck did you do?"

Tim shrugged his shoulders. He went on. "I learned a lot about living and dying that night. I drove the truck to the aid station. I was hysterical. I got the medic up and told him what happened. He didn't blink an eye. He had served two tours in 'Nam. I wanted him to hurry up, but he took his time getting dressed. He told me to relax. If Garter had left half of his head in his helmet, he said, the other half wouldn't care by now if he was a little late getting there.

"We walked out to the deuce and the medic went in. He came out about five minutes later. He looked at me and said 'You're right, he's dead.' In fact, he said something like 'You can't get much deader.'

"We went back into the aid station, and he put on a kettle of water for coffee and turned on the space heater. He called the BOQ and told the captain. Then he called the battalion surgeon on the FM radio. The duty officer at the other end asked for a report. The medic told him what happened. The duty officer wanted to know Garter's vital signs. Everything was zero. Heart rate, respiration, temperature, blood pressure."

"What did the duty officer say?"

"He asked if we needed oxygen!" Tim started to laugh.

"Oxygen!" And Patty started to laugh.

Tim raised his hand to stop while he gasped for breath. "Do you know what the first sergeant did? He told me I'd had a bad night, and told me to go back to the barracks and get some sleep. I started to leave, and he said that before I went to bed I had to clean out the truck. For the rest of the night I scraped brains off the bed of the truck with a putty knife. That's army compassion."

"That's army bullshit!" Patty said in anger.

"Not really, when you think of it; it was just what I needed. If they would have made a big deal of it, I might have been traumatized. I think it went the way it should have gone. I can tell you one thing, though."

"What?"

"There ain't no glory in suicide."

— **Chapter 17** —

Patty felt someone shaking his shoulder. He opened his eyes and tried to figure out where he was. Looking around the room, he remembered that he was up on the hill. Everyone was up and moving except for him. SSG Brown was still standing by his bunk, looking at him. "Come on, Fallica, we got six-hour checks," he said.

Patty shook the cobwebs out of his brain. He had been up almost all night, talking with Vitaman Tim. He just got to sleep less than two hours ago. He looked at the clock on the wall, 6 AM. Too goddamn early, he thought. He sat up on the bunk and started to pull his boots on. SSG Brown, seeing that he was up, walked out of the ready room. Patty had the urge to just lie back down and go back to sleep.

He didn't do it, though. He was kind of looking forward to pulling the six-hour checks on the TTR. Yesterday, Larson wouldn't let him touch anything. Today would be different. Larson was on guard duty, and he would get to do it by himself.

Patty left the ready room and walked into the corridor.

Three men were sitting at the table in the center. They were still playing Risk. That game had been going on for hours. Five guys had started it; now there were only three. It looked like Wagner was going to win.

The coffee pot was on, and the smell almost gave Patty a hard-on. He was only eighteen years old, but his coffee habit was strong. He poured himself a cup and walked into the van.

The elevation operator was a big help. He was almost ready to be a TTR operator. He helped get Patty through the checks, and showed him the small differences in this particular radar. Checks were completed in half an hour.

When Patty went into the corridor, Wagner was just finishing winning the Risk game. Everyone else was milling about; each person had a coffee cup in his hand.

Today was Friday. They were supposed to attend a formation in the afternoon. Monday morning and Friday evening were reveille and retreat formations. It was just a formality. Part of the army tradition, Patty was told. Patty couldn't care less. Back in New Jersey, they had formation every morning. Two a week was all right with him.

The truck pulled up in front of the corridor and blew its air horn. The crew on duty grabbed for their jackets and other gear they had brought up with them. Everyone made a dash for the truck.

The other crew was coming into the corridor as they were leaving. The different operators would exchange short bits of information with their counterparts: This works; this doesn't. Watch out for this, don't worry about that. Patty was glad when he was seated in the truck and on the way back down the mountain. He was hungry, and the mess hall would be his first stop.

As it turned out, the mess hall wasn't his first stop. Nobody wanted to eat breakfast. He didn't want to eat alone, and more important, Vitaman Tim had told him the night before that he would show him around Inchon, and Tim was leaving as soon as he showered and changed.

Patty showered and changed, too. His houseboy had done all of his civilian clothes and had them hung up in his locker. He was informed by his houseboy that he would require a kimchee cabinet for the rest of his things. For a nominal fee of $10.00, this could be acquired directly from the aforementioned houseboy.

Patty agreed. The deal was done.

Tim was ready and waiting when Patty knocked on his door. They took off down the hill. Patty had trouble keeping up with Tim. He didn't want to start complaining, for fear that Tim wouldn't want him around. Still, Patty couldn't understand why or how he walked so fast. It was such a pace that Patty almost had to break into a trot to keep up with him.

They walked out of the gate and started through the village. Tim told him that the village was called Moonhak. If he wanted to go back to the battery, all he had to do was tell the taxi driver "Moonhak," and he would be taken to the battery.

The village was poor and dirty by Patty's standards. There were no sidewalks, and the road, too, was mud and dirt. The houses had cinder-block walls and corrugated-tin roofs. Some huts further off the road were actually made of hardened earth with straw roofing. They were quite comfortable, Tim explained. The floors were heated by a charcoal stove. There were ducts that ran under the floor to distribute the heat.

Patty was told to sleep with the window slightly opened, because sometimes the concrete floors, as well as the ducts, cracked–and carbon monoxide would seep in. Tim told Patty that he had known at least five guys die from it.

As patty walked down the road, he noticed that what the guys had told him was true. All the dogs in the village did look like Fred. He mentioned this to Tim.

He just shrugged his shoulders. Patty figured that it was a stupid remark. Probably all Korean dogs looked the same.

At the end of the village, they reached a main road. This too was dirt. Tim turned a corner and went inside a doorway. He motioned for Patty to follow. Patty did.

Inside was a room with a dirt floor. A charcoal heater was in the center. Around the heater were wooden benches. Tim sat down on one of these, and Patty followed suit. A door slid open at the side of the room, and a small old Korean woman stepped out. "Bitaman! Onya Hashimnika! You go PX today?"

"Nay, Mamasan. Go ASCOM. You need?"

She shook her head, obviously delighted that Tim had stopped at her place. Tim turned to Patty and told him that they were in a "moklee" house. A moklee house, Tim explained, was a Korean version of a bar. Moklee was the stuff they made out of rice. It looked like milk and tasted something like stale beer. It fucked you up real good, but gave you a terrible hangover.

The woman, Tim explained, was the local black marketeer. If Patty wanted to sell something from the PX, this was the woman he should deal with. She also bought sleeping bags, field jackets, and anything else he could glom from the supply room. She paid the best prices, but she wouldn't deal with everybody. As far as Tim knew, he was her only supplier. If Patty wanted to, Tim told him, he would fix it so he could take Tim's place when he left. Patty said okay, not knowing what else to say.

Tim introduced Patty to the old woman. She smiled at him.

Patty noticed that she had a gold-capped front tooth. She looked friendly enough, so he smiled back.

She talked rapidly to Tim in a mixture of English and Korean that leaned heavily toward the Korean. Tim seemed to understand perfectly, but Patty could only make out a word here and there. When the conversation was over, Patty had no idea what they had talked about. He told Tim this, and again Tim shrugged his shoulders.

Outside, it was raining lightly. The sky was gray and threatening. Tim leaned back against the wall under the overhang. Patty was anxious to get going, and asked Tim what they were waiting for.

"The bus," was Tim's answer.

"They got buses?"

"Of course they got buses. Most of the guys use taxis. I use the bus. If you know where they go, you can save a lot of money. Most of the guys are too lazy to learn how to use the bus system."

Patty thought about it. Tim seemed to know what he was talking about, even though at this particular moment he was dying to get moving. Still, Tim was the authority, and Patty would respect that.

The bus came rumbling down the road before Patty had too much time to think about it. The door opened, and a girl in a blue uniform called out "Inchon" in a whining voice. Tim climbed on, giving the girl some coins he had fished from his pocket.

"How much did you pay?" Patty asked.

"Forty won," Tim replied.

"I'll pay you back when I change my money," Patty vowed.

"Don't bother. Do you know how much forty won is?" Tim

asked, looking at Patty as if he were retarded.

"No," Patty replied.

"About eight cents. I can afford to treat." Tim was smiling.

"How much is a cab?" Patty asked.

"Usually about twelve hundred won, which is almost four dollars. You can get laid for twelve hundred won. I know for a fact that you can get drunk."

The bus swayed with the ruts on the road. It was raining pretty hard by now, and the road was a sea of mud. After about a mile, it turned to pavement. Patty and Tim had taken a seat toward the back.

The bus stopped about every thousand feet or so. At each stop, two or three passengers would board. It only took a short time before the bus was completely full. Still the bus stopped. Patty couldn't believe that any more people could possibly fit in. The mamasan standing next to him in the aisle was pushing against his shoulder. He, in turn, was pressed up against Tim, who was pressed against the window. Patty thought for sure that soon the mamasan would be in his lap.

The bus kept stopping. By this time, the blue-uniformed girl would disembark, and after the last people who wanted to get on were on the steps, she would push against them until the driver could close the door. At times, she actually braced her legs against the door jamb and pressed with her back. Meanwhile, people were rammed together like sardines. It was strange the way the Koreans responded. In fact, they didn't respond at all. By the look on their faces, they could have been in their living rooms watching TV. It was unreal.

Patty could smell the kimchee. It was sickening at first, but after awhile his nose kind of died or just became overpowered. He became immune to it by the time the bus reached the station.

After leaving the bus, Patty noticed that they were now in a city. The buildings around the station were at least ten stories high. Patty hadn't seen anything like a city since he had arrived. He asked Tim what the population of Inchon was. Tim told him that it was about five million.

"How many GI's are stationed here?" Patty asked.

"About two hundred and fifty. There's us, and a detachment of MP's that guard the warehouses," Tim replied. "That's the greatest thing about this place."

Tim proceeded to tell Patty why it was so great. He explained that the Koreans in Inchon thought of the Americans as a curiosity. They received special attention. There, at least, they were considered guests. Other parts of Korea that hosted large contingents of Americans thought of them as a pain in the ass.

Also, Tim explained, the types of Koreans who lived near an American army camp were more than likely dirt bags that made their living off of GI's.

Another great thing about Inchon was that it was a big seaport. That meant sailors. Wherever sailors were, there were red-light districts. Inchon had a great red-light district. The girls there were some of the finest in the country. What was really nice, though, was that the sailors came and went, but the GI's there were a constant. The girls liked to have GI boyfriends to party with when the sailors weren't around. They also liked the fact that the Americans could get them things from the PX and take them to the American movies at ASCOM.

Patty liked to hear this kind of talk. He wished that they would get moving so that he could sample a few of the local women. He told Tim this. Tim told him that he had the rest of his tour here and that he should be a little patient.

Tim led Patty around the station until they came to a large Mercedes-Benz bus. To Patty, it was magnificent compared to the bus they had arrived on. Tim bounded up the steps, and Patty followed.

The bus was extremely comfortable. Not so many passengers got on. It was an express, to boot. They arrived in another city thirty minutes later.

"Where are we now?" Patty asked.

"Bupyung, about ten minutes away from ASCOM."

Tim started walking, and Patty hurried to keep up. It had stopped raining, and the sun was peeking through the clouds. Patty noticed that this city seemed a little different than Inchon. The buildings weren't as tall, and the place seemed a little poorer. Patty wanted to know why they were going to ASCOM to begin with.

"To go to the class-six store and the PX," Tim explained. "Mamasan hasn't seen me for almost a week, and she needs some things."

"Do you mean we came all the way over here so Mamasan could get some things from the PX?" Patty asked incredulously,

"Trust me, newbie," Tim replied. "Didn't I say I'd show you the ropes?"

Patty didn't say any more. He had asked Tim to show him around, and he was doing that. Besides, Patty had nothing better to do, and the sun had come all the way out from behind the clouds and it had turned unseasonably warm. Patty felt cheered. It was a good day.

They came up on the base. Walking through the gates, Patty felt as if he had stepped into another world. It was like a piece of America had been shipped over. There were stretches of green grass and even a football field! They walked past the football field to a large building.

"This is the PX, NCO club, and the class-six store. Not to mention the movie theater. This is going to be your main head-quarters. Be nice to the people here, especially the Koreans; it'll pay off in the long run," Tim said.

As if to make a point, Tim stepped over to the class-six store window. It looked like a bank teller's cage, but instead of cash being the commodity, booze was.

"Hi, Jimmy, long time no see," he said with a salesman's smile on his face.

"Bitaman! Hey how you been? You short?" Jimmy asked.

"I'm so short I have to look up to look down. What you got for me?"

"For you, anything."

"That's my man. How 'bout five bottles of Johnny Walker Black and four cases of Falstaff?"

"You got ration card?'" Jimmy asked, eyeing Patty suspiciously.

"Hey, no sweat. I don't need a ration card, Jimmy. Besides, I've used up all my liquor rations." Tim knew that Jimmy was hesitant to do business with Patty around. "This is my chingo. Patty, meet Jimmy."

They exchanged greetings.

"Jimmy, when I leave, Patty is going to take over. He knows the score, okay?" Jimmy smiled. "You got what I need?"

"Don't I always?"

With that, Tim slipped a folded wad of twenties to Jimmy. "You know what's there. I'll pick up the stuff on my way out," Tim said.

The next stop was the PX. Patty watched as Tim bought a rice cooker and two frying pans. He also purchased four jars of Noxzema and four cartons of Marlboros. When they were finished, they went over to the NCO club.

They sat over in a corner. The club was not very busy. Patty could smell food cooking, and he became hungry. They ordered fried chicken and beer.

Patty was impressed at the way everyone treated Tim. Every Korean he came in contact with seemed to be a close friend. Tim spoke fluent Korean, too. It looked funny to see him sound like a Korean. Patty had no idea what he said to them, but the Koreans seemed to have no trouble understanding. Everybody was all laughs and smiles. Meanwhile, Patty was rapidly getting buzzed on the beer he was drinking.

"Let's cutachoagie," Tim said.

"What is cutachoagie?" Patty asked.

Tim explained that it was a Korean-American slang word. "Choagie" meant "to go" in Korean. Therefore, to "cut a choagie" was a different way to say "let's go." Patty nodded his head. Patty was not sure about this Korean stuff. It all seemed difficult. He told Tim this, but Tim said he'd pick it up in no time.

They took a taxi back, and Patty was relieved. Tim explained that a taxi back was not just a luxury. Getting the stuff back to the village without being followed by Korean CID was easier if they took a taxi. Besides, he told Patty, he wanted to party.

When they reached the village, Mamasan was waiting. They went into the moklee house and made the transaction. Patty couldn't believe how much money she gave Tim. He shoved the money in his pocket, gave Mamasan a little kiss on the cheek, and they left.

They took another bus back to Inchon. Patty started to ask Tim how much he made, but Tim put his finger to his lips. Patty shut up. After a ride exactly like the first trip they had made in the morning, they arrived in Inchon.

As they walked down the sidewalk, Tim explained to Patty the art of black marketeering. The frying pans he bought for nine dollars at the PX sold for sixty dollars on the market. That was a profit of one hundred two dollars.

The rice cooker cost thirty-two dollars in the PX and one hundred on the market. The Johnny Walker was eight dollars a bottle at the class six and thirty when resold. The Noxzema was two dollars and sold for five; the beer was two dollars forty cents a case and sold for ten dollars. The Marlboros were a dollar ninety and sold for eight dollars. All in all, Tim explained, they had made a gross profit of three hundred forty-one dollars and eighty cents. After expenses, they'd netted two hundred eighty-five dollars and forty cents.

"What expenses?" Patty asked.

"The twenty I slipped Jimmy, the twenty I slipped Choe at the PX, the lunch, the beers, and the bus and taxi fares," Tim replied. "I got it down to a fine art. Not a bad morning's work." He smiled and winked at Patty.

"I didn't see you give anything to the girl at the PX," Patty said.

"You weren't supposed to," Tim replied.

"How much Korean money did you get?"

"One hundred thirty thousand five hundred sixty-seven won. That means you get sixty-five thousand two hundred eighty won. Give or take a couple."

"I get? How come I get?" Patty asked.

"Because you went with me. You took a chance same as me. You helped me carry the stuff. You would have been busted right along with me if we got caught. Understand?"

"I guess."

"Don't guess. It's fact. Guessing gets people in trouble. Let's get fucked up," Tim said.

"That's a capital idea!" Patty exclaimed. He was already half drunk.

"No, this is a capital idea," Tim said, as he thrust a huge wad of bills into Patty's jacket pocket.

— Chapter 18 —

Tim took Patty to a teahouse called "The Frog." It wasn't really called The Frog, but it had a picture of a frog on the sign. The rest of the sign had Korean lettering that Patty couldn't understand.

The place was big, and very busy. There were several floors with an open center surrounded by balconies from which you could see all the patrons. Tim was welcomed like a regular, and they were taken to a table upstairs. It was a luxurious place. The people who sat at the tables were all well dressed.

Patty had seen nothing like this since arriving in Korea. After being seated, a pretty girl in a traditional Korean costume came to the table. Tim ordered rapidly in Korean. The girl smiled and nodded, and soon returned with a kettle of tea, and two glasses of something else.

"What's this?" Patty asked.

"Try it and see," Tim said. Noticing that Patty was hesitant, he added, "Trust me."

Patty raised the glass to his lips. It was warm to the touch.

He tilted his head back and let the liquid pour down his throat. It was Scotch. Good Scotch, too. But it was warm, almost hot.

"Chase it with the tea," Tim said.

Patty took in a mouthful of tea. His stomach started to get warm, and then hot. He could feel the blood rush to his head and he began to feel giddy.

"Good, huh?" Tim said, more like a statement than a question.

"God, that's great," Patty said.

"I thought you'd like it," Tim said. He raised his head and drained his glass.

They ordered another, finished it, and ordered another. Soon they both had half a load on. Patty was really relaxed. He was wondering what kind of person was sitting across from him. Back at the unit they had called him burned out, but here in Inchon, and earlier in the village and at ASCOM, he had been dynamic. A real personality. It was like the difference between night and day. Patty wondered what made him tick.

"Why do they call you 'Vitaman Tim?' " Patty asked.

Tim looked at him and smiled. A twinkle was in his eye. "It's like this. One day I was in the Yellow House with one of my girlfriends."

Patty interrupted. "What's the 'Yellow House?' "

"The 'Yellow House,' my friend, is a five-city-block whorehouse not far from here. Sooner or later, maybe sooner than you think, you will visit the Yellow House," he said. "As I was saying," he continued, "I was in the Yellow House with this girl I saw occasionally, and some hits of speed fell out of my pocket as I was taking off my pants. The girl, not realizing, asked me what they were. I didn't want her to find out that I was doing speed, so I told her that they were vitamins. She asked me to write it down on a piece of paper. You see, every time she came across a new word, she made me write it down so she could study it. She was learning how to read English. Anyway, I wrote it down.

"Later on in the day, she asked me how to spell my name. I told her how to spell it. That, too, she asked me to write down, which I did. Later, one of my friends came over to the room to smoke a joint with me. He picked up the paper and read it. 'Vitamin Tim,' he said. He started laughing because I was known to indulge in speed. Well, to make a long story short, he started calling me 'Vitaman' Tim. Some of the guys back at the battery picked it up and started calling me that, too. For awhile they called me 'Vitaman,' but mostly 'Vitaman Tim.' The name has stuck with me ever since. That's it."

"Do you still use speed?" Patty asked.

"Not so much anymore. It burns you out," Tim replied.

"Can you get me some?"

"Sure. Want some?"

"I wouldn't have asked if I didn't," Patty said.

Tim reached into his pocket and pulled out a small envelope. He reached inside and took out three white pills. These he slid across the table toward Patty. "Today I think I'll indulge," Tim said, and proceeded to pull a couple more out. He put them in his mouth, drank a mouthful of tea and swallowed. Patty did the same.

They ordered another drink, and then Tim decided that they had spent enough time at the Frog. It was almost four in the afternoon, and they were both getting hungry. Tim suggested that they go down to the United Seaman's Service downtown, and eat before the speed took their appetites away.

They took another cab. It was only a five-minute drive. Patty was amazed at the size of the city. It was pretty drab, of course: the buildings were all made of concrete stucco, and were mostly gray. The roads were all paved, though, and the city had most of the modern conveniences.

The United Seaman's Service was located in the harbor district. It was a small place with a sign done in English. Inside, it was decorated with a nautical slant. Pictures of merchant ships, buoys and ropes hung on the walls. On the left was a bar. To the right was a dining area. Patty noticed immediately that the two waitresses were stunningly beautiful. The smell coming from the kitchen made Patty's mouth water.

They were led to a small table, and the waitress, obviously flirting with Tim, asked them if they knew what they wanted. Tim ordered a steak with onions and mushrooms, and Patty did the same. They ordered a couple of beers, and shots of whiskey.

Patty was feeling lightheaded. He realized that he was losing his appetite. He began to feel nervous and fidgety and started to sweat. "I think I'm starting to feel the speed," he said to Tim.

"Yeah, me too," Tim replied.

By the time the food arrived, they weren't hungry at all, but they attempted to eat anyway. The waitress came over to the table and wanted to know if there was anything wrong with the food. Tim told her that the food was fine. She told Tim that he should eat more and drink less. She said that he needed a woman to take care of him. Patty could see that she wanted to be that woman. Tim just grunted at her, and she walked away.

"Don't you see that she likes you?" Patty asked.

"Yeah, I know."

"How come you don't ask her out or something?"

"Because she is a good girl. If I wanted to get her into bed,

I'd have to promise to marry her, or at least be her boyfriend," he whispered to Patty.

"So?"

"So, if I hooked up with her, I'd never be able to do shit around here. She knows just about everyone. In fact, the local gangsters around here would break my legs if they found out I was screwing her around. Her brother is the number-one gangster in Inchon."

Patty let it drop. He wished that it was him instead of Tim that she liked. He would be glad to be her boyfriend.

"Do you want me to introduce you to her?" Tim asked.

"Yeah, guess so," Patty said, trying to act nonchalant. Meanwhile, his heart was beating like a jackhammer.

Tim caught her eye and waved her over. She started walking toward the table.

Patty watched her as she moved across the room, sure that he had never seen a girl so lovely. She had a white skirt on that ran a little short, and Patty got a good look at her long, well-formed legs. He noticed how gracefully she moved between the tables as she approached them. His gaze wandered to her chest, and he was surprised to see that she was blessed with firm, ample breasts, which struck him as a little strange for a Korean girl. They seemed to press at the sides of her loose-fitting blouse, which was made of a frilly cotton material. It was her hair that made Patty realize that she wasn't a full-blooded Korean. It was brown, not black, with golden highlights, which suggested that one of her parents had been a blond. As she stood at the side of the table, Patty noticed that her eyes were blue.

Patty was beside himself. He thought he had found an angel.

"Miss Im, I'd like you to meet a friend of mine, Patty Fallica."

Patty, turning scarlet, extended his hand. She took it and

gave a light squeeze. "I pleased to meet you," she said.

"I'm pleased to meet you, too," Patty said, wishing he could think of something witty to say.

"Patty's from New York, like me," Tim said. "He thinks you are beautiful," he added. Patty wanted to sink under the table.

"Thank you, Patty. I think you beautiful too," she said.

Turning toward Tim, she asked him when he was going to go back stateside. Tim told her that he had a couple of weeks left. Miss Im seemed obviously upset by that information, and she turned and walked away toward the kitchen. Patty thought that she was going to cry.

He felt bad for her. He wished that Tim would get up and follow her, but he seemed disinterested in the drama going on before him, of which he played a central character. "I know she likes you, now," Patty said. "If I were you, I'd snatch her up before she knew it."

"Well, you're not me!" Tim said testily.

Patty realized that he had touched a nerve. He was surprised to see that Tim reacted this way. Maybe, he thought, Tim wasn't as emotionally uninvolved as he thought he was.

"Let's cutachoagie," Tim said, leaving money on the table.

They walked out of the door and into the street. Miss Im had not reappeared to say goodbye. A taxi pulled up at the curb as if by magic. Tim waved him away and motioned for Patty to follow him. They walked down the street for a few minutes, turning left into a side street.

Tim led Patty down the side street for a few more minutes. The street eventually joined with a main street and Tim turned onto this. Patty was startled.

The buildings were very well lit. Neon signs blinked out the names of bars: "The Top Hat Club," "The Black Cat," "The OB

Club," and down at the end of the block, "Whiskey Mary's," with the brightest sign of all.

Patty couldn't see any GI's like he did at K-6. It was just getting dark, and the area wasn't really crowded. It seemed kind of quiet and peaceful. They walked up to the bar and entered through swinging-type doors. They reminded Patty of the old westerns.

The inside reminded Patty of the same thing, except instead of cowboys seated around a round table in the corner, there were Koreans. It had an atmosphere. There was a pool table just like the one in the bar he frequented in New York, except instead of the balls dropping into the holes and rolling down toward a collection shelf, they fell into nets.

The people playing cards looked up as Patty and Tim entered the bar. A short Korean with a black leather jacket waved. "Hey, Tim, you wanna pray cards?" he asked.

"Jimmy, how many times I gotta tell you, people don't pray cards, they play cards," Tim quipped.

The Korean laughed. "You pray someday, Tim. Wait, I get rid of these idiots and we talk and drink, okay?"

"That's why I came, Jimmy. Get prenty fucked-up stinko," Tim said with a Korean accent.

They sat by the wall near an old Rock-Ola jukebox. A girl came over and they ordered beer. Patty noticed that Tim was relaxing again. The speed they took made Patty feel a little hyped up, but it didn't have the same effect as the stuff he had taken at home in New York. That was okay with him. He didn't want to get high as a kite; he just wanted to get a little buzz on.

Tim got up and put some Korean coins into the jukebox. Led Zeppelin came through the speakers, telling them that they had a whole lotta love. Patty tapped his fingers and feet in time with the music. Tim walked back to the table.

"I remember when this song first came out," he said. "It drove the lifers crazy. Back in Yoju, all they had were country and western music. I slipped this in the jukebox and turned it up all the way. The bastards didn't know what to make of it. I think it scared them at first, you know, with all them zoomin' sounds and stuff. It was a pisser."

Patty was glad that Tim was talking again. He wanted to party. One thing was certain in Patty's mind: he would never again bring up the subject of Miss Im. It just ruined Tim's conversational ability.

Tim seemed to be on a roll. He told Patty about a time back in Yoju that he and a friend put on Jimi Hendrix's "Star-Spangled Banner." The unit was holding retreat formation in front of the barracks. They turned the sound all the way up, and when the music blared out of the speakers, the first sergeant almost had a heart attack. He yelled toward the barracks to whoever had that "hippyshit" playing to turn it the hell off. Somebody yelled from in the formation that it was the national anthem. The first sergeant, under military regulations, then had to bring the company to attention and to salute. Tim told Patty that he laughed so hard that he fell on the floor. He didn't even get in trouble for it, because they couldn't word the charges right. I mean What the hell, he said, you can't court-martial somebody for playing the national anthem.

Jimmy finished the game and walked over to their table. He was counting money as he walked. He had a big shit-eating grin on his face.

"You never lose, do you, Jimmy?" Tim said.

"Nobody good card prayer like Jimmy," he replied.

"You're not good enough to win all the time. Those guys are

just afraid to beat you. Why don't you save them the trouble of playing cards and just make them give you the money?" Tim teased.

"I not make those people lose," Jimmy said, feigning hurt feelings. "They lose all by themselves."

"Then how come you don't go to the Olympus and play? You could make bigger bucks there," Tim countered.

"They cheat at Olympus!" Jimmy said.

"And I know how you hate cheaters, Jimmy," said Tim.

"I buy drinks." And with that, Jimmy ordered three whiskeys.

Over drinks, Tim introduced Patty to Jimmy. Jimmy was impressed that he came from New York. Jimmy told Patty that he always wanted to go to New York. They had the toughest gangsters in the world there. He asked Patty if he was a gangster stateside.

Patty was about to tell him that he wasn't, but Tim kicked at him under the table, and he caught himself and told Jimmy that, yes, as a matter of fact, he was a gangster.

Jimmy asked him if that was why he had to join the army. Patty told him that he was a very smart man. Yes, he told him. That was the reason. He had to get out of the country for awhile.

"Tim too!" Jimmy exclaimed. "Now heat blow over and Vitaman go back—correct, Vitaman?"

"Correct, Jimmy," Tim said gravely. "Now I can go back and get the gang that killed my brother."

"Tim go and fuck 'em up!" Jimmy said. "Tim numbah hanna gangster."

"Jimmy numbah hanna gangster in Korea!" Tim said. They both raised their drinks to that, and Patty followed suit.

They talked and drank for a few hours. Patty was high, but

not really drunk. Between the excitement and the speed, he seemed to be able to drink like a pro. The conversation was like something out of a comic book. Tim would compliment Jimmy, and Jimmy would compliment Tim. Jimmy was the one who got plastered. He told Tim over and over that he was his numbah one chingo. He told him how if he ever needed anything–and he meant anything–when he got to the States, that all he had to do was write to his friend Jimmy.

Patty was itching to move on. The bar had filled up by now. He recognized some of the guys from the unit. They must have been from another section, though. The girls who were there didn't particularly catch Patty's fancy. He told Tim that he wanted to go somewhere else.

They left the bar and headed out onto the street. It was transformed. People were everywhere. Sin was a big business all over the world, and here in Inchon it was no exception.

The honkytonks were all out to make an impression on the sailors of various nationalities. The neon signs and the music that crept onto the sidewalks beckoned them to come in and let their hair down. Girls walked between the bars in their short miniskirts, brazenly flaunting their wares. It was good to be alive, Patty thought.

Tim flagged down a taxi. Patty wanted to know why they were leaving. He really didn't want to leave, he explained; he just wanted to get out of Whiskey Mary's.

It was after 11 PM. Tim explained to Patty that they had to be off the street before curfew.

"Are we going back to the compound?"

"Were not going back there. The Vitaman doesn't sleep at the compound," Tim said drunkenly.

"Where we going?"

"Sit tight, newbie, you'll see."

The taxi was picking up speed. The lights of the city became a blur through Patty's window. Traffic was fast at this time of night. Drivers were in a hurry to get to their destinations before curfew. Taxis were in more of a hurry than most, trying to get as many fares as possible before business came to an abrupt halt.

This particular taxi driver seemed to be a distant cousin of Mario Andretti, dedicated to the Evel Knievel school of safety. The little Toyota he drove groaned and screeched as it took the corners on two wheels. The driver was like most others in the country: he hadn't the foggiest notion of what that pedal next to the accelerator was. "Stop" was a forbidden word in the Korean driver's manual. In this country, the brakes were replaced by the horn. It was common custom to honk your way out of an accident.

Patty was not amused. He gripped the back of the seat and peered over the driver's shoulder with his eyes wide open in horror. A couple of times he tried to scream as the taxi would pass another vehicle on a blind corner, but no sound would clear his fear-constricted throat. A few times, he managed to slap the back of the seat repeatedly as different threats loomed in the windshield.

As hysterical as Patty was, Tim was just the opposite. He was stretched out with his head back, lolling from side to side, as the taxi took the turns.

Just as Patty was nearing hysteria, they came to a screeching halt in front of a group of what looked like apartment buildings. Tim paid the driver. Patty opened the door and stepped out on wobbly legs. Tim came around the taxi and motioned to Patty to follow.

They walked down a nondescript alleyway that cut through the center of the complex. As they walked, Patty saw that each building had a large picture window in front. Inside, he saw to his surprise that all of the rooms contained between three to fifteen girls, all dressed in either lingerie or evening clothes. As Patty stopped and stared at one of the windows, the girls giggled and blew kisses. A few beckoned him inside. He turned to look at Tim, who wore a wide grin.

"Pick one," he said.

Chapter 19

Patty looked at the girls. The more aggressive ones were also the ugliest. He looked past them and saw a girl sitting along the side of the wall with her make-up case in front of her. She seemed oblivious to the goings-on with the two Americans.

Tim was busy talking to a well-built older woman. They joked around like they knew each other. Patty couldn't make out what they were saying because they were speaking in Korean. Patty broke into the conversation and asked Tim how he could get the girl's attention. Tim said something to the woman he was with. A minute later, Patty was following the younger girl up the stairs to the second floor.

The corridors were narrow, with small doors that opened up to small one room apartments. It seemed that this building was built to be exactly what it was: a whorehouse. The girl stopped in front of one of the doors and slipped a key into a small padlock. She opened the door and motioned Patty inside.

Fallica wasn't shy at this point; the booze had lowered his inhibitions, and he was extremely aroused. She motioned him to the bed, and Patty sat down at the edge with his hands in his lap. The girl squatted in front of an old record player and put on an album. The sounds of Sam and Dave singing "Soul Man" filled the small room.

Patty looked around and saw that basically all the room contained was a small stereo and a bed. There were a few pictures of people cut out from magazines. A few he recognized, but most were Orientals. Elvis Presley was there. He saw a young Elizabeth Taylor. The rest were unknown to him. He took a good look at the girl who was now sitting cross-legged on the bed. She was young. Patty couldn't believe she was out of her teens. She had looked so much older sitting in the room with the other girls. Her expression was one of embarrassment and curiosity. Patty suddenly wanted to leave. He felt as if he was using this girl. He felt like the typical "Ugly American." "You speak English?" he asked.

She smiled and shook her head. Patty rubbed his hand over his face and looked at the floor. She looked at him, her expression now one of concern. "Cinchana," she said.

Patty looked up at her. She was on her knees now, looking down at him. He thought she was going to cry. Patty was on the edge of panic. He felt so uncomfortable, so out of place. He didn't have any idea of what he was doing there. He wanted to find Tim and get back to the compound.

The girl raised a finger and quickly left the room. Patty figured that she meant she'd be right back. He looked at his watch. It was almost one AM. It felt like an hour, but five minutes later the girl returned. Another girl was with her. This one was older, and frankly, Patty thought, she looked like a slut.

The new girl looked at Patty and giggled. Patty got irritated. Now he was embarrassed. He had no idea of what he was supposed to do. He felt like a monkey in a cage with these two girls looking at him. They both started talking to each other in Korean, sprinkled with excited giggles. Patty felt that they were laughing at him, and flushed.

The older girl stopped babbling and turned to Patty. "You no likee girl?" she asked.

Patty was speechless. He had no idea of what to say. He just looked at her with a blank expression on his face.

"You no likee, I stay with you," she told Patty.

Patty took a good look at her. She was a little overweight, and seemed just a little drunk. Her make-up looked like it had been applied with a trowel, and her eyes were bloodshot and red. Still, Patty thought, her breasts were bigger than any he had seen since arriving in this country. The girl saw where he was looking and slid across the floor toward him. She reached up and pulled Patty's face toward her. She whispered in his ear. "You likee big tits, Cherry Boy?"

Patty was shocked. In spite of the situation, he could feel himself getting aroused. He wanted this big-breasted girl. He wanted her, but he didn't want to offend the younger girl. The situation was unreal. Patty started to believe that he had entered the twilight zone.

The young girl said something to Miss Big-Tits. She didn't look happy; in fact, she looked downright angry. Big-Tits said something back to her, and that didn't sound like happy talk, either. Patty suddenly thought that there was going to be a fight. Words Patty couldn't understand picked up in tempo and volume. The fat one looked like a witch now. She definitely did not look like anyone Patty wanted to sleep with. The other one, though, looked absolutely beautiful. Her color was up and her back was straight.

She looked almost regal. In contrast to the older girl's high-pitched screams, she spoke firmly and seemed to measure her words. Even though Patty had no idea of what they were saying, he could tell that the older girl was being outclassed by the younger.

Just at the moment that Patty thought one of them would take a swing, the door opened and an old lady walked in. The two girls stopped their argument immediately. The chubby girl bowed her head and looked at the floor, while the younger girl stared at her, eyes still blazing. Mamasan said a few words in Korean, and the chubby girl left. Patty imagined himself watching a play. He couldn't understand the words, but he could figure out just what went on. He felt completely detached from the situation until Mamasan spoke to him. "You want new girl?" she asked.

"No," Patty said.

"How come you got problem?"

"I don't know what to say to her," Patty replied.

"You no have to talkee. You boom-boom. You know boom-boom?" And, with the question, she made an obscene gesture with her hands. Patty was mortified. He looked over at the girl and he could see that she was, too. Her face was even redder than it had been during the argument.

The old lady looked at the both of them, and an understanding smile appeared on her face. "You first-time sleep with Korean girl?" she asked gently.

"Yes," Patty lied. Well, it was almost the truth, because he couldn't remember anything of the first time. He didn't even know if he had done anything.

"This funny. This taksan funny," she said.

"What's so funny?" Patty asked. He didn't think it was so

funny.

"It funny because you cherry boy. It more funny because she cherry girl. Cherry boy and cherry girl go to boom-boom together. You cannot speakee to her, she cannot speakee to you. Nobody know how to say hello, nobody know how to boom-boom." She was laughing now.

Still laughing, she turned her head and spoke to the girl. The girl listened, and a smile turned into small giggles at what the old lady was telling her. Soon, both were wiping tears out of their eyes. Patty realized exactly what he had gotten himself into and started to laugh, too. The tension eased out of his body and he finally found himself comfortable in the presence of these two Korean ladies.

The old lady said something to the girl, and the girl left. Patty was hoping that she would be back soon. He was a little afraid that Mamasan would try to put some moves on him. Mamasan had no such intention, though, and Patty's fears were short-lived. "Her name is Miss Lee. First name hard for you. You call her Yobo. 'Yobo' mean 'darling' in Korean. She bring tea for her. Whiskey for you. You drink tea, and then you takee drink whiskey. She takee off clothes, you takee off clothes. Go to bed. That's it. Oddaso."

"Oddaso," Patty replied.

"What's your name, Cherry Boy?"

"Patty."

The girl returned with a small teapot and a bottle of Four Roses. She took a shot glass out of her pocket and poured Patty a drink. She put it on the floor in front of him. She also poured a cup of tea for him and a cup for herself. Mamasan quietly left the room, closing the door behind her.

The girl reached up and ran a finger across Patty's cheek.

"Epa," she said.

"I don't understand."

"Moolah?" she asked.

"Moolah," Patty replied.

She reached down and took Patty's hand. She took his finger and ran it across his cheek. "Epa," she said. She took his finger and ran it across her own cheek. "Epa-ni?" she asked.

Patty looked at her. She looked so pretty.

She ran Patty's hand across her cheek again. "Epa-ni?"

Patty ran his fingers along her cheek and down her neck. "Epa-ni," he said.

She smiled. He smiled. They drank tea. Patty felt not the least bit self-conscious anymore. They drank tea, and Patty tossed back the whiskey. Two or three times he tossed back the whiskey. He felt the warmth in his stomach and the warmth of the room. Suddenly he felt very relaxed. Relaxed and sleepy.

The girl stood and pulled back the cover of the bed. She started to disrobe, and Patty did the same. One thing troubled Patty, though; he had to take a leak. He didn't know how to ask her where the bathroom was.

Miss Lee got into the bed and motioned for Patty to lie down. He knew that once in the bed he would have to pee even more. He was drunk enough to ask her. "I got to take a leak," he said.

"Moolah," she replied.

He started to get frustrated. He looked at her and tried again. "I got to pee," he said.

"Pee? Moolah."

Patty knew he was going to have to try another way. He reached down to his crotch and made a hissing sound. She understood. The girl got up and reached under the bed. She pulled a small pot out from under it. She pushed it toward him.

Patty looked down at the pot. He couldn't believe what she was asking him to do. It was bad enough pissing in the latrine with somebody using the urinal next to you; this was impossible. He couldn't piss into this thing with her standing next to him. "No way!" he said.

"Moolah," she replied.

"I said no way. I can't do this. You've got to have a bathroom somewhere; I'd rather piss in the street."

The girl looked at him. She got up and put on a robe. She slid a pair of rubber slippers that looked like canoes to him and she beckoned him to the door. Patty followed.

They walked down the hall and she pointed at a door. Patty went inside and saw, to his relief, a commode in the corner. He used it and left. She was gone. He walked back toward the room.

Patty made a left when he should have made a right. He walked down to the third door and opened it. The room was empty. He realized that he had made a mistake: this didn't look like her room at all. He walked back from where he had come.

As he passed the stairwell, a girl came into the hall. She was tall with long black hair and a red miniskirt. She had a white blouse on that was unbuttoned in front. Her breasts jiggled as she walked. As she passed Patty, she gave him a lewd look and patted his ass. Patty almost turned and followed her. She went into the room he had mistakenly thought was his. Next time, he thought.

He passed the latrine and counted down three doors. He opened the door and saw that he was in the right room. The girl was in the bed. Patty hurriedly took off his shirt and pants and slid into the bed next to her. She was asleep. He thought of waking her but didn't have the heart. He also thought of going down the hallway and knocking on a particular door three doors from the latrine, but he didn't have the nerve. He thought about it awhile and drifted off to sleep.

— Chapter 20 —

Patty was dreaming. Peter was teaching Wendy how to crow. He was on a rock below her, and Wendy was up on a small cliff above. It was almost like the play, except Wendy was Korean. Peter looked like Vitaman Tim. Patty opened his eyes and realized where he was.

The window above the bed told him it wasn't very late in the morning. The sun was hardly illuminating the dawn. A rooster crowed from somewhere out in the distance, causing him to dream of Peter Pan. Patty wondered where they kept roosters in a crowded city.

The girl was sleeping next to him with her head on his shoulder. His arm was around her shoulder. Patty moved his fingers, and realized that his entire arm was asleep. He gently removed it and she stirred, turned over away from him and continued sleeping.

Patty flexed his arm. Pins and needles told him that the circulation was coming back. He looked at the girl.

The blanket was just covering her hips. Her shoulders and

back were bare. Long black hair was spread across the sheets and over her arm. Patty pulled the blanket up and pulled her close.

He could feel her warmth against him. He reached down under the blanket and felt how full and smooth her buttocks were. Full, smooth and warm. He quickly became aroused. He felt himself grow against her. He moved his hands under the blankets and cupped her breast. He sought her nipple and gently rubbed it between his fingers. It grew hard.

Patty's other hand stroked her side. He thought he felt her shiver as he traced the outline of her thigh ever so lightly with the tips of his fingers. He got bolder as his passion increased. His hand slowly moved over her soft, fleshy thighs and traveled between her legs. He gently stroked and probed. He moved his fingers and found that she was wet. As he slowly explored her, he felt her tremble and heard her breathing become deeper and faster. His hand took the cue, and it too became deeper and faster. He kissed her neck, and his other hand became more possessive of her breast. She turned and locked her arms around him.

As the rooster crowed in the distance, they shared each other's bodies. Twice they made love with not a word passing between them. Patty wanted this to go on forever, but a knock on the door and Tim's voice telling him that they had better get to the compound told him that this particular adventure was at its end. Reality was something that came at dawn, and it looked like Vitaman Tim.

— Chapter 21 —

Tim was inside the taxi by the time Patty came out of the building.
He looked terrible. His face was lined and swollen, he had horrific bags under his eyes, and his hair looked like something on a drowned rat. In fact, if Patty didn't know who it was, he would never have guessed. "Didn't sleep at all," Tim said wearily.

"How are you going to work today?"

"Same way I always go to work, kemo sabe. I takum party cure." With that, Tim said something to the cab driver. Patty was starting to realize that almost every conversation started with "Yobosayo." He didn't know exactly what it meant, but he gathered that it meant something like "Hey, you."

The cab driver stopped in front of what looked like a drug store. Tim jumped out of the cab and told Patty to wait. Patty started to feel the effects of drugging and drinking all night. He probably looked as bad as Tim. Patty wished he hadn't indulged quite so heavily. Tim came back to the cab a few minutes later with a small bag. He opened it and showed Patty the contents.

Inside the bag were four small bottles of what looked like rough syrup. The labels were in English. They said TUSSU-PRIN-C. Patty reached into the bag and pulled one out. "This is cough syrup!" Patty exclaimed. "What the fuck are we going to do with cough syrup?"

"Look, kid, trust me. This stuff is fifty percent codeine. It'll cure what ails ya. Drink these down with the first bottle."

Tim handed Patty three white pills. Patty looked at them. All they said was CIBA. "What are these?"

"Doriden. Goes good with the codeine. You'll feel mellow as a Jell-O. Take my word for it. You'll pull the most contented set of dailies you ever pulled."

Patty started to unscrew the cap on his bottle. Tim stopped him. "Don't take it now. Wait until we get to the village. That way it'll start on you just when you get to the shower. Great rush."

Patty looked out of the window while Tim closed his eyes. As the taxi left Inchon, the scenery grew worse. Between Inchon and the missile battery, the taxi passed an industrial area. Patty looked at the buildings. The whole area seemed gray. A cold fog seemed to wrap itself around the structures. This is gloomy, Patty thought.

Looking out the window, Patty felt his spirits being crushed. He wished that he could be back in the States. He wished that he could be in his own kitchen, drinking hot coffee while the friendly sun threw light on the clean, even streets of Long Island. He didn't want to be in this place. More than ever before, it felt foreign and hostile.

He saw people moving out on the streets in their layers of clothing. They seemed to move as if in their own depressions. Puffs of vapor came out of their mouths and noses as they walked. Old people walked with a stoop, and young men hurried past them. Patty noticed that there were very few women out and about this early in the morning.

"Makes you wish you were back in the World, doesn't it?" Tim said. Patty looked over at Tim, who was awake now and seemed to be studying him. Patty suddenly felt waves of depression slide over him. He had a hard time trying not to let Tim see it. He swallowed, and he could feel the constriction in his throat.

"Don't let it get you down, partner. You're going through cultural shock. It'll pass. The speed you took last night isn't helping you feel any better, either. You'll be all right," Tim said gently.

"I'll be all right." Patty said.

"Yeah, you'll be fine," Tim said.

The taxi started down the dirt road that led to the battery. Tim grabbed a bottle out of the bag, opened the top, popped three pills in his mouth and chugged the syrup down. Patty did the same, except that as he took a giant pull on the liquid, he started to feel like he would vomit. He resisted the urge to puke all over the cab and managed to get it down. He wiped his mouth with the back of his hand.

"You forgot to finish your medicine," Tim said.

Patty looked at the bottle. It was only a little more than half empty. He took a deep breath and gulped the rest. He was surprised to find that the second half of the bottle didn't taste so bad. In fact, he didn't find the taste half bad at all. His belly warmed as the liquid made its way down. "This stuff isn't so bad," Patty said, and he grabbed another bottle out of the bag.

"Don't drink another one," Tim warned. "You'll get fucked up. Besides, you'll need it for a pickup later on in the morning."

The cab stopped at the gate. Tim paid and they walked up the hill toward the barracks. Patty cursed under his breath as they walked. He didn't like mountain climbing so early in the morning. Why couldn't the army find a nice piece of flat land to put the battery on?

Patty undressed and headed toward the latrine. He wished he could have just stretched out on his bunk for a few hours. Damn that curfew. It didn't leave you a choice, he thought; you had to be back at midnight, or you had to stay out all night.

The latrine was, as usual, a crowded, boisterous place for so early in the morning. The showers sent out bales of steam. He hung his towel up and walked into the shower room. It felt good to have the hot water splash onto his skin. He washed the night off his body and felt the warmth of the water penetrate into his muscles. It felt great. Patty realized that he really did feel great. It was amazing that he could feel like this with all the drugs and booze and just a few hours' sleep.

Suddenly he felt a rush, and remembered the pills and the cough medicine. His head was light, and the sound of the water seemed far away. He walked out of the shower, grabbed his towel and headed toward the sinks. It felt as if he were walking on air. Somebody said Hi, but when he glanced up to see who it was, the guy was already in the shower. Patty felt as if he were moving in slow motion.

Shaving was a bitch. He could hardly feel his face. He didn't mind the cuts, though; in fact, they were kind of interesting. It was neat how the rivulets of blood kind of crisscrossed each other. Other guys came and went at the sinks next to him, but Patty kept on shaving. This was the closest shave he had ever had.

Brushing his teeth took some time. Everything took some

time. It wasn't long before he realized that he was the only one left in the latrine. He grabbed his towel and skipped off to the barracks.

The guys were already dressed and headed out to the porch to smoke their morning bowl. Patty let his houseboy dress him. "Wassa matter you?" asked Kim.

"Wassa matta me? Wassa matta you?" Patty asked, laughing.

The houseboy just shook his head. He put Patty's boots on. He was ready for work.

The steps leading down to the mess hall didn't seem as long as usual. The cold nip in the air actually felt good this morning. Patty thought that this was a great day to be alive. He opened the door to the mess hall and the smell of bacon and eggs made him think of Sundays back on Long Island. He looked over at the food and decided that he wasn't really hungry. He walked over to the coffee pot and poured himself a cup.

Everybody in the mess hall looked so friendly this morning. He wanted to stop at each table and tell the people sitting there how much he enjoyed their company.

This was a great place, Patty thought. This was just a great day to be alive. He walked over to the IFC table and sat down. A few of the guys had come down early and were surprised to see this new guy with this shit-eating grin sit down next to them. Patty nodded hello to each one individually. They just looked up and stared.

"How you doin,' Fallica?" asked Staff Sergeant Brown.

Patty was glad he had somebody to talk to. He felt like talking. He wanted to let his new section chief in on the prior evening's events. He wanted him to know just how happy and pleased he really was. It came out in a long giggle.

Everybody just looked at him. Drool started to run down

his chin. Patty's eyes seemed a little cockeyed. He realized that they were staring. He felt the drool run down onto his hand. He looked down at it. He must look like a jerk, he thought. He started to giggle more.

"Did you have a good night, Fallica?" Brown asked. "You must of had a good night. You're sure having a good morning, or do you always drool at breakfast?"

Vitaman Tim stepped up to the table with his breakfast tray in his hands. He looked at Patty and immediately knew what was going on.

Brown looked up at Tim. "Do you have something to do with this?" Brown asked.

"As a matter of fact, Sarge, I do," Tim told Brown. "I was just coming over here to inform you that I believe Fallica is the victim of some Korean hanky-panky."

"Hanky-panky!" Fallica repeated.

"Hanky-panky?" Wagner said.

"You got it," Tim said gravely, "hanky-panky."

"You do the hanky-panky and you turn you turn yourself around, that's what it's all about," Fallica mumbled, and started into another fit of laughter.

Brown frowned. Other men in the mess hall started looking over at the table.

Trying to avoid any more attention, Brown asked Tim to take Fallica up to the barracks and to try to straighten him out.

Tim told Patty to follow him outside. Patty did just that. Once outside, Tim gave Patty three hits of speed. "Take these: they'll straighten you out."

"I feel great!" Patty protested.

"You're not going to feel too great if you can't get to work. You're completely fucked up," Tim said.

Patty popped the pills into his mouth. Tim walked up the stairs to the barracks. Patty followed. When they arrived at the barracks door, Tim started back down.

"Where you goin'?" Patty asked.

"Back to the mess hall. Come on."

Patty followed back down. As they arrived at the mess hall door, Tim turned and started walking toward the stairs leading back up to the barracks.

"Where are you going now?" Patty whined.

"Back to the barracks; I forgot something."

"I'll wait here," Patty said.

"No, come with me. I hate to walk by myself."

Patty followed Tim back up the stairs. At the top, Tim stopped and looked at Patty. "How do you feel?" he asked.

"Okay. How do you feel?"

"Like a babysitter," Tim said tiredly.

"Did I make an ass out of myself down there?"

"Yeah."

"Am I in trouble?" Patty asked. He had a worried look on his face.

"Not if you are straight enough to go to work."

"I can make it to work," Patty said.

"Good. That's good. You see, Patty, it really doesn't matter what you do over here, as long as you can get to work. Understand?"

"No sweat, GI. I can make it. Thanks." Tim could see by the embarrassed look on Patty's face that he did understand. They both trudged off to work.

— **Chapter 22** —

The guys were cutting Z's in the ready room. Patty had pulled his tour of guard duty and was in the rack adding to the assorted snores and muttering of sleeping men. He was dreaming he was home in New York. He was driving with Gayle in his dream. They were heading down Main Street in his brand-new car. In his dream he heard a siren. He looked into his rear view mirror and saw a police car. Damn he thought, you can't get any peace anymore. The cop had pulled him over and was shaking him. He kept screaming at the cop to leave him alone. He opened his eyes and saw Rope standing over the bed.

"Get up, man! Crew drill. Drop your cock and grab your socks!" Rope screamed.

Patty threw off the blanket and reached for his boots. The siren was screaming in his head. Damn, he thought, another goddamn crew drill! Why can't they let us alone? Even though Patty had only been in country less than a month, this seemed like his hundredth crew drill. He shoved the laces into his boot and ran toward the corridor.

The crew was all there. As he ran into the radar control van and donned his headset, he heard the tracking supervisor report tracking station present, and heard the battery control officer roger his report. He started on his checks.

All the checks came from rote. He was hardly aware of what he was doing. It seemed like only minutes later when he shut the cabinet doors and seated himself in the center chair of the three-man radar console. He fired up the B scope that showed him a quadrant of the larger acquisition radar that was in the next van. The tracking supervisor took the missile tracking operator's ready-for-action report, and reported to the BCO that the tracking station was ready for action. The BCO rogered that, and Patty listened in as the launching area reported.

Everyone was ready for action, Patty thought. He prepared for the command of "Blazing Skies!"—the simulated command for battle stations. All dressed up and nowhere to go, Patty thought. He heard the BCO click his headset, and he unconsciously fingered the toggle switch that would automatically slew his radar to the same place the acquisition radar operators and the BCO were looking at. The light above him clanged red, and the BCO reported, "Red status, battle stations!"

Patty's finger moved on the toggle switch as soon as the designate buzzer sounded. He was stunned. "Battle stations." There had to be a mistake. The BCO meant "Blazing Skies." He turned and looked at the track sup. Tim looked at him. His teeth were showing, and sweat dripped off his forehead. Battle stations it is, thought Patty.

The B scope showed them what the BCO was looking at. Patty noticed that the azimuth was north. He grabbed an overlay and slipped it over the scope. He could see the north-south border. On the south side he saw two or three targets.

The north side had about two hundred! The trails on the blips showed that they were heading south. Patty felt his intestines crawl up into his stomach. "Holy shit!" he said.

"Un-key your headset!" Tim said.

"Keep it together!" The BCO roared.

They slewed onto a target. The elevation operator searched, and the target popped into the gate. The range slewed onto the target and they locked it up.

"Locked on one AC inbound, 75K. Negative ECM," Tim reported.

Patty looked at the target. Suddenly the scopes got fuzzy and looked almost like a bad TV.

"ECM condition two, BCO," Tim reported.

They had a difficult time tracking. They went to manual tracking mode and managed to hold on. Patty could see on the B scope that there were now almost as many targets in the south as there were in the north. They were heading north.

The targets in the north were heading south.

"Track sup!"

"Track sup."

"Give us range and azimuth."

Tim reported range and azimuth once every thirty seconds. The border was getting closer and closer. Sweat coming off Patty's scalp made the headset itch against his ear.

The van was deathly quiet. The usual banter was absent. The B scope showed the two opposing forces getting closer to each other. Tim continued to give reports. Azimuth continued steady and range decreased. It would be less than a minute before they were over the border.

Patty noticed that his error line started to move. He turned his azimuth to keep it straight. Tim reported the azimuth change. Looking over at the B scope, they noticed that all the aircraft in the north were turning. The ECM that blurred their scopes abruptly stopped. Range started to increase as they changed direction northward. The aircraft coming up from the south started an orbiting pattern near the DMZ.

"Stand down to Blue Status!" The BCO ordered with relief in his voice.

"Blue Status received, Track Station," Tim said, also with a sigh of relief.

"Jesus," said Patty, "what the fuck was that?"

"That was the way the mother fuckers up north see if we are on our toes. It's also a good way to make us spend a lot of money sending up all those airplanes," Tim replied with a note of disgust.

"What would have happened if we didn't respond in time?" asked Phillips.

"That's anybody's guess. All I know is that I hope that I have my ass back home when that happens. You newbies will have to take that responsibility. Let's do post-firing checks and get out of here sometime tonight." Tim sounded tired.

The crew went about its business. From outward appearances, it seemed like any other night, but this night seemed a little different to Patty. He knew he did his checks with a little more attention to the small details. He also noticed that the others were not rushing through their checks, either. After tonight he would think a little differently.

This was not a game like he thought it was. This was for real. It was real for him, for the other guys on the crew, and for the pilots in those aircraft.

Everyone else was sleeping, not knowing what was happening in the cold black sky above Korea. He knew, though, and that was enough for him. There was a reason to be here. Whatever the North Koreans wanted to achieve out of this little exercise, all they accomplished was to make the men on the south side of the thirty-second parallel believe. Believe that they had an enemy to the north.

When Patty left the van to collimate his radar, the sun was making its way over the mountaintops. The horizon was a brilliant shade of red. He remembered a poem that his mother used to recite to him:

"Red sky at night, sailor's delight.

Red sky at morning, sailor's warning."

Patty looked over to the north. Less than fifty kilometers away was the DMZ. He wondered if a North Korean soldier was doing the same thing or something similar to what he was doing. He figured probably so.

By the time checks were complete, the other crew was already on the hill. They would perform another set of checks. Yesterday it seemed stupid to pull the same checks twice. Today it didn't seem stupid at all.

The section chiefs briefed each other while both crews listened in. When the briefing was over, Patty walked out of the corridor and climbed up the tailgate of the deuce and a half. He was grateful to see the light of this day.

— Chapter 23 —

The next few weeks passed by quickly. Tim was really short. He taught Patty a great deal. Patty was only in country a little more than a month and a half, and he already knew the black market prices for almost everything in the PX, what drug store clerks spoke enough English to know what he was talking about, and how to use the bus system to go just about anywhere he wanted.

Patty also learned a lot of Korean. Besides the language, he learned a great deal about the people and their customs. Tim was a great teacher, and he never tired of explaining things.

Miss Im also took Patty under her wing. She called him "brother." She introduced him to her cousins in Inchon, and a few that lived in Seoul. Patty enjoyed the excursions with her. Tim refused to go, telling Patty that he didn't want to forge any more ties than he already had with her. When he told Patty this, he seemed sad somehow. Patty thought for the second time that there was more to this story than met the eye.

The day Tim was supposed to DEROS rapidly approached.

Patty convinced the other guys on the crew to throw a party for Tim at the NCO club the night before he left. They protested at first, but reluctantly agreed. The biggest obstacle to having the party was that nobody except Patty really knew him. He won the argument by reminding each and every one of them how Tim had shared his knowledge of the system with them all, at one time or another. SSG Brown readily agreed with this assessment.

It was to be a surprise party. The crew was in charge of the details, and Patty was tasked with inviting the Koreans that Tim would want to come. Patty was also given the responsibility of making sure Tim showed at the right time. Patty accepted this assignment.

The day of Tim's party found Patty and Tim at the Frog. Tim was remembering all the guys he had served with and all the good times. He was getting pretty drunk.

Patty noticed that Tim didn't mention the World at all. Normally, somebody on his last day in country would be thinking about home, but not Tim. Patty had the feeling that he really didn't want to leave.

It was about seven PM, and Patty put his plan to get Tim back to the compound in effect. He told Tim he wasn't feeling well. Tim seemed concerned, but Patty knew it wasn't enough to get Tim back. That's when Patty told Tim he was feeling faint. Tim watched Patty slump over in his chair and fall on the floor. It wasn't long before Tim had Patty in a taxi, and they were both headed toward the compound.

Patty noticed that Tim seemed preoccupied. Patty surmised that Tim didn't really want to go home. After all, what was home to Tim? For the last four years he had called this place home. This was where his friends were, this was where his world was, and here he was a king. Back home he would be just another guy. Patty couldn't imagine Tim being just another guy. Everyone over here thought of him as something of a legend.

The taxi pulled up to the gate, and they weaved toward the club. Patty asked Tim if he would go in and have a farewell drink with him.

"I thought you were sick," Tim said.

"I am," Patty replied. "I thought a little food might make me feel better."

Tim looked at Patty with a hint of understanding on his face. "You dipshit," he said. "You got me here for a goddamn party. Don't you know I party alone?"

"Just this once, Tim. Come on," Patty pleaded.

"All right, asshole. Just this once."

They walked toward the club entrance and Tim walked in. Over Tim's shoulder, Patty could see everyone. There were just as many Koreans as there were Americans. The guys from the hill had two tables by the bar. Jimmy the gangster was leaning against the jukebox. Miss Pak, the black-market mamasan, was there. So were a couple of waitresses from the Frog.

Tim scanned each and every face, and gave them all an almost imperceptible nod. He stopped at every person almost as if he were committing them to memory. Which, Patty thought, he probably was. Tim continued to check every face. Some he waved to, some people got a nod.

Everyone seemed to want to be acknowledged. Tim was an institution, and he was leaving. It seemed to be the end of an era. Toward the back of the room was a girl. Tim's eyes fell on her. She waved, and a look of infinite sadness showed on her beautiful face. Tim looked away. It was too much for him to bear.

Someone launched into a version of "For He's a Jolly Good Fellow," and the entire club followed suit. After the song, a few guys yelled for a speech. Everyone quieted down and all eyes went to Tim. He was out of his element. Panic seemed to grip him, but Patty saw him shake it off and get his emotions under control.

"I want to thank everyone for coming to this party. I'm not used to being the center of attention. I just want to tell you all that I'm going to miss each and every one of you." Tim looked over at the first sergeant and scowled, "Well, not all of you." Everybody laughed.

"These have been the best days of my life. I know a lot of you guys count the days until you go home. I used to count the days I had left. I wish I were staying, but I can't. Now I'm so short I got to look up to look down. Let's do it one more time, bartender."

The crowd went crazy. You'd have thought General McArthur had delivered his farewell speech. Even the battery commander was standing and clapping. He was short, too. His party would be at the BOQ with four or five officers and the same amount of senior NCO's. It would be a nice quiet party for a nice quiet guy.

The party broke up sometime after midnight. Patty looked around for Tim, but he was nowhere to be found. In fact, Patty reflected, he hadn't seen him for awhile. Patty had faith that he'd show: Tim could take care of himself.

Patty hoped that Tim hadn't headed off for Kimpo alone. That would mean he wouldn't see him again, and it would also mean he couldn't go with him to Kimpo. SSG Brown had given Patty the day off as long as he was back by six-hour checks.

He didn't want to miss that time off.

Patty staggered up the stairs toward the barracks. The guys were pretty much asleep when he walked in. Looking over at the door to Tim's room, he saw the padlock secure on the hasp. Tim hadn't come back here; that was certain. Patty crawled into his bunk and didn't think for the rest of the night.

Kim the houseboy shook Patty's bunk. He was concerned that Patty hadn't gone to work. The barracks were empty, his crew having left for the hill and the other crew still on the way down or in the mess hall. Looking at his alarm clock, Patty saw that it was after seven. Tim had better get up here soon, or they were really going to be stretching it. His flight left at one, and he was supposed to be there at least an hour before.

Patty dressed and showered and headed for the mess hall. The other crew was there. They wanted to know how the party was. Patty told them, and they all felt bad because they had missed it. That was the way it was when you worked twenty-four on and twenty-four off. The other crew might well have not existed. The only thing his crew shared with the other crew was the equipment.

Breakfast was over, and Patty still had no idea where Tim was. It was after eight now, and he was getting worried. He got up and headed for the gate, not knowing where he would look for Tim, but anything was better than sitting around. He was approaching the gate when a kimchee cab screamed around the corner and slid to a halt with its nose just grazing the chain-link. Tim stepped out, obviously in a hurry.

Patty was relieved to see him. He ran up to the taxi and noticed that Tim had a girl in the back seat. Typical, he thought: right up to the end he was running true to form. Patty dismissed the girl from his mind and accompanied Tim to the barracks to get his things.

They returned a few minutes later with two suitcases. The driver got out and put the suitcases in the trunk. Patty got into the front passenger seat and Tim got into the back. They were heading down the village street at a brisk pace when Patty turned around to talk to Tim. He got the shock of his life.

Sitting beside Tim was Miss Im! She was nestled into Tim and holding his hand. Patty must have looked surprised, and Tim just smiled and shrugged his shoulders. "I saved the best for last," Tim told Patty.

"I'm jealous. Jealous and glad at the same time," Patty said.

Their destination arrived all too soon. Miss Im and Patty escorted Tim to the terminal. Miss Im kissed Tim and cried. Patty felt a lump in his throat. He tried to say goodbye, but Tim stopped him. "Friends don't say goodbye," Tim told Patty.

"Then what the fuck do they say?" Patty asked.

" 'I'll see you later,' " he said.

"Yeah, 'see you later,' " said Patty.

Tim turned and walked toward the boarding area. Patty watched him as his figure got smaller. Tim suddenly turned around and yelled to him, but Patty couldn't make out what he said. He turned to Miss Im and asked her if she'd heard what he'd said. She nodded her head Yes.

"Well, what did he say?"

"He say don't fuck everything up for him."

"What the hell does that mean?" he said.

"That mean he come back," she said simply.

Chapter 24

Fred came back from the village early. He was hungry for some-thing other than fermented cabbage. If he was lucky, they would serve mystery meat on the hill and there would be lots of leftovers. He crawled under the fence and made his way to the ready room. He had arrived right on time. Mystery meat it was, and everyone was glad to give him their portions.

There were more people on the hill than usual tonight. The new battery commander and the fat first sergeant were up there. Fred didn't like either. The first sergeant smelled bad to Fred. He wanted to bite him, but the fat bastard always kept his distance. The new BC was mean-looking, and Fred figured that he kicked.

It was best to know what he was like, so Fred went over to where he was eating, and sat down and just looked at him. He was ignored. Fred didn't like to be ignored. In fact, this asshole was lucky to be on this hill. After all, it was Fred's hill. He had been here longer than any of them. He growled at the intruder.

The battery commander jumped. He looked at Fred. Fred

looked back at the battery commander. Stalemate.

"Don't be alarmed, sir; Fred just wants some of your meat," SSG Brown said to diffuse the situation.

"I don't give a shit what he wants, Sergeant. That mutt growls at me again and I'll have him thrown off the hill," the BC said testily.

Rope came over and grabbed Fred by his collar and dragged him out of the ready room. Fred looked at the BC all the way out.

"You really should try to make friends with him, sir," Phillips said. "He's really a good dog. He keeps us company on guard duty and he doesn't let any slickie boys in."

"Real fine, son. That's real fine. Just understand something, soldier: when I want your opinion, I'll ask for it. Meanwhile, that fuckin' dog is up here on probation. One more fuck-up like he just pulled, and he's out of here." The captain went back to eating his food.

Rope whispered to Patty, "That bastard don't want to share his mystery meat with Fred. I guess he don't know it'll get you sick."

Patty laughed.

"What's so funny, Fallica?" asked the first sergeant. "Want to share it with us? Are you telling New Yawk jokes or something?"

"No, First Sergeant; heard this one in Texas. It was so stupid we laughed."

The first sergeant turned beet red. He was from Texas. "You're a wise-ass, son. Do you know what happens to wise-asses?" he asked.

"Yes, First Sergeant," Patty answered. "They put them on a godforsaken hill in the middle of Korea."

"It could be worse," the first sergeant said between gritted teeth.

"Yeah, Patty, you could be sleeping with Mrs. Marshal in El Paso," Rope whispered in Patty's ear.

Patty choked. He ran out of the ready room and spit his food out on the sidewalk. Fred came over and ate it. After regaining his composure, he returned to the ready room, cleaned his tray and walked out to the guard shack.

Murphy was out there. He was stoned again. Patty wondered if Murph really gave a shit about anything. He asked him if he did. Murph said he didn't. Patty rolled a joint and smoked it with Murphy. He waited awhile until the smell went away, and went into the corridor for six-hour checks.

It was cold out. Cold and windy. Fred couldn't go into the ready room, and he didn't want to go into the corridor because of the four-hundred-cycle noise the vans put out. It hurt his ears. Fred just decided to lie down on the sidewalk.

The battery commander walked out of the ready room and headed toward Fred. Fred was lying on the sidewalk directly in front of the steps leading to the corridor. The BC would have to step over him if he wanted to get into the corridor. He did just that.

Fred bit him. On the ankle, just above the boot. Hard. Hard enough to make the BC scream. By the time the crew came out to see what the commotion was all about, the commander was lying on the ground with his foot in the air, and Fred was gone.

"What happened?" asked SSG Brown.

"That fucking Fred bit me!" the BC cried.

"Are you sure it was Fred?" Phillips asked.

"Shut up, you imbecile!" said the battery commander as he

got up and limped towards his jeep. "Drive me to the aid station!"

The first sergeant hopped in the jeep, gunned the engine, and headed down the hill. "Fred's in trouble," SSG Brown said.

Later that evening, the medic called the hill to report that the BC had to have three stitches. It would have been worse, but the largest part of the bite got the top of his boot. They needed Fred down at the aid station so they could test him for rabies. If they couldn't find him, Captain Williston would have to have a painful series of rabies shots.

Fred was nowhere to be found. It was almost as if he knew he was a fugitive. He just disappeared. The captain disappeared for awhile, too. He went to the hospital in ASCOM to get a painful series of rabies shots. The guys on the hill just assumed that Fred got off on the wrong foot with the captain.

— Chapter 25 —

It wasn't long after Fred bit the captain when Murph had his problem. It was well known that Murphy liked the ladies. Any ladies. Fat, skinny, pretty or ugly, old or young: Murphy liked them all. They seemed to like Murphy, too. Patty had seen from going out with Murphy that he knew every whorehouse or blowjob palace in the area. The girls knew him, too. They would actually fight over whose bed he would sleep in. Patty asked Murph what the secret of his success was, and Murph would invariably grab his crotch.

Murphy was grabbing his crotch again in the shower. Patty and he were the only guys showering, and Murphy walked over to Patty with his dick in his hand.

"Murph, I don't want to see your dick," Patty said with annoyance.

"What a minute, I want you to check something out," he said.

Patty was ready to come down on Murphy, but he caught the concern in Murphy's voice. That was really odd, because

Murphy was never concerned about anything. Still, Patty decided to act cautiously. "Okay, Murph, I'll bite—but you better be serious. What's wrong?"

"It's my pecker. I got something wrong with it. I noticed a sore on it a couple of weeks ago, and I ignored it. Now it won't go away, and it's getting worse. I'm worried."

Patty looked at Murphy; he looked scared. "Let me see," Patty said.

Murphy showed Patty his pecker.

"I don't see anything," Patty said.

"Look," Murphy said, and he turned it over and showed Patty the underside. There, Patty saw a chancre sore the size of a dime. It really looked terrible. He tried not to, but he made a sound of disgust anyway. "Jesus, Murph! That looks like shit! If you don't get that fixed, your dick is going to rot right off!" Patty exclaimed.

"Oh, shit! I knew it! My dick's gonna fall off. I knew it, I just knew it. I'm gonna kill myself." Murphy was serious.

"What a minute, Murph. Don't do anything rash. You probably got the syph. If you get to the hospital, they'll be able to clear it up. But you gotta go." Patty tried to be reassuring, but he knew that Murphy wouldn't do anything if he thought the consequences would be anything less than having his dick fall off.

"Yeah, okay, I'll go tomorrow and get it checked out," Murphy said nervously.

"Yeah, you better do that. Who'd you get it from, anyway?" Patty wanted to know who was carrying syphilis.

"Beats me," Murphy replied.

"Who did you bang lately?"

"About twenty or thirty girls in the last month. How do I

know who gave it to me?" he said. "Do you think I got the Black Syph? Do you think they'll put me on that island off the coast of Japan for the rest of my life? Oh God, Patty! I don't want to go there! I swear to God, if they don't put me there I'll promise to never fuck anyone again! I'll swear to God, I really will!"

Patty could see that Murph was about to come unglued. "Murph, that's a rumor. That story about that island is bullshit! They can cure you if you just get to the hospital." He added, "If you don't go, though, it'll kill you sooner or later."

"I'll go. I'll go tomorrow. I promise."

All that day on the hill, Murphy was quiet and moody. As far as Patty could tell, Murphy didn't mention his problem to anyone else. After chow, Murphy volunteered to take Big O's guard duty. Nobody thought anything about it; Murph liked it out in the guard shack. Usually, that was where the party was at night anyway. It was no different this evening.

Half the crew crowded around the space heater. If pot were plentiful, the usual custom was to throw a fistful on top of the cherry-red space heater and just breathe. That's what everyone was doing. Breathing pot and telling stories.

Sometimes the stories could get interesting. They ranged from confessions of past sins to stories of the supernatural. Some of the tales revolved around Foxtrot. Some were about women. Most were entertaining. Still, more often than not, most were pure bullshit.

Reeger was telling a story about how he caught his old girl-friend cheating on him. Everyone was engrossed in this inti-mate tale of betrayal. Patty was leaning against the guard-shack door, hanging on every word that Rope said. The story was about to climax when Murphy tapped Patty on the shoulder.

Patty turned around and saw Murphy peering intently out of the guard-shack window.

"Here, take these and my weapon, and let me out the gate," he whispered to Patty, handing him the keys to the gate and his M-16.

Patty did what he was told. Nobody really noticed them leaving the guard shack.

It was cold, dark, and windy on the hill tonight. The only light on the hill was coming from the mercury lamps that ringed the perimeter. In reality, they were tactically useless because they only lit up the inside of the fence. The guys used to laugh and say that the enemy could see in, but they couldn't see out. A whole battalion of North Koreans could be outside, and nobody would see them on a moonless night.

Patty took the padlock on the gate and slipped the key into it. He slowly opened the gate, and Murphy slipped outside as soon as the space was wide enough for his body to clear. He turned and put his finger to his lips, signaling Patty to be silent. All Patty could think of was, what the fuck was Murphy up to?

Murphy slithered around the perimeter to Patty's left, in a crouch. Patty could barely make him out in the darkness. The only light illuminating him came from the few stars that weren't covered by clouds. He saw Murphy look down at one of the bunkers, coming up at it from the rear. Patty was surprised to see Murphy suddenly take a flying leap into the sandbagged foxhole.

Patty had no idea what was happening. All he knew was that Murphy had to have a reason to do what he did. Instinctively, he brought the rifle down from his shoulder and locked a round into the chamber. He pointed it at the bunker and saw Murphy come up to view through the sights. But it wasn't just Murphy.

Somebody was there with him–and Murph had him around the throat with one arm, and was forcing one of the person's arms into a hammerlock with the other.

"I got you covered, Murph!" Patty yelled.

"Don't shoot me, asshole!" Murphy yelled. "I got him!"

The guys came out of the guard shack to see what the yelling was about. They saw Murphy bring his prisoner through the gate.

"What you got, Murph?" Wagner yelled from the guard shack.

"I got me a spy!" Murph yelled back.

The guys swarmed around Murphy. The man from the bunker was dressed in camouflage fatigues and had a pair of binoculars around his neck. "Better get the duty officer," Patty said.

The duty officer, Lieutenant Moore, came out and told Murphy and Patty to bring the man to the ready room. They frisked him there, and found a pad and a pencil, but that was all–no wallet, no ID. The duty officer called the battery commander, who in turn called the MP's from ASCOM.

The MP's from ASCOM turned out to be CID, who in turn brought along their Korean counterparts. They exchanged no pleasantries with the guys on the hill, instead going directly to the ready room and forbidding entrance to anyone while they interrogated the prisoner.

Patty and Rope decided that they would peek through the windows of the Quonset hut and see what was going on. Standing on a box, Patty peeked through the corner of the Plexiglass window, and had full view of the sleeping area.

They had the Korean in a chair with his hands bound behind him. A Korean CID man would ask him something in Korean. The prisoner would just look straight ahead in silence.

The CID man would then strike him along the side of the head, knocking him to the floor. This continued a couple of times until Patty decided that he'd seen enough.

Rope climbed up on the box and took his turn at the window. He, too, didn't stay up there long. They both headed back to the guard shack, where the rest of the crew waited for their report.

The CID people used the ready room for about two hours. They left with the prisoner, and the crew started six-hour checks on the equipment. The XO called to report that the man had been identified as a North Korean, and they believed he was an intelligence officer. The guys congratulated Murphy on capturing him, but Murphy didn't seem to care one way or the other. To him, it might just as well have happened last year.

The rest of the evening was uneventful. Morning came, checks were pulled again, and they went down the mountain after briefing the other crew about what had happened.

The guys were pretty much silent about the spy they had caught. Patty couldn't believe the brutality he had witnessed in the ready room. The other guys had seen the man's face when he came out, and it wasn't a pretty sight. They didn't talk about it much.

Murphy actually went on sick call. Reeger went with him for moral support, and came back just before lunch and told the crew that Murphy had gotten admitted to the hospital. Everyone decided to go up there and pay him a visit. They could also eat dinner in the NCO club there and use the Class Six store.

They took the bus to the Inchon bus station and got on another bus to Bupyung. The Bupyung bus was an express. It had white linen on the seats and a stewardess. The windows were large and clean. In reality, it was pure luxury. As they rode, Patty looked at the countryside. It was close to winter outside, and the rice paddies were brown and frozen. Smoke came from the small chimneys of each hootch, and the land looked very peaceful.

The bus dropped them off at the ASCOM gates. They were soon at the hospital.

Patty was amazed that the other guys didn't know how to use the buses. They had wanted to take cabs out of Inchon, which, to Patty, was a complete waste of money. Patty realized that he had become a kind of guide for them. That was interesting, because he was the newest in country. Tim had taught him a lot.

The hospital was old, left over from the war. There was a newer hospital in Yongsan, and this place was slated for demolition soon, but it was still in use.

They had Murphy in the hospital bay. He looked all alone in the center. The bay was made for perhaps twenty-five patients, but today there were only three or four. They walked over to Murphy's bed and he turned and smiled.

"How ya doin,' Murph?" asked Wagner.

"Great, Kool. They're really takin' good care of me here. They said I'd be out of here in a couple of days," Murphy said happily.

"What's in the IV?" Big O asked, pointing to the bag hanging at Murphy's left.

"Pure penicillin. High-test. Gotta take it for awhile. They said I had one of the worst cases of syph they ever saw," Murphy said proudly.

"Lucky they didn't cut it off," Patty said.

"Yeah, right," Murphy said with relief. "Check this out." He threw back the blanket and showed them his pecker. It was covered with bandages wrapped from top to bottom like a wounded snake. On top, the bandage was tied off in a bow. "See, guys, one of the nurses put a bow in it for me. Looks great, don't it?"

"Yeah, Murph, now you got the fanciest dick in Korea," Rope said. Everyone laughed.

Just at that moment, someone yelled "At ease!" from the entrance of the bay. They all turned and looked. Down the center of the aisle came General Emerson and an assortment of aides, and people with cameras following behind like baby ducks following their mother. "Which one of you men is Murphy!" the general bellowed.

"I am, sir!" Murphy yelled.

General Emerson walked over to the side of Murphy's bed. "So you are the soldier who captured the North Korean spy last night?" It was more like a statement than a question.

"Yes, sir," Murphy answered.

"Fine job, son. Real fine job. We need more dedicated men like you. You are certainly a credit to us all. I can only hope that the other men in my command can follow your shining example." With that, he extended his hand to Murphy. "I want to shake your hand, son, and congratulate you for a job well done!"

Murphy had been cradling his injured pecker with the bow on it with his right hand, and so he reached out for the general's hand with his left. Halfway there, he realized that he was reaching out with the wrong hand, and brought his left hand to his family jewels and reached out again with his right. The general seemed a little flustered by Murphy drawing his hand back the first time, but recovered, and was now pumping Murphy's outstretched hand and smiling at the camera.

The photographer snapped a few pictures of the general and Murphy shaking hands. The general continued to pump Murphy's hand as he turned his face toward him. "By the way, son, what are you in here for?" he asked casually.

"Syphilis," Murphy answered simply.

The General finally looked down and saw Murphy's bow-wrapped pecker. He must have realized at that point why Murphy had switched hands at the beginning of the handshake. He quickly dropped Murphy's right hand as if it were radioactive.

The entire crew and all the people who had come in with the general looked at the floor. Patty felt himself trying to stifle a laugh that started from the center of his guts. He couldn't look at any of the others, afraid that he wouldn't be able to control himself if he saw even the slightest hint of a smile. Thankfully, the general turned on his heels and quickly walked down the center of the bay and out the door. Everyone broke into laughter. Soon they all had laughed themselves to tears.

" 'Real fine, son, real fine. You certainly are a great example to the rest of the men in Korea,' " Phillips mocked.

"A fuckin' shining example!" Rope screamed through laughter.

"Yeah, we really should have more like you!" Wagner added.

Murphy was neither embarrassed nor ashamed–he was hysterical.

— Chapter 26 —

Fred was a fugitive, and he knew it. Nobody could understand how a dog could know such a thing, but Fred knew. He was no longer seen around the admin area. The only time the crew saw Fred was after dark, on the hill, when he would slither under the fence and come looking for handouts. He even looked like a fugitive. His eyes were bloodshot and he was dirty. He looked exhausted. He was a dog on the run.

Captain Williston had posters all over the compound. They were simple and to the point. He wanted Fred, dead or alive. He even offered a reward of a three-day pass and one hundred dollars. So far, two dead dogs had been brought to him by the guys from the launching area, but they weren't Fred, and the BC wanted Fred.

The crews up on the hill wouldn't turn Fred in. Some of them pleaded with the captain to grant him a pardon, but he wouldn't. He was determined to see the dog dead. He even took to wearing a forty-five, vowing that he would shoot Fred on sight. Looking at the captain's face made you believe him.

He wanted to see that canine's corpse.

This entertained the guys on the hill. It made for great conversation. Wagner wanted to turn him in. He saw it as a way to get rid of Fred and his pecker tracks. The others told him that they would never forgive him if he turned him in. Patty wanted to find another dog who looked like Fred and give him to the BC, but the others thought that it wouldn't work because the BC would see Fred sooner or later and figure it out.

Phillips wanted to take Fred to Delta Battery and let him stay there until the heat was off. They had thought that this was a good idea, and they had even made a phone call to the IFC section over there. Arrangements had been made, and the plan was about to be executed, when Rope had found out, by overhearing the captain at the club, that the BC over at Delta was one of his best friends.

Murphy had come back from the hospital. The experience hadn't changed him. He had a project he was working on in the maintenance shed that he wouldn't let anyone know about. Murphy was always into something.

Patty had been put in for promotion. He was now a qualified tracking supervisor, and SSG Brown thought that he deserved to be a sergeant. He still had to go to K-6 and stand in front of a promotion board, and he was looking forward to it.

Christmas came to the hill. It wasn't much different from other days, except that the mess hall sent up turkey loaf, cranberry sauce and stuffing. The army played Christmas carols on Armed Forces Korean Network. The North Koreans played race-to-the-border again. Foxtrot won. The other crew had a pretty good dinner in the mess hall, and they had a USO show. The Red Cross donut dollies were supposed to come up on the hill and play games with the crew, but they never made it.

It snowed a little, but not much. The other crew went to see the BC to try to get a pardon for Fred, but he didn't seem to be in the Christmas spirit. The next day was no longer Christmas, and Patty was relieved. He had gotten homesick, and a little depressed.

Three days later it snowed a lot. The hill looked almost like the Alps in The Sound of Music. Looking at the mountain from a distance, it was hard to believe that in reality it was a craggy mess of rocks and boulders. The sides looked smooth and soft with their two-foot covering of snow.

Murphy was excited this morning. For two weeks, he had been busy at work in the maintenance shed with his "project." He told everyone on the way up the mountain that it was done, and that they would all get to see it after dailies.

The deuce and a half couldn't make it up the hill that morning. The dirt road was too choked with snow. Halfway up the hill, the crew dismounted and finished the trip up by foot. By the time they reached the top, they were exhausted. The departing crew bitched and moaned at the prospect of walking down the mountain.

Meanwhile, while the grumbling crew was getting ready to begin their trek down, Murphy, Wagner, Rope and Big O were on top of a small cliff overlooking the nearest turn from the guard shack. At their feet were piles of snowballs. They crouched down in the snow until the departing crew was directly below them, and let loose with a flurry of hard-packed balls. The crew below didn't have a chance. The attackers kept up the volley until the last member of the other crew was out of sight. Then, laughing at their victory, they proceeded up the hill.

When the checks were called into battalion as complete,

Murphy took off for the maintenance shed. The others followed soon after. Murphy was waiting for them at the door. He motioned for them to come in.

In the middle of the floor, elevated by two handmade wooden horses, was what could only be a toboggan, complete with ropes tied to both sides. It was about six feet long and curled in the front. "What do you think?" asked Murphy.

"It's fantastic!" Rope exclaimed.

"Yeah, it's great," Phillips said. "When do we get to try it?"

"Right now!" And with that, Murphy motioned to the others to give him a hand.

"Wait a minute," Wagner said. "Where do you think you're going to ride that thing?"

"Down the hill, where do you think?"

"Our hill?" Patty asked.

"Of course," Murphy said.

"You'll get killed," Wagner said.

The rest of the crew looked at Wagner. Murphy let go of the toboggan and walked over in front of him and put his hands on his hips in a defiant stance. "Since when did you turn into a candy-assed pussy?" he asked Wagner.

"Don't be an asshole, Murph. This hill is full of rocks and boulders from the top all the way to the bottom. You don't even know if you can steer that thing," Wagner stated.

"Bullshit," Murphy said. "I designed that thing. It'll steer. Trust me."

"Trust you?" Patty said. "I wouldn't trust you with shit, let alone my life!"

"Fuck you, dickhead," Murphy said to Patty.

"Fuck you, Murph, I'm with Fallica," Wagner told Murphy.

"Who's going with me?" Murphy asked the rest of the crew.

The rest of the guys looked at each other. Phillips said he would. So did Rope, Big O and Carson. They didn't talk after that; they just walked over to the toboggan and carried it out the door.

"They're gonna get killed," Wagner said under his breath.

"Better them than us," Patty said.

The men pulled the toboggan through the gate and toward the north slope of the mountain. Patty and Wagner followed. The area below looked smooth enough, but under the snow were small gullies and boulders. There seemed to be a path that looked almost navigable, if the thing would steer well enough. Patty thought that they just might pull this off. He almost wanted to join them, but the thing was only large enough for four.

"You know, Patty, they just might pull this off," Wagner said.

"I was thinking the same thing," Patty replied. "Maybe next trip we can do it."

The men were all sitting on the toboggan. Murphy was in the front, then Reeger, then Rope, and at the end was Carson. Murphy had the ropes in his hands as if he were holding the reins of a horse. He had the look of a madman on his face. The others, sitting behind him, looked like small boys putting their hands in a cookie jar.

Murphy didn't hesitate long. He shouted "Push!" and they pushed out with their legs. Patty had to admit, it looked pretty impressive. They actually looked like they knew what they were doing. The toboggan took off like a shot, heading down the hill at a breakneck pace. Patty and Wagner watched as it headed toward destiny.

The route they were on looked straight enough, but the toboggan was starting to drift right. Murphy started pulling on the ropes, but it didn't seem to matter. They heard him yell "Lean to the left!" but that didn't work either.

A huge boulder stood in their path. "Jump!" Murphy yelled. It was too late. The boulder refused to jump. The toboggan hit with such force that it catapulted the men off like Raggedy Anns being shot out of a cannon.

Murphy was the first to leave, and also the first to land. It was Carson who took the longest trip. Sitting all the way in the back, he shot at least twenty feet. It was very impressive. He actually flew over the others. Carson, the human rocket.

Looking down the slope, Wagner and Patty saw the carnage below them. For a brief moment, it looked like a battlefield. The guys were spread out on the snow, crumpled up in crazy positions, as if they were all hit by a well-placed mortar round.

Rope was the first up. Murph and Big O managed to lift their heads. Carson didn't move. Rope ran over to Carson. "Call the medic!" he screamed up to Wagner and Patty.

They ran into the corridor and called the medic. He came, picked Carson up in the ambulance, and disappeared with him off to ASCOM. SSG Brown was pissed. They had lost Carson for at least two months. The call from ASCOM revealed that he had suffered a compound fracture in his right leg.

Chapter 27

Winter in Korea was difficult. The cold, biting wind made time spent outside very unpleasant. The evenings were spent at work, either in the guard shack in small groups of two or three, or in the ready room, watching twenty-year-old reruns on AFKN TV.

Two games were popular on the hill. Spades, played with partners, was definitely the major time-killer. The guys on the hill had their own way of playing. They had their own way of cheating, too. Code words were the favorite way of letting your partner know what you had in your hand. The guys had their favorite partners, and it was tough to separate them. This type of cheating was acceptable, because everyone on the hill did it. Open cheating was deplored. The arguments usually ended up with the offending party admitting, in a good natured way, that they were wrong. It was a very rare thing for an argument to become heated during a card game.

The other game was different. More fights broke out on the hill from playing Risk than for any other reason. The guys who were regulars in the game were treacherous. The beginning of the game went quickly; weaker players were eliminated in the first hour, as a rule. Usually five or six men would start the game, two would soon be eliminated, and the remaining four would play until dawn.

Risk was a game of world military strategy. It was acceptable for treaties and alliances to be made. This is what caused the arguments. When a player would get too strong, the other players would gang up on him to make sure he was removed as a threat. Sometimes the play would be logical. If everyone was playing to win, you could predict who was going to be attacked, and when. But this was Foxtrot Battery in Korea, and nothing here was really logical. Resentments from days or weeks before could be resolved on the playing board. Sometimes treaties were made or broken with no regard to logic.

The most common complaint was that the person breaking a treaty did not give the other person a one- or two-turn notice that the treaty was over. Surprise attacks occurred constantly. The person on the receiving end of the attack would be outraged; it never failed to provoke moral indignation. The most famous line was "How could you do this to me? We were supposed to be allies!"

This tickled Patty. He couldn't believe how naive some of the guys could be. They actually believed that they could trust each other. Patty never forgot that this was a war game, and that all that mattered was who was left at the end. He loved breaking treaties. He loved looking into a face that had been betrayed, and hearing the whining complaints. He loved getting the confidence of somebody and ripping it apart when it suited him. All of Patty's aggressions came out in Risk.

There was one man on the hill who Patty feared. He was a

shade slicker than Patty was. This man could act completely innocently and gain the trust of all the other players. He would play like he really didn't give a shit who won or lost. This man acted as if he were just playing to kill time. He would remind everyone of how untrustworthy Patty was; and how, on numerous occasions, Patty would turn on anyone and everyone. It drove Patty crazy when the others would not realize that this person did exactly the same thing! His tactics were not as good as Patty's, but his manipulation of people were. He was Patty's mortal enemy on the gaming table. His name was Wagner.

Patty always knew what Wagner was up to. His basic strategy was to stay away from him during the game. Wagner did the same with Patty. They were always circling each other, watching and waiting. They made treaties with everyone but each other. The game, more often than not, turned into a six-hour battle of wits between the two men. The other players usually acted as pawns, and the most amazing thing about that was that they never even knew it. All they knew was that it was always Wagner or Patty who won. After the game, the two would talk about the things that had happened during the game. To Patty, it was the best part of playing Risk.

Wagner and Patty were partners at Spades. They had not lost a game since they teamed up with each other. It was getting increasingly difficult to get anyone to play with them. All the other guys knew that they cheated, but nobody could figure out how.

The pair ran the crew. SSG Brown knew this, too. No major decision was made without Brown explaining things to Wagner and Patty. The only crew member who didn't go along with everything they proposed was Murphy: he decided everything on his own. Brown would want something done, and the crew was made to think it was their own idea by Wagner and Patty. It was a marvelous way of getting things done with little or no resentments. This made the crew on the hill one big happy family.

The other crew was different. They were generally older, and the camaraderie wasn't the same. The section chief was SSG Dixon. He was a hard-bitten southerner who believed in authoritarian rule. He was six foot three inches tall, and he had a size twelve boot. He never tired of telling people that he could very easily put that boot up somebody's ass. Because of this, he was known as "Paddlefoot." He hated the nickname.

Paddlefoot's crew was much more experienced on the equipment, but they acted more like individuals than like a team. The older men on the crew had huge egos and were hard to take. It was common for a new man to ask for a transfer to Brown's crew. No one could blame them. Brown's crew was more fun.

The crew stayed pretty much together on their off days as well. The mornings were usually spent in bed. Patty never slept. He would go to the village while the others were sleeping and see Mamasan. If he weren't black marketing that day, he would be at the drugstore making his weekly purchases or visiting Miss Im. The only other crew member awake in the morning was Murphy. Patty always wondered where he went, but he never pried. He didn't want anyone prying into his life, either.

Patty led almost two lives off duty. His daytime life was full of wheeling and dealing but, unlike his tutor, he enjoyed the company of the crew in the evenings. He would show up at the compound at around four in the afternoon, and meet up with everyone at the NCO club. He never ate anything but breakfast in the mess hall. He claimed that the food gave him the shits.

The evening would start either at the Frog or the Seaman's

Service in Inchon. If they didn't eat at the NCO club, they would eat at the Seaman's Service. By six or seven they would all have a buzz on. The rest of the evening was usually spent in Inchon at one of the clubs.

Patty enjoyed going to the Olympus and getting a steam bath and a massage. For ten bucks, he would spend thirty minutes in the steam bath, and thirty minutes on a table having his body kneaded by a young masseuse. Sometimes he could convince her to give him some head, or at least a hand job. It always invigorated him, and he liked the feeling of being fresh and clean when he began the evening.

The time spent at the clubs was always fun. The crew could tell whether or not they would spend the night there before they left the hill. If there was a lot of traffic in the harbor, they knew that the girls would be busy with the sailors.

As said before, Inchon was a seaport, and the red-light district catered to sailors. The girls loved the GI's, but the sailors paid a lot more. A sailor would think nothing of dropping a hundred bucks on a girl, but the GI's would never pay more than ten. It was a matter of simple economics.

Although the girls would rather sleep with sailors, they liked the Americans better. Inchon had almost no American presence, unlike many other Korean cities. The only Americans stationed at Inchon were a small detachment of MP's who did customs work, and Foxtrot Battery. This was nice, because the Korean people in Inchon didn't feel overrun by drunken GIs. It was great for the soldiers, because the Koreans treated them well and the city retained its national flavor. The bars were not set up to fawn on Americans, as they were in the towns outside military bases. The police were real Korean police instead of MP's. In Inchon, they tended to look the other way if some of the men acted out—as long as they weren't hurting anyone.

The girls also liked the Americans because they were there all the time. It was common for a soldier to have a girlfriend who worked in the bars. During the day, he would spend time with her at her place, or they would go out sightseeing. During the evening, she would see sailors, unless none were in port. In that event, her GI boyfriend would go home with her and spend the night for free.

The arrangements worked out well. The girls would not only appreciate the Americans for the things they brought them from the PX; they also liked going to the Seaman's Club for dinner, or to the movies at ASCOM, or some of the places Americans went to that a Korean girl who worked the bars of Inchon could never expect to see.

Patty had a girlfriend in Inchon. Her name was Lydia. She was a big-boned girl who drank too much. Patty thought she was a lot of fun. She also knew how to read and write English. Lydia had a college degree in psychology. She told Patty that she could make more money as a hooker. Patty liked her for her intelligence; he also liked her because she had a great body. She didn't have the typical slight oriental body; she was stacked. Lydia was tall, too, with great hips and a firm, round ass. The girl stood five seven and weighed in at one hundred thirty-five. She was great in the sack, too. Patty learned a great deal from Lydia.

It hadn't been easy for Patty. He knew a fair amount about sex, but the knowledge had all been gained from books and magazines. The little he knew first-hand was all basic stuff.

Spending time with Lydia was an education in itself. The first time he had met her was at the Top Hat Club. Unlike the Top Hat Club at E-6, this club was your basic whiskey bar with a small pool table. Patty had been hot that night, beating sailors of varying nationalities. He hadn't particularly cared when Lydia had started playing until she leaned over the table to take her shot, and her ample breasts caught Patty's attention.

It had been awhile since he had seen breasts like Lydia's. Korean girls were not noted for their mammary development. In the drugged and drunken state Patty was in, he took this basic loin-stirring lust as love. He started a conversation with her and they drank bourbon for the rest of the evening.

She was taken with Patty, too. She liked his way of talking, and his youth. They found themselves touching each other before they left the bar. She invited him over to her house. This was a surprise to Patty, not because he ended up going home with her, but because he hadn't propositioned her first. They walked up two flights of stairs and entered the apartment.

The place was a mess by Korean standards. It didn't look at all like a Korean apartment. The first thing Patty noticed was that Lydia didn't take off her shoes when she went in. The second thing he noticed, besides the unkempt appearance of the place, was that it had regular chairs and a sofa in the living room, and on the floor, instead of the usual wood or linoleum, was a rug. Lydia led Patty into the bedroom, and he was again surprised to see a Victorian-style four-poster bed, complete with a frilled canopy. If he didn't know better, the apartment could be in England, not Inchon, Korea.

As far as Lydia's lovemaking skills went, they were direct and to the point. When she was drunk, all conversation stopped as soon as the first kiss took place. She was like a machine. Even her eyes glazed over and became almost vacant. Orgasms were not an issue for her. She clearly lost herself in sex. Attempts at any type of intimacy other than the physical kind were completely rejected. This would go on until early morning, when she would pass out from sheer sexual exertion. Even a sexually naive person, such as Patty was, could understand why she was attracted to him. He knew that it wasn't his looks or intelligence that mattered to her; it was his youth and sexual stamina, pure and simple.

Patty awoke the first morning feeling very aroused. He was in a dreamlike stupor and feeling some very strong sensations in his private area. He opened his eyes and saw that Lydia's head made a small hill in the blanket above his crotch. He smiled to himself. She never stops, he thought.

Slowly, Patty lifted the blanket to get a look at the ministrations she was employing. Sure enough, she was using her mouth in a way that Patty thought she used it best. This erotic scene turned Patty on immensely. He watched her as she went about her gentle sucking. It reminded Patty of an infant with its thumb in its mouth. That's when Patty realized that Lydia was fast asleep. Fast asleep with him in her mouth. He felt like a pacifier.

That didn't stop Patty from enjoying it, though. He started getting close to climaxing, and this woke Lydia up. She didn't let up, though, and Patty, for the first time, let someone know what he tasted like.

After it was over, he wanted to disappear. He didn't realize, or couldn't realize, that this girl knew exactly what she was doing. He felt like a pervert, and even after he went back to the compound and went to work, the feeling stayed with him. It was strong, this feeling of perversity, but not strong enough to stop him from running back to her the very next day he was off.

The things she showed him didn't end with that. He learned

things such as how to employ beads, ice, hot oils and other in-animate objects in lovemaking. Every time he would leave her, he would come back to the compound with the same feeling of self-loathing. This went on for most of the winter. He didn't dare tell anyone about it; he was too embarrassed. He felt like a whore. Lydia's whore. He was being corrupted, and he knew it. Still, he couldn't stop. He was addicted.

He finally told SSG Brown about it. Brown was very, very, interested. He not only asked Patty for details, but he also want-ed to know who this girl was, and where she lived. Later on, Lydia told Patty that SSG Brown had offered her fifty dollars to spend the night with her, and that she refused him. Patty knew this was true, because Brown admitted as much when Patty confronted him. He told Patty that she was just a hot ticket, and that he shouldn't worry about what they were doing. He told him something about consenting adults and how it per-tained to sex. Patty felt enormously relieved, but she refused to see him again. He had a big mouth, she said. He was crushed.

She stayed away from him for almost a month. He would go down to Inchon and linger in the same clubs that she fre-quented. It would kill him to see her walk off with a sailor. She never failed to wink or smile at him as she left. He wanted to beg, but he couldn't bring himself to do that. He thought she was being a real bitch, which she was.

Patty was surprised to notice that not only did he miss the sex they had, he also missed her company. They had a lot of fun drinking and playing pool. She had a good sense of humor, and he missed it. He was also surprised to find out that she would not go home with a GI. Sometimes he wished that she would, so that he could find out if she did the same things in bed that she did with him.

Patty found himself at Whiskey Mary's during a snowstorm. He wasn't paying much attention to the weather, finding drinking and bullshitting with Jimmy more interesting. By the time Patty decided to leave, no taxis were running; the snow on the roads was just too bad to permit travel.

Jimmy called one of the girls over. She looked good to Patty, and he decided to spend the night with her. They went to her place, which was not far from the bar. They were just settling down to business when the door burst open. Lydia stormed in, shoes on, no coat, with her hair down around her face. She went over to the girl, lifted her up, and literally threw her out of the bed. She told Patty to get dressed. He did and they left. Patty followed her through the storm, feeling like an errant schoolboy.

When they got to her place, she simply told Patty that girls in Inchon were off limits to him, if he didn't want his dick cut off. She didn't say anything about ignoring him; she just took him to bed and made love to him. He felt like a hostage, but he didn't mind. He was happy again.

— Chapter 28 —

Winter turned to spring. You could tell that the season was changing–not by the weather, but by the smell of the honey pots being brought to the rice paddies. The administration area and the IFC hill didn't get much of the aroma, but the launching area did. The guys used to say that any pilot could tell if one of the missiles was close to his aircraft by smell alone.

Patty went to the promotion board at K-6. He'd had his uniform refitted by the tailor at the compound, and SSG Brown helped him set up the promotions-board appointment. He helped him study for the board, too. Patty relearned his drill and ceremonies and first aid, and studied things they might ask him about his job.

The night Patty got to K-6, the night before he saw the board, he went out and got drunk. He again hooked up with his old friend Mr. Kim, but this time he didn't lose his pants to a slickie girl.

He did wake up late and with a hangover, however. A super hangover. He looked at his watch and saw that it was nine fifteen. He was supposed to be at the board at nine hundred hours. He jumped out of bed and ran toward the latrine with his shaving kit in hand. He shaved and ran a comb through his hair.

He didn't notice that he had cut himself shaving, and blood ran down the side of his neck. He put his uniform shirt on and succeeded in smearing the blood all over his neck. In his hurry, he still didn't notice. He took his spit-shined low-quarters out of the shoe box and finished dressing on the run.

The board was being held across the street from the transient barracks at battalion headquarters. He was still adjusting his tie when he entered the building. Looking around, Patty saw other soldiers standing in the hallway, waiting to enter the room where the board was in session. They looked as nervous as he felt. He wondered if they had hangovers as bad as he had. Taking a closer look, he noticed that some of the guys didn't look too good.

Patty asked some of them if his name had been called yet. Nobody knew. Patty was afraid to ask the sergeant who was calling out the names; he didn't want to bring attention to the fact of his lateness. So he waited as, one by one, nervous soldiers stood in front of senior officers and sergeants, trying to impress them enough to get a promotion.

Patty tried to find a way to talk to one of the guys coming out. They must have been told not to talk to anyone in the hall. He had a brilliant idea. He walked up to the sergeant who was calling out the names. "Excuse me, Sergeant, I have to use the latrine. I just wanted to know if I'm next."

"What's the name?" he asked.

"Fallica, Sergeant."

"No, Fallica," he smiled, "you're not next."

Patty thanked him, and when the sergeant walked back into the board room, Patty went out the front door and ran after the man who had just left. "Hey, man!" Patty yelled after him.

The man turned around and saw Patty running up to him.

"What did they ask you?" Patty asked.

"Why should I tell you? Find out for yourself," the other fellow replied testily.

"Why shouldn't you tell me?" Patty was on the defensive.

"Because they told me not to tell anyone what went on."

"So you won't," Patty stated with contempt.

"No, I won't." Now the other fellow was on the defensive.

"Yeah," Patty said, "they dangle a stripe in front of you, and you turn your back on everyone. I imagine that if you get promoted, you won't hang out with any of your old friends because you're too good for them." With that, Patty turned and started to walk away.

"Wait a minute, man."

"What?" Patty asked.

"What do you want to know?" the other fellow asked.

"Just what they asked you," Patty said.

"Okay." The man thought for a moment. "First they asked what special significance today has."

"Well?" Patty waited.

"How the hell do I know?" the other fellow complained.

"What else did they ask?"

"Well, they asked some drill and ceremony questions. Then they asked how many soldiers we have in Vietnam."

"How many do we have?" Patty asked.

"I didn't know that either, but they told me afterward that we have five hundred and forty thousand."

"What else did they ask?"

"They asked me what I thought about marijuana," he said.

"What did you say?"

"I told them that anybody that smokes that shit should be shot. I mean it, too!"

Patty could see that he meant it. "Anything else?" Patty was in a hurry to get back.

"No, except a couple of MOS questions."

"What's your MOS?" Patty hoped he was a 16C.

"I'm a 95B, MP," he said simply.

"That won't help me. I'm a 16C. But thanks a lot for all you've told me. I hope you made it," Patty said in his most sincere tone. He started to walk away.

"Wait a minute, there's something else I forgot to tell you."

Patty turned around. "What?"

"Well, after you report, you're supposed to look behind you, take three steps backward, and sit down. Don't make them long steps, because the chair is real close. Take half steps. I backed into the chair," he said with a red face.

"Thanks," Patty said. "I'll remember that."

Patty ran back to the building where the board was still in progress. He noticed that there were still about the same number of men standing around waiting for their turn. He felt jumpy, and wished that he had a cup of coffee. He was thirsty as hell from the drinking, and he made frequent trips to the water bottle. He walked up and down the narrow hallway, looking at the pictures hanging on the wall. A few were the typical army pictures. This or that division or regiment fighting at this or that place. All were pretty boring. He had seen most of them before. The only thing worth reading was a framed sheet depicting the honors and lineage of the battalion. He read it. Patty would read anything if he were bored.

Standing around waiting for his name to be called was agony. He wished he'd never said he'd do this. Getting promoted wasn't one of Patty's priorities. The only reason he said Okay was because SSG Brown had seemed so desperate. Another good reason was because nobody on the crew wanted one of the sergeants from Paddlefoot's crew reassigned to Brown's crew.

This was discussed because SSG Brown was getting short. Everyone wanted Wagner as a section chief. If a sergeant came from another crew, he would have more time in grade than Kool. Nobody wanted that to happen. If Patty were to get promoted, the crew would remain intact, with no personnel changes.

The time dragged on. Patty walked down the hall again. He kept going over the reporting procedure in his head. "Specialist Fallica reports to the President of the Board." He was supposed to salute and look over his right shoulder, and take three steps to the rear, and sit down at attention. He remembered what the other fellow had told him. Take three small steps.

He went over the questions they would ask him over and over again.

Five hundred and forty thousand troops in Vietnam. Marijuana. What could he say about that? He smoked it every day. What could he say about it, except that he thought it should be legal? He knew they wouldn't go for that. He wondered what significance today had. He stood in the hallway reading the battalion's lineage and honors again.

There it was! High in front of him. The battalion was formed on March 21, 1942. March 21 was today! Today was the battalion's birthday! What a stroke of luck. He'd freak them out. He'd probably be the only guy to know that. This was going to be a breeze.

The door kept opening, and the sergeant would call out somebody's name, but it wasn't Patty's. It wasn't until he was the last one left in the hallway that they finally called him. He had thought that he wasn't too nervous, but as soon as he heard his name, his heart started to pound, and he developed a slight ringing in his ears. "Don't be nervous; they're not so bad," the sergeant whispered in his ear as they walked into the room.

Patty saw the battalion commander and the sergeant major sitting at the long table. The others on the board he didn't really know. He walked briskly to the center of the table and stood at attention in front of the colonel. He saluted. "President Fallica reports to the Specialist of the Board."

The colonel looked at him and returned his salute. He shook his head and smiled. "Take a seat, Mr. President."

Patty realized what he had done. His face turned crimson. He wished that he were back at Foxtrot. This was going to get rough. He turned his head and looked over his shoulder. He couldn't really see the chair behind him, and he didn't want to turn around to find it. He remembered what the man had told him, and took three small steps to the rear and sat down. He landed on the floor.

The board members didn't laugh. The sergeant major looked at the ceiling. The captain looked at his hands, and the other members just looked embarrassed. The colonel broke the silence as Patty stood up. This time he did turn around, and he saw that the chair was at least three feet from where he thought it would be. He went over and sat down at attention. His ass hurt.

"Welcome, Specialist Fallica," the colonel began. "You have been recommended for promotion to the grade of sergeant

E-5. This board has convened for the purpose of either endorsing that recommendation or deciding not to endorse that recommendation. We will ask you a series of questions to determine your suitability to perform at the higher grade. Do you understand?"

"Yes, sir," Patty answered.

The questions started. Each member of the board would ask him a question. Patty found that he could answer almost all of their questions, especially the ones pertaining to his job, and he started to become comfortable. The sergeant major was next. "How many troops do we currently have in North Vietnam?" he asked.

"Five hundred and forty thousand, Sergeant Major," Patty replied.

The sergeant major shook his head. The next one to ask a question was the battalion XO, Major Pratt. "What is your feeling on the use of marijuana?"

Patty panicked. He didn't know what to say. The only thing he knew was that they disapproved of it. He couldn't defend it, because it was illegal. He didn't care.

Patty was going to take a stand and tell them that it should be legalized. He had already blown this board, and he wasn't about to compromise his convictions and tell them what they wanted to hear. He figured that he would start his defense of the practice by stating a simple fact, and go on from there. "I know it's illegal, sir," he began.

"That's the best answer I've heard yet," the major said, beaming. "I wish that other soldiers could be more like you, Fallica. It doesn't really matter what we think. The fact of the matter is that it's illegal."

Patty figured he would just shut his mouth. They didn't want to hear anything more. He wouldn't say anything more. He was secretly pleased it had gone this way. Maybe, Patty hoped, he might just pull this off after all.

"What is the significance of today?" the colonel asked.

Patty was waiting for this. It was his ace in the hole. "Today is the battalion's birthday, sir!" Patty said smartly.

The colonel looked at the sergeant major. "Is it today?" he asked him.

"Beats me, sir," the sergeant major replied.

"How the hell do you know that?" the colonel asked Patty.

"I read it outside in the hallway," Patty confessed.

The colonel chuckled, as did the other board members. "Today is also the first day of spring," he explained to Patty. "Do you know why you were the last one to appear before the board?"

"No, sir," Patty answered.

"Because we couldn't find you this morning, that's why."

— Chapter 29 —

Fred waited on the hill behind the officer barracks. He had been waiting there since before dawn. Captain Williston was making Fred's life miserable, and now it was payback time. Sooner or later he would have to come out. Fred would wait.

The BC, still carrying his .45, was as determined to get Fred as Fred was to get him. This was war on a personal level. Man vs. canine. To the BC, it was a matter of principle. He was the commander. He would not be intimidated by a flea-bitten dog. To Fred, it was a matter of just being pissed off. To the men on the hill, it was a matter of being completely disregarded by their commander. It didn't matter how they pleaded their case; he didn't want to hear it. The crisis was heating up.

Something had to be done. Fred was coming onto the compound less frequently these days, and he was looking thin and weak. This was too much for the guys to take, because as far as they were concerned, Fred was as much a member of the crew as they were. To them, he was another American.

A clandestine meeting was held between the crews. Even

though Paddlefoot's crew was older and more conservative than Brown's crew, they were also fond of Fred. Not everyone attended, certainly not the two section chiefs, but most did. The consensus was that no combat readiness evaluation would be successful until the BC stopped harassing Fred.

The word was put out. It consisted of telling Granny, the company clerk. He wasn't an informer for the BC; he was more of a barometer of attitudes within Foxtrot. He liked Fred, too. He let the BC know in a roundabout way that Foxtrot probably wouldn't be combat ready until the situation was resolved.

It wasn't long after the meeting that they had an evaluation. The guys were just finishing evening chow when the battalion evaluation team drove through the gate. They walked into the corridor with a stopwatch, and declared "Blazing Skies!" The crew had fifteen minutes to complete pre-firing checks, and another five minutes to lock onto a target and simulate firing a missile.

It didn't happen. Half the guys on the hill went suddenly dumb. Adjustments were done with heavy hands, and as far as locking onto targets went, an outsider would swear that the crew was blind. The CRE team left the corridor shaking their heads. They would be back within forty-eight hours according to the regulation, they promised; until then, they were non-combat ready, and were therefore in an out-of-action status.

The men put on an incredible show of feigning disgust with themselves. The BC didn't know whether to buy it or not. His military mind couldn't really conceive of soldiers actually shirking their duty because of a dog. He didn't say much after the drill, but his face told the crew what they wanted to know. Two or three failures would get him relieved. The crews would suffer with constant training drills and such, but this was important, and they were willing to sacrifice. They wouldn't get relieved. It wasn't their careers.

Captain Williston had all this on his mind this morning. He was so preoccupied with the Fred situation that he forgot to strap on his pistol. Today was not the day to forget to carry his side arm. Today was the day for revenge.

The door to the BOQ opened, and out stepped the captain. It was early in the morning; the compound was deserted. Most of the soldiers were either in the mess hall or in their sections changing crews. The captain wanted to get up to the hill early and supervise the training. The CRE team should be back sometime today, and he wanted to make sure the crew was on its toes.

Fred wanted to make sure that the captain was on his toes. As the BC walked around the corner of the barracks, Fred shot toward him like a lightning bolt. The captain never had a chance. One minute he was lost in his own thoughts; the next minute he was facing a large, snarling dog who was hell-bent on revenge.

The captain reached for his forty-five. It wasn't there. Fred looked up at the captain and saw the fear on his face. That was all Fred wanted to see. He sat down on his haunches and just stared.

Captain Williston didn't know what to make of all this. Fred made no move at him or away from him. This was a stalemate. They just stared at each other. After a few minutes of this, Fred got up and walked away. The encounter was over. The BC was confused.

On the hill, the crews were catching hell. The first sergeant had gotten there early. A formation was called, and the men resented it. Formations, in their mind, were for the admin area.

No formations were ever called on the hill.

SSG Brown called the men to attention, and the men listened as the first sergeant addressed them. "Gentlemen, I suppose you are wondering why I'm here. I'm here because I want to make some things absolutely clear. First of all, we know that you men are trying to subvert authority. Well, I want you to know that we know, and that it won't work. You men are shamming. That's right; shamming."

Murphy poked Wagner, and whispered "What the fuck is 'shamming?' "

The first sergeant went on:"We know that you have sabotaged the combat readiness of this unit. We won't tolerate it. From this day, until we are declared combat ready, no man will leave the compound. You are all restricted."

A groan went up from the formation.

"I hope that you men see the light, and work with us instead of against us. Remember, no more shamming!"

A voice, just loud enough to be heard inside of the formation, could be heard. "What the fuck is 'shamming?' " It was Murphy again.

The formation was dismissed, and the men headed off to the corridor. Murphy asked Wagner again what the fuck shamming was. Wagner told him that it meant goofing off. Murphy wanted to know why he didn't say that in the first place.

All that day, the men made fun of the first sergeant. Conversations would start out with "I want you to know that we know that you know..." and everyone would laugh. Nobody said much about the restriction. Nobody except Murphy. Murphy had something to say about everything.

The CRE team came that afternoon. They failed again. The team promised to come back within another forty-eight hours.

The battery was still out of action.

Captain Williston came up to the hill that evening.. He had the first sergeant with him. He called a meeting with the crew in the ready room. To his credit, he asked the first sergeant to wait in the corridor. "Would somebody please tell me what the problem is up here?" he asked.

The guys just looked at each other.

"We can't get anything accomplished without some kind of dialogue," he complained.

The men stayed silent.

"Murphy, you've always got something to say; what's the problem?"

"The problem, sir, is that you've got it in for a member of this crew," Murphy
replied.

The captain looked perplexed. He looked at the crew and tried to recall if he had been particularly hard on any of them lately. Normally he wouldn't really care if he was or not, but his command was on the line. The colonel had called earlier and had let him know that he was on the verge of being relieved. "Three strikes and you're out," were the words he had used. He couldn't figure out which one of the crew had the beef. "Who?" he asked.

The men shuffled around in their chairs, glancing at each other. Most of the men looked at Wagner. Wagner looked at Patty, and the rest of the crew, noticing the direction of Wagner's gaze, did the same. Patty guessed that he had been elected. "Fred, sir," Patty said simply.

"This is about a fuckin' dog?" The BC asked. "A fucking dog is responsible for putting the security of a whole country at stake? A lousy, nasty, flea-bitten dog is responsible for ruining my career? I can't believe this. You can't be serious."

"We're serious," Patty said flatly.

"I can have you people charged with mutiny. This is the most serious breach of discipline I have ever experienced in my career," the captain remarked.

"It's pretty hard on us, too. We've never flunked two CRE's in a row, sir," Wagner added.

The BC just sat there thinking. He could either charge the men with something like dereliction of duty, or submit to their demands and take the damn dog off the hook. If he made a case out of this rebellion, the colonel would think that he was running some kind of circus. He had no choice. He could make them pay for this later. Especially that wise-ass Fallica. The one with the brass balls and the big mouth. "Okay," he said quietly. "You win. Fred gets a second chance, but if he bites me again, I'll kill him. Go to work."

The crew did their best not to shove their victory up the captain's ass. They somberly rose from their seats and walked toward the corridor. They practiced crew drills and post-firing checks for the rest of the evening. As they were walking into the corridor, the first sergeant called out to Patty. "How do you think you did the other day at the promotion board, Fallica?" he asked.

Patty turned and answered up. "I have no idea, First Sergeant."

"The major called me from K-6 the other day," he said. "He wanted to know how the hell you ever made Spec Four. He told me to give the president his regards. He also wanted to know if you still have a sore ass."

Patty glared at the first sergeant. The first sergeant glared back at Patty. There was no love lost between them. Patty didn't know it then, but he had more to worry about than the first sergeant. The battery commander didn't have him high on his all-time favorite list, either.

The CRE team came back again in the morning. The crew passed with Superiors in both performance and equipment readiness. The men had mixed feelings about it. They were glad that they had gotten Fred out of trouble, and they were happy to have rehabilitated their reputation. They were also a little sad, because they really did want to see the BC relieved.

— **Chapter 30** —

The next day, Patty did his usual black marketing. He stopped off at the Frog and got an early start on his drinking. It was sunny, but extremely cold and windy. He couldn't believe that it was spring–it felt more like midwinter. So the stop at the Frog was a necessity: his body was almost numb from the cold. The hot whiskey and tea he drank not only gave him a slight buzz, but also returned some of his circulation.

Besides the tea and whiskey, he popped some speed. It wasn't long before he was ready to party. It was too early to party in town, so he decided to go back to the compound and get some company. At this time of day, the majority of the crew would be down at the NCO club, so that's where he headed.

The crew was in the club celebrating their previous night's victory over the BC, but the party was officially for passing the CRE. It really could not have been any other way, because the BC was the one buying the drinks. The launching area men were there, too; after all, they had been the other half of the crew on duty.

A few air force officers were there as well. The commander had invited them to stop in. They were TDY from Vietnam to do a stint at the local bombing range to the northeast of Foxtrot. They were also buying drinks. By the time Patty arrived at the club, everybody was well on their way to a good hangover.

The guys were happy to see Patty. His stature had gone up with the crew for standing up to the BC. As much as the crew liked him, the BC and the First Shirt disliked him. That made him even more popular among the guys.

Patty was sitting at a table near the bar with Wagner, Big O, and Phillips. He was drinking cans of Falstaff and shots of bourbon. He was feeling no pain at all. The guys were complaining about the country music on the jukebox, so Patty got up from the table, walked over to the machine, and reached around the back and hit the reject button. Hank Williams stopped singing about being so lonely, and Led Zeppelin started in with "Whole Lotta Love."

This freaked the officers out. They hated that hippie shit. They told Patty to turn that shit off. Patty acted as if he didn't hear them, and sat down at the table. The commander walked over to the jukebox, rejected the song, and some other cowboy began to sing about his pickup, or horse, or whatever it was that cowboys sing about.

The conversation at the table was getting good. Phillips was telling about how he had gone to bed with his girlfriend's mother. They had all heard this story before, but Phillips just got funnier each time he told it. The air force officers were telling war stories to some of the officers of Foxtrot, and Patty couldn't help but overhear.

One of the officers, a young captain, was particularly offensive. He not only talked louder than the others, but the things he said were really disgusting. He really seemed to be in love with his job, and his job was bombing North Vietnam.

Not that bombing North Vietnam offended Patty; it didn't. What bothered Patty was the way the air force captain described it. When one of the army officers asked the captain how they managed to avoid civilians, he answered that they didn't; that it was, in fact, one of their prime objectives. "Not officially, of course," he laughed.

"You're kidding, aren't you?" asked Lieutenant Collins.

"No I'm not, lieutenant," the captain answered. "Fuck them little gook babies. Fuck all them slimy gooks. Every time I drop a bomb I see a little gook arm go flying in the air. If it were up to me, I'd nuke the whole fuckin' place."

Patty looked at the man. He was drunk, and so was Patty. The war offended Patty because he felt that it was useless. He had been for it in the beginning stages, but when he saw that the politicians had no intention of going all out for victory, he was sickened by the senseless slaughter for no apparent reason. He wanted the US to pull out. This captain talking about killing gook babies represented all of what he had learned to despise. "Is that what you wanted to be when you were a kid, Captain? Did you tell your mother you wanted to grow up and be a baby killer?" he asked sarcastically.

"Who the fuck said that?" asked the captain.

"I did," Patty replied.

"You're a real wise-ass, aren't you, sonny?" said the air force captain.

"No, I'm not a wise-ass, I'm just sick of hearing about your heroic exploits in babycide," Patty said defiantly.

"You never been to 'Nam. You don't know shit, kid. If you went there you would understand," he said.

"I hope I never understand the things you understand. Killing enemy soldiers is one thing. Killing innocent civilians is another," Patty said.

"Nobody is innocent over there," the captain replied.

"And who the fuck are you–God? Who gave you the right to decide who should live and who should die?" Patty was pissed.

"Fallica, at ease!" the BC commanded. "Sit down and shut up. This man is a guest at our club."

"Yes, sir," Patty said and sat down.

The air force officer glared at Fallica. Patty sat at the table and glared back.

"I guess the army sent all the punks to Korea," the air force officer said loudly to no one in particular.

Patty rose from his seat and turned to the BC. "I don't have to take that shit from this asshole, sir!" he yelled.

"Who you calling an asshole, punk?" said the air force captain.

"Who do you think?" Patty answered.

That was all it took. The air force captain came off of the bar stool and toward Patty. Fallica didn't expect it, and took a hard right under his left eye. He fell back over the table, knocking drinks and cans of beer onto the floor.

The air force officer stood over Patty in a fighting stance. The blow had sobered Fallica up considerably. Rage seemed to consume him. He picked himself up off the floor, and out of the corner of his right eye he saw the captain's foot coming toward him. He dodged to avoid the blow, and found himself on the floor again. Instinctively, he kicked out at the captain, and his foot caught him just below the knee, on the leg he had his weight on. He went down, too. As they were both getting up off the floor, Patty took a swing, and landed a blow against the captain's cheek. Patty got up, the captain went down. The next thing that Patty knew, the BC and some of the other men were restraining him.

Patty was being held from the back and he couldn't move. The air force captain was being helped up. Suddenly, the air force captain pushed the person away, and lurched towards Patty, punching him in the right ear. Patty heard his ear ring loudly. He tried to break free of the man holding him. He later learned that it was Lieutenant Collins. He was held too tight to break free. Some of the guys from IFC grabbed the air force captain before he could inflict more damage to Patty. The club was silent. All eyes were turned to the combatants.

The BC was glowering with rage. "Leave the club, Fallica. I want you in my office first thing in the morning!" he screamed.

Patty walked away in a furious rage. He'd be there tomorrow, he thought; and if the captain wanted to press charges against him for the fight, he'd press charges of his own against that asshole air force captain.

The next morning, Patty reported to the captain. As he expected, the captain had drawn up an Article 15. Patty refused to sign it. The captain told Patty that he would bring it to a court-martial. Patty explained to the BC that the air force captain had hit him first. The BC disagreed, and told Patty that he had four officers who would testify that it was Fallica who had thrown the first blow. The BC also explained that he could also charge Patty with insubordination. He promised Patty that if he signed the Article 15, he would not restrict him to compound, nor would he reduce him in grade. Patty signed.

Fallica was called down from the hill later on that day. He was read the punishment. Restriction to compound for thirty days, a fine of two hundred dollars, and reduction to PFC. Patty stared at the battery commander with his mouth open. "You promised no restriction and no bust!" he protested.

"Do you have anything in writing?" the BC asked.

"No; all I had was your word," Patty replied.

The battery commander looked at Patty with disgust. "Fallica, you're lucky I didn't charge you with mutiny over that dog thing on the hill. Consider yourself lucky to have any stripes at all," he said.

"I want to appeal to the colonel!" Patty said.

The captain stared and started to turn red. "Don't threaten me, Fallica!" he screamed.

"I'm not threatening you, sir. It's my right to appeal," Patty replied.

"Go ahead and appeal. You just go ahead. Do anything you want to do. Just be prepared to face reality," the BC said coldly.

Patty went up to the hill and drafted his appeal. In his letter to the colonel, he explained exactly what had happened. He made two carbons. One of the carbons he kept; the other one he sent to the colonel in a letter. He delivered the original to the captain the next morning.

As Patty was leaving the orderly room, the first sergeant waved him over to his desk. He reached into the drawer. "Put these on," he said.

Patty reached out and took a small package from the first sergeant. He opened it. Inside were PFC pins. He put them on.

Back at the barracks, the crew was furious at the situation. SSG Brown had even come up to see how Patty was taking it. Brown told Patty he should have taken a court-martial. He offered to speak to the colonel. Big O wanted to put a contract out on the BC. He thought that he could have his arm broken for less than fifty bucks. This worried Patty because he knew that it was possible, and he was in enough trouble, so he told Big O not to do it.

The weather cleared up and the days were getting warmer. Suddenly, in a matter of days, the vegetation turned green, and life around the compound became busier. Patty wanted to get the hell off compound. Besides driving him crazy, this restriction was really bad for business. Murphy was doing some errands for Mamasan, and Patty was worried that he might take the whole operation over.

The nights were still pretty cold. A few of the space heaters on the hill had taken a shit. Patty enjoyed taking them apart and putting them back together. Everyone congratulated him on his mechanical expertise when he fired them up and they actually worked, but Patty had no idea why they worked. He figured that they just needed cleaning.

Fallica was knee-deep in carbon and diesel fuel when a call came up to the hill ordering him to come down for Friday retreat formation. This incensed Fallica. He asked SSG Brown why he had to go. Brown told him that they would probably read his Article 15 to the battery, and the captain would want him to be there. Patty was fit to be tied. He put on his field jacket and took the truck down to formation.

The formation had already started when Patty drove up. He jumped out of the cab and fell in with Paddlefoot's crew. Paddlefoot asked him why he was so dirty. Patty explained that he hadn't had time to wash up. He really felt disgusting and out of place.

The first sergeant addressed the formation. He accused the unit of shamming. He told them that, from this day forward, there would be no more shamming at Foxtrot. Somebody in the formation wanted to know what the hell shamming was.

He was told to shut up.

The first sergeant then turned the unit over to the BC. The captain came out with his lieutenants, and they replaced the platoon sergeants and the first sergeant. The captain yelled out for persons to be decorated front and center.

Patty was pissed. He couldn't believe that he had actually been called down from the hill to watch this. He wished that the captain would have a stroke or something.

Fallica was lost in his reverie of revenge when he felt a nudge at his elbow. He turned toward the nudge, annoyed. It was Paddlefoot. "Go on, Fallica," he said.

"Go on what?" he asked.

"Go on up to the front of the formation," he said impatiently.

"Yeah, right. Real funny," Patty said.

"I'm serious. Get up there." Paddlefoot said this loud enough so that more than a few people looked at them.

Patty guessed that Paddlefoot was serious. He couldn't believe they were actually going to read his Article 15 with him standing in front of the whole formation. Fallica was mortified. Besides his shame, he looked like a hobo, covered with soot as he was.

He walked to the center of the formation and stood at attention. Inside, he wanted to hide. He actually wanted to cry, he was so embarrassed. The BC came in front of him and stood at attention also, with Lieutenant Collins at his left. Lieutenant Collins started to read from a paper he had in his hand. "To be promoted to Sergeant E-5, Specialist Four Patrick J. Fallica," he proclaimed.

Patty was dumbfounded. He turned his head and looked at the lieutenant, who smiled at him and winked. Patty then turned and looked at the BC, who was not smiling at all. "You look like shit, Fallica," the BC said under his breath to Patty.

The battery commander and Lieutenant Collins stood on both sides of Patty and removed his PFC pins and, in their place, put on the sergeant's chevrons. "I'll get these back before you leave, Sergeant Fallica," the BC whispered.

"No you won't," Patty replied confidently.

Formation was over after the playing of retreat. The flag went down, and the battery was dismissed. Paddlefoot came over to Patty and told him to report to the orderly room. Patty wondered what the hell was going on now. He felt that he lived in the orderly room lately, and almost told Paddlefoot he should move his bunk in there.

He saw the colonel's jeep parked in front. The first sergeant told him to report to the colonel. He walked toward the BC's office, knocked on the door, and waited until he heard the colonel tell him to come in. "Sergeant Fallica reports," Patty saluted, and after the colonel returned the salute, Patty dropped it and stood at attention.

"Sit down, Sergeant," the colonel said gently.

Patty sat down. He was acutely aware that he looked terrible with his sooty black fatigues and his black eye.

"I received your appeal, Fallica," the colonel said. "I received your appeal, and I amended the punishment. That's why you got promoted today. As I said, I amended the punishment so you could get promoted. I saw your name on the promotion list. By the way, you just barely made the board." The Colonel paused and sat, looking for a reaction from Patty. He didn't get one.

"I didn't want you to lose two stripes over this affair. I figured that one was enough. You see, your orders were cut before you received the Article 15. I still had a dilemma on my hands, because the captain doesn't have the authority to bust an E-5 or above. That authority rests with a field grade officer. Since you were promoted before the bust, the captain couldn't impose the reduction. It's a 'catch twenty-two.' Am I making any sense?"

"Yes, sir." Patty could see what had happened.

"I came out this afternoon to administer the Article 15 myself. After I read the charges, I felt that promoting you to E-5 was not in the army's best interests. I was going to remove the fine and the restriction, and leave the reduction in place. The reduction, by the way, would have been from E-5 to E-4," he said.

"So am I busted back to E-4?" Patty asked.

"If I hadn't talked to Lieutenant Collins, you would be giving me the stripe back at this moment, but it seems that there was a difference in opinion about who hit who first."

"The air force captain hit me first, sir," Patty said defensively.

"That's what Lieutenant Collins said. He volunteered the information, by the way. I

believe him. I'm going to throw out the Article 15 entirely."

"Thank you, sir."

"I want you to understand something, Fallica. I want you to understand that because we have a democratic government doesn't mean that we have a democratic army. We do the job that the commander in chief asks us to do. We don't vote on it or have individual opinions on it. That part of an issue is left up to the citizenry and the government. We are only instruments of that government. Other countries have military establishments that get involved with issues. Since the military establishments have such raw power in those countries, it inevitably ends up in a military dictatorship, or a government that no longer bends to the will of the people, but to the will of their military."

"I understand, sir."

"I want you also to understand that the man you fought with was sent out of Vietnam because he is suffering a major depression after missing his military target and hitting a civilian-populated area. The flight surgeon has sent him to ASCOM to be evaluated because they believe him to be suicidal. Part of what he said in the club was no more than an act. He is a deeply troubled man who will probably never be the same again. I would like you to draft a letter of apology. Not for defending yourself, but for butting into a conversation that you didn't belong in."

"I'll do that, sir," Patty said earnestly.

"I also want you to think about what I said on a democratic army. Do you know that the Russians got their asses kicked in Finland because they elected their officers by a popular vote? It seems they elected them by popularity instead of military skills. They scrapped that procedure. I know about the incident with the dog. If anything like that happens again, I'll have your balls. Do you want to keep your balls, Sergeant?"

"Yes, sir."

"Then get out of here and fix the rest of those space heaters. If I ever hear your name again it had better be about something good."

"Yes, sir." Patty saluted and hurried out of the BC's office. He winked at the first sergeant as he walked past his desk. "Fuck up and move up," he thought. He got into the truck and started up the hill.

The crew was enthusiastic about the promotion. Patty was the center of attention as the crew slapped him on the back and shook his hand. He had to excuse himself after awhile to head to the latrine. Once inside, he turned to make sure that nobody followed him. When he was sure he was alone, he walked up to the mirror and looked at the stripes on his collar. "Sergeant Fallica," he thought. "Hot shit!"

Chapter 31

The weather was getting warmer. Patty could no longer do his
parka routine. The parkas issued in Korea had fur-edged hoods.
Heavy wire ran under the fur so that a soldier could squeeze
both sides together and close the hood, thereby keeping his
face protected from the Korean winter. Patty would close the
hood and bring his arms inside the parka. Using his fingertips,
he would open the hood from the inside and slowly push his
head out inch by inch. "I'm being born!" he would exclaim. It
always got a laugh.

Fallica found another routine. He called it "driving the first
sergeant crazy." The crew had been playing with a Frisbee on
the hill. Murphy had told Patty the next day, as they were walking through the admin area, that he wished he had brought it
down from the hill so they could play. Patty ran to the side of
the BOQ and made believe that he was throwing the Frisbee
to Murphy. Murph didn't understand until Patty exaggerated
the next throw and yelled at him to catch it.

Murphy caught on, and simulated a spectacular catch over

his head. "Great catch, Murph!" Patty yelled.

At just this moment, Granny and the first sergeant were leaving the orderly room for the mess hall. Granny saw them playing. "What are you guys doing?" he called.

"Playing catch, Gran, what the hell does it look like?" Patty said.

"What the hell are you playing catch with? I don't see anything."

"You can't see anything because there is nothing here." Patty was suddenly inspired. "It's all a big sham. We're shamming."

Murphy caught on immediately and started to laugh. "Yeah, Gran, we're throwing the sham. Were shamming," he said through his laughter.

The first sergeant glared at them, then turned and walked briskly toward the mess hall. Granny called to Patty. "Throw it to me!" he cried.

Patty made an imaginary throw toward Granny, and he simulated making the catch between his legs.

"Check that style!" Murphy shouted.

"What a sham artist!" Patty exclaimed.

The first sergeant turned and saw his company clerk throw the so-called sham over to Murphy.

"You're really shamming now, Gran!" Patty called to him.

The practice of shamming spread throughout the battery like a rumor. It wasn't long before it had developed into an art. People were shamming on duty and off, catching the sham behind the back, in the air, and even upside down. Shamming was a very imaginative sport. It was adopted quickly because it could be played anywhere, anytime, and because it drove the first sergeant crazy.

First Sergeant Marshal could do nothing to stop the practice, and this just added another reason for him to drink. He drank more now than he had when he'd arrived at Foxtrot. He told himself it was because this was by far his worst assignment. He swore in letters to his wife that it would also be his last.

This just wasn't his type of army anymore. The younger soldiers asked "why" all the time. He wasn't used to soldiers questioning authority. His way of doing things left no room for questions. He had put in his paperwork for retirement to be effective at the end of this tour.

Captain Williston didn't appreciate this new game, either. He noticed that even his officers were playing. He knew that unless he could find a reason to stop it, any protest against shamming would be interpreted by the unit members as just another way to break their balls. He was also worried about the first sergeant. He noticed the drinking. He also noticed that Marshal would sometimes go into a fog. The captain talked about it with the battalion commander. He described it to him as "going vacant"–one minute Top would be there, and the next minute he wouldn't. He had seen him do this a couple of times.

Once, in the BC's office, they were talking about this new thing that the men had invented. The first sergeant thought that Fallica had started it. The Captain replied that he wanted a reason to outlaw the game. The First Sergeant didn't reply. He just stared out into space. The BC tried to get him back by yelling his name. Nothing happened. He was gone, somewhere in the ozone layer. Captain Williston stared at him for a few minutes, and as if by magic, the first sergeant just resumed the conversation as if nothing had happened.

During a telephone call with battalion, the BC caught him doing it again. He seemed to be getting flustered with the questions they were making him answer. He saw the first sergeant rummaging around his desk, looking for different papers and talking a mile a minute. Suddenly, he just stopped talking in mid-sentence and started staring at the wall. It made the BC nervous. Williston worried that one of these days he might not snap out of it.

Shamming went on. It was amazing how seriously they played. The men had actually invented rules and regulations. Most of the rules were as simple as the game itself. The number one rule was that the action had to look as real as possible. For instance, you couldn't just throw out a hand if somebody yelled "Catch!" Also, if a sham were thrown at two people, one of them had to catch it; they both couldn't. Another odd rule was that if a person missed it, that person had to go get it. This could be hysterical when it landed somewhere like the orderly room roof, and a player had to climb up to retrieve it.

The Koreans started playing it, too. The security guards started throwing shams on guard duty. The people in the village had fun in the streets with their own shams. Sometimes visitors from K-6 or ASCOM would think they had entered a lunatic asylum. They would stand open-mouthed as men leapt in the air and made fantastic catches. The attraction of this game was that you could be as good as you wanted to be. Every heroic catch you could imagine could be made with a sham. After a little exposure, the visitors also became converts to the sport.

Shamming epitomized a tour of duty in Korea. Playing this game with something that wasn't really there to begin with was similar to playing with weapons that you couldn't really shoot, or making love with women you couldn't really love. The whole country was a contradiction.

Everyone walked around with spit-shined boots they didn't have to shine, lived in squared-away barracks they didn't have to clean, and did a job that very few people back in the World appreciated. It all made as much sense as catching a sham.

— **Chapter 32** —

SSG Brown called Wagner and Fallica into the maintenance shed for a meeting. Patty had asked Kool what the meeting was about, but Wagner refused to tell. He told Patty that it was a "little surprise." Patty didn't like surprises at work.

Brown was already there waiting for them, leaning back on a stool. Patty always felt that he was at a meeting of the underground, because it was always so dim in the shack. He had meant to replace the undersized light bulb, but it had always slipped his mind. Brown smiled and asked Wagner and Fallica to make themselves comfortable. This meant pulling up a five-gallon paint can.

"I'm getting short, boys," he stated. "Going to go back to the World. I never thought I'd see round-eyed women again, but I guess they can't live without me."

Wagner and Patty laughed politely. This was as close to humor as SSG Brown ever got.

"The crew has to have a new section chief. I've been thinking about this for a long time. I've discussed the situation with

Lieutenant Moore, and he told me that he would accept any decision I make," he continued.

"I thought that this was all decided!" Patty interjected. "Kool is going to take over. That's what we planned. That's why I took this stripe!"

"Wagner doesn't want to be section chief," Brown countered. "Can't make him do it. Besides, he's getting short, too."

"Then who's going to do it?" Patty asked. "I can't do it. I'm only eighteen years old, for Christ's sake!"

"Well, I thought about it. I figured that you didn't want all that responsibility, even though I think you'd make a great section chief. I'm going to get Adams to come over from the other crew," Brown stated.

Patty looked at Wagner. He was just looking at Patty, and Patty knew that Kool knew about this already. "You're an asshole, Wagner. You're really letting the crew down. Adams is an asshole. He won't fit on this crew. He's all fuckin' army. He'll be a pain in the ass!" Patty was angry.

"Fuck you, Fallica!" Wagner replied. "Why don't you do it?"

"Because nobody will listen to me; I'm just a kid compared to everybody else."

"So what?" Wagner asked.

"So, they won't take orders from a kid!" Patty said.

"They'll listen to you because you're a sergeant, Fallica, and that's all they'll see," Brown told him. "Wagner will be your assistant; he'll help you out."

"That's exactly what I mean. Kool would be the last one to take orders from me. He's got more time in the chow line than I got in the army!"

"I'd take orders from you. I might argue with you from time to time, but not in front of the crew," Wagner said.

Patty looked at Wagner again. He could see in his face that he was being serious. He looked at Brown; he was serious also. Patty couldn't believe that this was really going down. He'd never expected it. "I don't think I could pull it off," he said quietly. "They'd crucify me."

"Then we better get Adams over here so he can get to know the crew before he takes over," Brown said with a deep sigh.

"Anybody but Adams!" Patty pleaded.

"Anybody?" Wagner asked.

"I know what you're doing, Kool," Patty snapped.

"Then it's got to be Adams," Wagner shot back. "Just remember what happened today when you start bitching about him."

Patty knew he was cornered. This was a setup, and he knew it. He knew that nobody on Brown's crew had any use for Adams. Fallica's next statement was inevitable. "Okay, I'll do it," Patty said, his voice filled with resignation. "But you better help me, Kool. You still got four months in country; you're not getting off the hook for four months."

"See, Fallica, you're already sounding like a section chief," Brown said happily.

Patty left the guard shack with very mixed emotions. He had always wanted to be a section chief, but he thought it would be at a much later date. It had never occurred to him that he could actually handle a section now. He wondered what the crew would say. He also wondered if he could really do it. He had two weeks to get used to the idea. He had told Brown he was only eighteen years old. He was lying. He was eighteen and a half, with no time in grade. Big O was twenty-five, Murphy was twenty, even Phillips was twenty-two. He was the youngest guy on the hill.

The next day was incredibly sunny and warm. It seemed as if spring was going to be pre-empted for summer. The crew didn't want to hang around the admin area after work; they wanted to get right into town and party. It was only nine thirty when they walked out the gate for Inchon.

Patty was the one with the ideas. He told the crew about an open-air market near the Frog that sold nothing but toys. He asked the crew if they wanted to check it out. They did. Phillips said he wanted to try some of that hot whiskey, so the guys decided to hit the Frog first.

They took the bus to Inchon. It felt good to feel warm, dry air on their faces. Everybody was in an extremely good mood. Patty was surprised at their reaction to the news that he would be the new section chief. They didn't seem to care. They were just happy it wasn't Adams.

Moving through the alleys in Inchon always fascinated Patty. Korea, especially Inchon, was like a giant Disneyland. Little things, such as a drug store or a bar, were like new experiences he could sample. Fallica was still amazed that drugs were sold over the counter. He would sometimes buy drugs when he didn't even want them. It was the thrill of the purchase that excited him.

They were greeted warmly upon entering the Frog. The waitresses there knew that they would spend a lot of money. Some places in Korea didn't want the American business because it wasn't worth the hassle they had to put up with. Inchon was different. The few Americans they had in this city of five million didn't show up enough to make a pain in the ass of themselves.

It didn't take long to get a good buzz. Patty and Wagner had taken some speed before they got too blasted. It was almost one in the afternoon when they left the Frog.

Big O was pretty drunk. It was really easy to tell. Since he had no teeth, he would spray everybody he talked to. Big O never wore his false teeth when he was drinking. The way he slurred his words with no teeth made understanding him nearly impossible. Every once in a while he would crash into the side of a building. Nobody really cared, though; somebody would always get a little more drunk than the others.

One of the best things about being drunk in Korea was that you really couldn't offend the Koreans. This was because most of the Koreans couldn't understand slurred, drunken English enough to be offended, and the rest of them thought that Americans were all crazy to begin with. It was hard to get in trouble unless you actually hurt somebody.

Seeing all the toys in the market brought out the kid in most of the crew. Phillips was intrigued by the different multi-colored kites. He bought a box kite, a ribbon kite, and a few kinds he had never seen in his life. Rope thought that the little battery-powered toys were fabulous. He bought a bag of various toys he claimed he was going to send to his nephews.

The Korean shop owners took pride in their wares, and seemed to have a great time showing them to the Americans. Patty got a kick out of watching the guys paying the full asking price. They had no idea that things weren't done like that in Korea. The shop owners fully expected to negotiate on the price. Haggling was part of shopping. Tim had taught Patty the art of haggling. It was almost second nature to him now.

Everyone but Patty had a bag full of toys. Fallica figured that he was just too busy to play with any he might purchase. Besides, he didn't want to lug them around for the rest of the day. He had no intention of going back to the compound until the next morning.

Just as they were about to leave, Big O spotted the guns. Tucked away in a corner of the market was a stall that specialized in toy guns of every type.

They were really amazing. If you didn't know that they were toys, it would be easy to mistake them for the genuine articles. Reeger wanted to buy them all. He looked at each and every one of them. He almost bought a replica of an M-16 until the shop owner brought out an AK-47. It was love at first sight. The only difference between the real rifle and the toy was that the bullets were red plastic, as was the clip that held the magazine in the rifle.

Big O loved the way it came apart in three pieces. He assembled it and disassembled it three times. The crew watched Reeger as he screwed the receiver group onto the stock, and then screwed the barrel onto the receiver group. It wasn't the rifle that was so interesting to the crew; it was Big O's face.

Watching "O" playing with the rifle was like watching a man possessed. Finally they grew tired of him playing with it, and told him to buy it and play with it later.

They took taxis to Whiskey Mary's. The place was pretty quiet during the day. Jimmy had a big poker game going on, though, and it must have been for pretty high stakes, because the Koreans were watching every move the players made. The money on the table was a sizable amount. Patty figured that Jimmy wasn't going to be available to party with them for awhile.

They sat and drank beer and flirted with the few girls who were there. The front door was open because of the warm weather, and the sunshine poured through the windows. It was really turning into a mellow afternoon.

Nobody noticed Reeger pulling the bag up from under the table except Murphy. From the look on Big O's face, it was apparent that he was into mischief. He had on that weird smile and darting eyes that signaled, to those who knew him, that he was about to pull something off.

Murphy watched Reeger as he pulled the stock of the rifle from the bag. He bent down and came up with the receiver group. Some of the others noticed him screwing it onto the stock. Nobody said anything as he reached down under the table again and came up with the barrel. A girl who had been watching the game noticed Reeger screwing the barrel onto the receiver group, and quietly nudged one of the girls standing next to her. Patty and Wagner were deep into conversation, and hadn't noticed anything until the place grew deathly quiet. They stopped talking and looked around.

Every person in the place now had their eyes firmly fixed on Reeger. By this time the weapon was completely assembled, and he stood up and rammed the magazine into the slot. It came together with a loud click. He then smiled that crazy man's smile and pulled the bolt back, and then let it slide forward, chambering a round with another loud click that made some of the Koreans jump.

The crew looked at each other as Reeger slowly walked over to the table where, a few minutes before, people had been playing poker. The Koreans seemed to shrink with every step that Big O made. Patty realized that they thought the rifle was real, and felt a wave of panic rise from his belly. He wondered if anyone at the table had a gun. He wanted to call out to Reeger, but he was afraid that the noise would spook somebody into blowing Big O's head off.

Reeger walked right up to the table. One of the players

pushed the money toward him in a panic. Big O just laughed. It was a killer's laugh. Patty believed that, in his drunken state, Reeger really believed he had a real gun. "I don't want your money!" he said drunkenly.

Big O was drooling and weaving from side to side. Murphy could be heard in the background trying to stifle laughter. The Koreans fully believed that this crazy American was walking around with an AK-47. Wagner tried to diffuse the situation. "Reeger, put that gun down!" he yelled.

Wagner was scared that somebody was going to shoot Reeger, too, but it didn't stop him from appreciating the ridiculousness of the situation. Every person on the crew was vacillating between hysterical laughter and fear that Big O would get shot. It immobilized them all.

"Get the fuck up and get against the wall!" Reeger cried.

The Koreans obeyed. Even the girls who were standing around the table went over and stood against the wall.

"Put your hands behind your heads!" Big O ordered the frightened people, moving his gun as he talked.

The scene in the bar looked like a scene off a Hollywood lot. The Koreans were standing against the wall with their hands behind their heads. Patty noticed that Jimmy was as scared as any of them. In spite of the potential seriousness of the situation, Patty was hard put not to fall apart with laughter. Tears were actually running down his cheeks. Some of the guys couldn't hold back the laughter. It sounded like groans when it did escape.

"Turn around and face the wall!" Big O ordered them.

The Koreans turned and faced the wall. "Don't kill me!" one girl sobbed.

This was too much for Patty. "O, put that damn gun down!"

he yelled.

This command from Patty actually made things worse. It seemed to add just the right amount of realism. Almost all the Koreans were moaning and pleading now.

"Shut up! Shut up or I'm going to let you have it!" O yelled at them.

They didn't shut up.

"Okay!" he screamed, "Get ready; here it comes! Bang, mother fuckers! Bang!"

The people against the wall screamed as two little red plastic bullets looped out from the barrel and bounced against the wall.

By the time the Americans had regained their composure, and the Koreans had realized what had just happened, Big O had walked out of the bar and was now on the streets of Inchon.

Patty recovered from the scene in the bar and was the first out after Reeger. Wagner followed close behind. Big O was nowhere in sight. The two didn't know which way to give chase, but it didn't take long to figure it out.

Over to the right, the street ended in an intersection. A cop in the middle was jumping up and down while hysterically blowing his whistle. The traffic there was stopped. Patty and Kool took off in that direction. As they passed the intersection, the cop was still waving his arms and stopping traffic. Cars, cabs and buses were stacking up all over the place.

Rounding the corner, they expected to see Big O, but he wasn't there. They continued to run down to the next intersection a short distance away. Looking first to his right, and then to his left, Patty saw Reeger on the sidewalk. He was standing and staring at a drunken beggar who was puking on all fours next to the curb. Wagner called out to Big O. Reeger turned and faced them. "Hey, guys, this guy's drunk!" he shouted, and with that, he gave the old bum a small push with his foot.

The drunk fell over. Big O then put his foot in the man's back and turned toward Patty and Wagner, rifle resting on his hip. He looked like a big-game hunter posing with his latest trophy. "Go ahead, take my picture!" he called out drunkenly.

Just at that time, the cop from the other intersection rounded the corner. He took one look at Big O in his pose, and must have thought that Reeger had shot the drunk. He went right into his traffic-stopping routine. Later on, Patty and Wagner figured the reason he didn't shoot Big O was because he was worried that Reeger might start a massacre, and he wanted to keep people away from him.

Wagner saw a taxi coming from the opposite direction. He ran out into the street and flagged it down. The driver, unaware of what was happening, stopped. Patty grabbed Reeger and pulled him over to the cab. Wagner had the back door open, and Patty threw Reeger into the seat. "Munhak!" Wagner screamed at the driver.

The taxi driver, aware that something was going on, screeched his tires and headed for the compound. Wagner and Patty kept glancing toward the back until they were out of Inchon, and were sure that nobody was following them. Once they were sure they were in the clear and the pressure was off, they started laughing. The taxi driver was laughing, too, even though he had no idea what he was laughing about.

Reeger was in a daze, half asleep and half awake. Looking at him, Patty was aware that even though he was responsible for the situation, he didn't have a clue as to what was going on. He was that drunk.

The cab stopped outside the compound gate. Wagner and Patty talked to the driver and split the fare. While this was going on, they didn't notice that Reeger had let himself out of the taxi, slipped inside of the gate and was walking toward the orderly room.

Wagner was the first to notice that Reeger was gone. He nudged Patty, who turned around. Wagner pointed toward Reeger. Patty took off, trying to get to Reeger before he made it to the orderly room.

Patty was a couple of steps too late. Reeger was inside before Patty got there.

Wagner followed behind Patty. The first sergeant was doing paperwork at his desk when Big O burst into the room. He looked up from his work. "What do you want, Reeger?" he snarled.

"I want to see the pig," Reeger slurred.

The first sergeant started to get up from the desk with murder in his eyes, until he saw the rifle in Reeger's hands. He sat back down. In a soft calm voice he asked Reeger what it was he could do for him. Patty started to tell the first sergeant what was going on, but the first sergeant told Fallica to shut up.

Patty figured he would shut up.

"I don't want to see you. I want to see the head pig!" Reeger snapped.

The BC opened his office door to see what the commotion was all about. He looked ready to voice his displeasure at the noise going on outside of his office, when he saw the rifle in Reeger's hand. He quickly shut his office door. Nobody could blame him.

"Get out of there, you fucking coward!" Reeger yelled.

The BC stayed inside of his office.

Patty noticed that Sergeant Lance, who was coming onto charge of quarters, was slowly inching his forty-five out of his holster. Reeger saw it, too. "Put that pistol on the floor!" he said.

Lance put the pistol on the floor and gave it a kick toward Reeger.

This was too much for the first sergeant, who was sweating profusely. He had a look of sheer terror on his craggy face. Patty imagined him dropping to his knees at any moment, begging Reeger to spare his life. That was pretty close to what he did. "Reeger, put that rifle away. Please, Reeger, put it away and we'll forget this whole thing," he pleaded.

"Not a chance!" Reeger replied, spitting as he talked. "Get ready, Top, here it comes!"

Marshal shut his eyes tight as he prepared for the bullet to enter his skull.

Reeger stood over him with a look of mad glee etched on his face. Slowly he squeezed his finger, and the little red bullet popped out of the end of the rifle. It bounced against the bald spot on the first sergeant's head. He looked up. Reeger fired two more shots that hit him in the chest. "What the hell?" the first sergeant asked. "What the fuck is this?"

He looked down at the top of his desk and saw three little red bullets sitting on it. A smile started to appear at the corners of his mouth. Reeger still stood above him with the rifle pointed. "You're history, Reeger. I'll make sure you pay for this forever," he said menacingly.

Chapter 33

Fred was back. He was up to his old tricks, like leaving pecker tracks on Wagner's bed. Everybody on the hill was happy to see him put on weight and act like his usual cantankerous self.

SSG Brown left, and Patty took over as section chief. The first few days it felt odd. Trying to keep track of everything that was going on was confusing. Wagner helped him, and for that, Patty was grateful. He had to make sure that the checks were pulled and the different details completed, and that guard rosters and commo guard rosters were done every morning.

Since the weather had warmed up, more outside work had to be done. The unit was preparing for a defense combat evaluation, and that took a lot of work. Bunkers had to be repaired from the effects of winter, the fence had to be mended, and commo wire to the different positions had to be checked and replaced if necessary. In short, everything on the hill had to work.

This meant sandbagging. The army had a fetish about sandbags. The bunkers were sandbagged. The walls of the vans were sandbagged. If the army could invent some kind of floating or airborne sandbags, vehicles and people would be sandbagged. The platoon sergeant had tasked Patty's crew with filling at least five hundred bags a day. The plan was to fill sandbags every working day until seventeen hundred hours, or until the five hundred were done. Since they were down on a deep maintenance status for the next two weeks, this meant physical labor for a complete eight-hour day. This was strange to the men on the crew who were used to working only on the equipment.

The first day of the detail, Patty gave the men a little speech. He tried to motivate them by promising them they could knock off after five hundred bags were filled. He wasn't expecting the reaction he got. The crew told Patty that five hundred would take all day. They didn't think his incentive was any big deal.

Filling sandbags wasn't the hardest job in the world, but it was boring. Patty took the crew into the sand pit on the western side of the mountain. Reeger, who was now a private after his escapade with the rifle, held each sandbag open, and Patty filled one after the other with shovelfuls of dirt. They did about ten of them in twenty minutes. The rest of the crew watched them.

"This isn't so bad," Patty said.

The crew said nothing. They all just sat on the sidelines and watched. Reeger and Patty filled about ten more sandbags.

"You know," Patty said casually to no one in particular, "this is a pretty good way to get in shape. I'm working up a pretty good sweat."

The crew didn't even acknowledge him. Patty and Reeger filled about ten more sandbags.

"Would somebody come down here and relieve Reeger?"

Patty asked.

No one volunteered. Fallica looked up at them. They were all looking away. "Rope, get down here and relieve Reeger," he said.

Larson slid down the bank and relieved Reeger. Patty was grateful that he hadn't protested. They went back to filling more sandbags. This time, Larson held the bags open while Patty shoveled. They filled about ten more sandbags.

Patty was getting tired, but he wanted to lead by example. He didn't want the crew to think he wouldn't do the same things he expected them to do. He wanted one of the men to offer to take his place, but it didn't happen. He started to get angry. "Anybody want to take my place?" he asked.

The only answer Sergeant Fallica received was silence. He filled about ten more sandbags with Larson. He was getting really angry now. He tried to shame the men into participating. "You know, guys, we got three more shovels and about four hundred and fifty more sandbags. It would be nice if some of you guys decided to be part of this instead of letting a select few do all the work." Patty couldn't keep the anger and irritation out of his voice.

Somebody snickered. Patty looked at each one of the crew and tried to tell which one of them did it. It was impossible to tell, because they all had smug looks on their faces. He lost his patience and threw down his shovel. "Goddamn it! Get your asses down here and start filling these fucking sandbags! I'm the freaking sergeant here, and I shouldn't have to do all the work!" he screamed at the crew.

The men started to smile, but said nothing. Phillips started to clap. They all started clapping. "It's about time you told us to do something," Murphy said. "We were getting sick of you trying to bullshit us. Nobody likes a sergeant who begs."

Patty flushed. He was confused at first, but then he thought about it. They were right. He was the sergeant. He was, after all, paid to tell them what to do. He wasn't being paid to do it himself.

The crew jumped into the pit and started filling sandbags. The normal chatter returned as they went about their business. Patty had tried to relieve Larson, but Larson refused. He had called Patty "Sarge." It was the first time anyone on the crew had not called him Patty or Fallica. It sounded a little weird to him, but it made him feel good.

The work went very slowly. The crew was detailed for two thousand sandbags a week for two weeks. At the rate they were going, it would take a month to fill four thousand bags. Patty would have rather had the other crew's job of painting and replacing worn sandbags. Sitting at the edge of the pit, he tried to come up with a way to speed things up.

After a full day's work, they just barely came up with the five hundred sandbags. The other crew drove up in the deuce and loaded them up. Patty noticed that some of the guys had developed blisters. He would have to get them some work gloves. The blisters also meant that the work would go even more slowly tomorrow than it did today.

Patty went to the village that evening. He still had the sandbags on his mind. Mamasan had asked his houseboy to tell Patty to stop by the moklie house, so that's where he went.

The moklie house reeked of kimchee and sweat. The local farmers had been working in the rice paddies all day, and were rewarding themselves with some liquid refreshments. The place was crowded. Some of the men outside were playing a game with some sticks. Patty had seen Koreans play the game before, but he could never make any sense out of it. To him, it just looked like they threw the sticks on the ground.

Mamasan was telling Patty that she needed a few fans from the PX. She promised Patty triple what they cost. Of course he said he would oblige her. He was just about to say goodbye when they heard a commotion outside. Mamasan went out to see what was happening, and Patty followed.

Two Korean men were arguing about something. They were yelling loudly at each other and pointing to the sticks that Patty had seen them playing with when he walked in. The shouting grew louder, and suddenly one of the Koreans punched the other in the head. The man who was punched fell down. That was it. The fight was over.

Patty had seen this before. He never saw Koreans get into fights like the ones he had seen back home. It seemed that, over here, they would argue with each other until one would throw a punch, the one who got punched would fall down, and that would be it.

Patty asked Mamasan what it had been all about. She told him that they had argued over the game they were playing. They had bet five hundred won, which was a full day's wages. The loser had protested, and the fight broke out. Mamasan also explained that the man who threw the punch had lost face for losing his temper. In other words, the man who got smacked won the argument. That was the Korean way.

Later that evening, sitting in the Seaman's Service after a massage at the Olympus Hotel, Patty got a brainstorm. Tomorrow he would try something very unorthodox on the hill.

Patty stayed with Lydia that night. He had a great time as usual, but he got the feeling that something was wrong. She didn't joke around with him as she usually did, although the sex was better than ever.

When Patty arrived at the mess hall the next morning, he wasn't surprised at the crew's lack of enthusiasm about going to work and filling sandbags. The only person on the crew who wasn't bitching was Wagner. He would do the same thing as he did the day before. He was helping the maintenance crew tear down his radar.

Instructions were given to the crew. Patty wanted them to get up to the hill and start filling the sandbags. He told them he would be up there in a little while. There was something he had to do in the admin area.

The crew left without him. Patty borrowed the platoon leader's jeep and headed out the gate. He was back in less than an hour. He headed up to the hill.

Down in the sand pit, the men were filling sandbags. They had only finished about fifty so far. Patty figured as much. He walked over to the side of the pit and told them to take a break. They didn't have to be told twice. He asked them for their attention once they had relaxed a bit.

They gave it to him. "What would you give to get out of this detail?" he asked.

"Anything," Phillips replied.

"Would it be worth a couple of bucks to you guys?"

They all agreed that it would be worth it.

"Everybody dig into your pockets and come up with some scratch," he told them.

"What the hell are you doing, Sarge?" Rope asked him.

"I got some hired help coming up," he replied.

As if on cue, four middle-aged Korean men came into view. They walked over to Patty.

"Is this your hired help?" Murphy asked. "They don't look

like much to me."

"Give them a chance," Patty said as he peeled off bills and paid them. "They have to do better than we're doing."

The Koreans took the money from Patty and jumped into the pit. They started to work immediately, chattering good-naturedly with each other. The crew watched them critically for a few minutes. They worked at a good steady pace, and in fifteen minutes, they had matched the pile of sandbags that the crew had filled in the previous hour.

"They're doing pretty good," Rope said, lighting a joint.

"The two on the left are faster than the other two," Murphy pointed out.

"I bet that the ones on the right fill more than the ones on the left," Phillips said.

"How much are you willing to bet?" Murphy asked.

"Five bucks," Phillips replied with a grin.

"You're on," said Murphy.

"Wait a minute," Phillips said, looking at his watch. "We'll start at fifteen after and go until fifteen to eleven. Half an hour."

"Okay."

Phillips jumped into the pit. He walked over to the papasans he had bet on, and explained what was going on. He told them that he would split the money with them. They smiled and nodded their heads.

Murphy saw what Phillips had done, and jumped into the pit and did the same with his papasans. The rest of the crew gathered around the pit to check out what was going on. Everyone wanted in on the action, and started placing side bets on the papasans. Patty marked off the areas in which each team of papasans would stack their bags. At ten fifteen he dropped his hand and the race was on.

The men stood at the sides of the pit and cheered the papasans on. They sweated and filled sandbags like men possessed. The crew urged them to go faster, and the papasans responded. It was close. The two teams of sandbaggers alternated the lead: one team would start to surge ahead, and the other team would notice and pick up the pace. It was a real race. At the end of the half hour, Phillips's team had won. Murphy handed the money to Phillips, and Phillips jumped into the pit and split it with the papasans. To the Koreans, it was worth it. To them it was a lot of money.

Larson counted the sandbags. By eleven thirty, they had over three hundred of them. They broke for lunch, and told the Koreans to come back at thirteen hundred. They got on the deuce and went down to the mess hall. When they came back, the Koreans had finished another hundred sandbags. They apparently didn't want to eat lunch.

The races went on throughout the day. Sometimes the guys would team up with the Koreans and make four teams. They had a ball. The Koreans would shovel, and the GI's would hold the bags open and tie them off. By the end of the day, they had the whole week's quota.

Patty figured that they had better hide some of the bags. He didn't want the platoon sergeant to know that they had finished. He figured that they could milk this detail all week. He asked the papasans to come back the next day. The other crew came to pick up the five hundred bags they left out, and the crew finished the day by smoking joints and walking down the hill. Patty was a hero, and the crew was getting the job done. It had all worked out.

The next day was even better. Patty brought up three cases of beer and ice. Between the Koreans and the crew, they filled more sandbags than they did the previous day. They had almost two weeks of work done in just three days. They continued to bring the Koreans up to the pit for the rest of the week. By Friday afternoon, they had over six thousand sandbags. The next week they just sat around and drank beer and smoked joints. Every afternoon they would pull out five hundred sandbags for the other crew to pick up, and they would knock off.

Thursday they didn't even go to work. After the other crew left with the bags on Wednesday, they stacked up the bags for Thursday. This was the best detail they had ever pulled. It would be a long time before they would forget the "papasan races."

— Chapter 34 —

A few new men came onto the hill. One of the new men was a tall black soldier from California named Mannik. He was different than any black man Patty had ever known. He didn't give a shit about anyone's color, or anybody's idea of how a black man should act. This included the other black soldiers, who had a tendency to be militant at times.

Mannik was in love with his rock and roll, especially Led Zeppelin and Black Sabbath. He had a huge poster of Jimi Hendrix over his bunk. Nobody had to ask Mannik if he did drugs. It was taken as a matter of course.

Mannik fit in with the crew immediately. His sense of humor was always right on target. The first sergeant singled him out immediately for persecution. To the First Shirt, he was another wise-ass assigned to the IFC.

McCoy, on the other hand, was a little more reserved than Mannik. He was from Texas, and was as tall and thin as Mannik was. He was older than most of the others on the crew, even though he had been in the army less than two years. He was a target-tracking operator, and Patty could see that he was really good at it. Patty also realized that McCoy was an alcoholic. He didn't drink much on the hill, but Patty knew he was drinking.

Drinking on the hill was something that Patty had never encountered. He could accept the pot smoking; the guys had a way of overcoming it once they got on the equipment. Drinking was another story altogether. He doubted as to whether anyone could get sober from alcohol on cue.

Patty didn't want to turn McCoy in. He really liked him and respected his intelligence. He had a wry, cynical sense of humor that could crack Fallica up. He was also one of Patty's biggest supporters on the hill. In the space of a month, he had shown the ability to manipulate the crew into following Fallica's every idea. In this respect, he was a bigger help than Wagner.

Warner was from New York. Unlike Patty, he was from upstate. Upstate was like being from another country to Patty. Warner was nineteen years old, and he'd left his wife and two-year-old son back in the World. He was happy to get away. Warner liked to party, and he and Mannik were inseparable from the time they first met.

Some of the crew was also getting short. Wagner didn't seem to go out with the guys much anymore, preferring to stay close to the barracks. He had less than a month left, and he was scared of getting the clap or being run over by a kimchee bus. Murphy had less than two months left, but it didn't stop him from doing anything. Rope had already left, and, like anything he did, he did it quietly. Patty missed having him around.

The crew had a reputation. Lieutenant Moore affectionately called them "Fallica's gang." He liked the crew and would switch with other officers so that he could pull duty officer on the hill with them. The other crew knew about this and resented it. They were an older group, top-heavy with rank, and they considered themselves more mature and professional.

When the battery was selected to go to Annual Service Practice, the other crew was chosen to go, based on their professionalism and experience. They went to B Battery and did poorly, scoring eighty-six percent. ASP was a once-a-year event, when a battery would fire a live missile at a simulated target. The other crew's stature was considerably diminished after their poor showing at ASP. Patty didn't miss the opportunity to remark that they should have sent his crew instead.

One warm Sunday in late June, Patty was walking through the IFC area. He noticed most of the crew behind the generator building, and he walked over there to see what was up. As he approached the group, he noticed a box behind Mannik. Next to the box was a can full of diesel fuel. "What are you guys up to?" he asked.

"Nothing," Mannik said, too soon to satisfy Patty.

"I know you're up to something. You answered too fast, Mannik."

"We're having rat races," Murphy told him.

"Rat races?" Patty asked. "What the hell are rat races?"

"You promise you won't tell anyone?" McCoy asked.

"I'm not a snitch, McCoy."

"Yeah, I know you're not, Sarge, but you might not like this. It's not exactly humane, if you know what I mean—but after all, they're rats, you know. Slimy, disgusting, disease-infested rats," McCoy explained.

"Yeah, Patty," Reeger added, "the fuckin' things that make it sound like it's raining when they get together on top of the hootches in the vill."

"I know what rats are," Patty said. "How do you race them?"

They crew looked at each other, waiting for somebody to speak. It seemed to Fallica that nobody wanted to make the first move. "I'm waiting," Patty said, crossing his arms and tapping his feet like his father used to do when Patty was a kid. "We'll show you," McCoy said. He slipped on an asbestos glove, and Warner did the same. They put their hands into the slit in the bowl where the flaps were folded over, and the two came out with medium-sized adult rats. Patty flinched. They were disgusting; he hated rats. They were all over this country. Sometimes he believed that Korea had more rats than people.

Warner took his rat and dunked it into the can filled with diesel fuel. Mannik did the same. They took them out, dripping with diesel. Murphy stepped over and took out his Zippo. Mannik and Warner dropped to their knees, holding the rats on the ground. Murphy put the lighter to the tail of Warner's rat. Reeger came over and put his Zippo to the tail of Mannik's.

The rats both started to ignite at about the same time. They were thrashing wildly as the flames grew larger and started to travel up their tails toward their backs. They were squealing like, well... rats. Patty was appalled. He couldn't believe what he was seeing.

Murphy yelled, "Go!" and they let their rats go at the same time. When they were released, they took off running in a straight line. The flames were traveling up their backs and consuming their bodies. They ran right down the path to the lower forty until the flames had consumed them. Warner's rat fell over first, with Mannik's rat still running, until it, too, rolled over on its side.

"All right!" Mannik yelled.

"Double or nothing!" Warner challenged.

"You're on," Mannik said.

Patty had had enough. He didn't say a word as he turned around and walked back to the corridor. Fred was in his usual position lying in the sun next to the steps.

"Stay away from those new guys, Fred," he said, and patted the dog's head as he walked into the corridor.

Wagner was in the corridor pulling commo guard.

"Hey, Kool, do you know what the guys are doing outside?" Patty asked.

"Having rat races."

"Yeah, you know about it?"

"Sure," Wagner said. "They've been doing it every day for a week. They pay the houseboys a dollar a rat."

"God," Patty said, shaking his head. "It's disgusting."

"I know," Wagner said, "but what can you say? They're rats."

"It's still disgusting."

"Are you going to make them stop?"

"Do you think I should?" Patty asked.

"No," Wagner replied.

"It would make me look like a jerk."

"It would make you look like a jerk," Wagner agreed.

"I hope nobody ever finds out about this," Patty said.

"What could they say?" Wagner asked.

"I know, I know," Patty said. "They're rats."

— Chapter 35 —

Lydia had moved away. Patty couldn't understand why. She hadn't mentioned it to him, or given any indication that she was going to leave. He went down to the Seaman's Service to pour out his troubles to Miss Im. She listened to him politely as he drank away his troubles.

Patty left just before curfew and spent the night at the Yellow House. He let himself be consoled by an understanding businesswoman, as they liked to be called. He awoke the next day with a terrible hangover. He took his usual cure and went to work feeling a little better, but he still couldn't understand why Lydia had just left without letting him know.

The more Patty thought about it, the more he realized that she had been acting strangely. She was getting quieter and more withdrawn when he had been with her.

Thinking back on it, she hadn't been with a sailor for quite a while. Her drinking had almost stopped, too. The only thing that had remained constant with her was her desire for sex, even though that had changed a bit also. He couldn't exactly explain it. The frequency of their lovemaking had stayed the same, but it had seemed more intense on her part. She still acted the same way, but when they were finished, she wanted to talk when they were through. She also wanted to hold him more. Once, he awoke to her stroking his face. He thought she was crying, but he wasn't exactly sure. He didn't mention it. He knew she would have denied it.

Missing her was different than before. He somehow knew she wouldn't be back this time. He also knew that she wouldn't be hooking. He didn't know how he knew; he just did. Leaving Inchon and hooking somewhere else would be really stupid for her. She had it made here. Nowhere else in Korea could she make the kind of money that she made here. She had told him that. But that wasn't the reason he knew she wasn't hooking. She had changed somehow, and Patty couldn't figure why.

Patty realized with surprise one day that he had only four months left on his tour. God, he thought; time really flies. His mother had written him a letter, slamming him for not writing. He knew she had a perfect right to be angry with him; he never wrote. He was always too busy. He wrote her a letter to make her happy.

Patty didn't miss anything by being here. He didn't miss his family, and he didn't miss his friends back home. He missed Tim at times. He hated it when people would leave. The new guys on the hill were great, but they weren't the same.

Murphy was getting short; so was Reeger. Everybody who was at the battery when he got here was getting short. Phillips had extended his tour, though, and that made Patty feel a little better. He debated at times whether he should do the same. He couldn't decide.

Murphy had to fuck up one last time. The crew was at the

Frog drinking something new called Black OB. OB was one of two types of Korean beer. The other was Crown. Patty hated Crown because he had a walking nightmare once after drinking it. He blamed it on the beer.

Black OB was really strong. Wagner had started drinking it, and had introduced Patty to it. Patty mentioned to the crew that it was strong, but they drank it the same way they drank regular beer. Tonight it was Murphy's turn to drink until he passed out. In fact, Murphy got drunk so early that nobody wanted to leave the Frog to escort him back to the battery. They decided to put him in a cab and pay the driver to just drop him off at the gate. They went back to their drinking after Murphy was safely in the cab.

The next morning in the mess hall, everyone was talking about Murphy. Granny told Patty that Murphy had come in last night drunker than shit and started throwing rocks at the BC's window. The BC came out and asked Murphy what the hell he was doing. Murphy told him to go fuck himself. Patty shook his head and started to walk away. Granny stopped him by pulling at his sleeve. "You didn't hear the best part!" Granny said.

"There's more?"

"Yeah. After the BC told Murphy he was going to get him busted, he asked Murphy if he had anything to say for himself."

"Oh, shit," Patty said.

"Shit is right!" Granny said.

"What did Murphy say, Granny?" Fallica wasn't sure he really wanted to hear this.

"He walked up to the BC, and told him that even though he was a real fucking asshole, he loved him anyway because he was his commanding officer. Can you imagine that?"

"What did the BC say?" Fallica asked.

"Before or after?" Granny asked Fallica.

"Before or after what?"

"Before or after Murphy walked up to him and kissed him on the lips."

"Get out!" Patty shouted, turning around with his hands over his face. "Murphy didn't do that!

"Swear to God, Fallica. I saw it. So did four or five other guys who were coming back from the vill."

"What did Captain Williston do?"

"He punched Murph in the mouth. Murphy passed out, and the BC told me to get the medic. But don't worry, Murphy's all right," he assured Patty.

"Where's Murphy now? He wasn't in the barracks."

"The BC sent him to ASCOM this morning with the medic for a psychiatric evaluation," Granny said.

"But he's not crazy; he was just drunk," Patty protested.

"I know that, you know that, but the BC thinks he's nuts. He thinks all you guys on the hill are nuts. He told me that watching those scopes causes brain damage. Especially the guys on your crew, Fallica."

They kept Murphy for over a week. The crew couldn't understand why they wouldn't let him come back. One afternoon, Murphy walked into the corridor like nothing had happened. The crew crowded around him. "What happened, Murph?" McCoy asked.

"How come they kept you so long?" Patty wanted to know.

"Because they thought I was crazy!" Murphy laughed. "They really thought I was nuts!"

"So how did you convince them you weren't?" Mannik asked him.

"At first, I couldn't. Every day they sent me to this shrink. He would ask me how I was feeling, and all that kind of shit. He wanted to hear all about my family, and about my upbringing, and all the rest of that crap that they want to know. He asked me how I got along with everybody, and if I liked the army. I told him that everything was fine. I told him that my family was fine, that the army is fine, and that I got along with everybody just fine."

"He didn't buy it," McCoy said.

"No, he didn't," Murph answered. "Every time the session was over he would tell me that if everything were fine, I wouldn't be talking to him. He kept telling me that he was there to help me, and that he was going to help me get better. I told him that nothing was wrong with me, and that I was just drunk at the time I kissed the BC."

"He didn't believe you," Patty said.

"Nope. The more I told him I wasn't nuts, the more he thought I was. Yesterday I figured out that if I really were nuts, I wouldn't know I was nuts. I went in this morning, and he started in with the same old line about how he was going to help me, and all that other shit. This time, though, I told him that I really did feel like I was crazy. I told him I was glad that he was going to help me. He was as happy as a pig eating shit. I could see it in his face."

"So how come he let you go?" Phillips asked.

"Well, after he quit smiling at me and writing things down in his book, he told me about how this was probably the best thing that ever happened to me. He was really laying it on. After he was done talking, I thanked him, and told him he was the best psychiatrist in the whole world. Do you know what I did then?" Murphy asked with a mischievous smile.

"What?" Patty said with mock exasperation.

"I kissed him. Right on the lips. He jumped up and told me to get the fuck out of his office and get back to work. He told me that I was beyond help!" Murphy laughed.

Everyone laughed with him. It just showed the crew, once again, that it was them against the army.

Chapter 36

The crew went to B Battery to practice tracking targets in an electronic warfare environment. Each crew from the five different batteries had to track ten targets with different degrees of jamming manufactured by a simulator attached to the radar van. Patty's crew scored two out of ten. They were the laughingstock of the battalion.

Fallica couldn't believe how his crew had fallen apart the instant the jamming got bad. McCoy was the principle offender. He was as shaken as Patty had ever seen him. Paddlefoot's crew had a field day picking on Patty's crew, even though they had only scored six out of ten. Foxtrot Battery had the worst score in the battalion.

The trip to B Battery had taken three hours over back roads that were mostly dirt. The newer members of the crew, after the long ride in the back of a deuce and a half, learned about the value of jockey shorts. McCoy left the truck bowlegged.

Staying the night was a different experience for the crew. They had to wait on the hill until late in the evening for their turn at the equipment. One of the section chiefs from B Battery, a short Italian from Brooklyn, showed Patty around. They were looking off the top of the mountain into the South China Sea, when Patty noticed the action on the beach. "What's going on down there?" he asked, pointing through the darkness at the beach.

Rossi squinted through the fence. "Oh, that," he replied. "There seems to be a firefight going on."

"What do you mean, a firefight?" Patty asked, not really believing he had heard Rossi correctly.

"Just what I said: a firefight. Happens all the time. Infiltrators. The North Koreans keep sending them, and the South Koreans keep killing them." He pointed down toward the beach. "Notice the tracers. Our side uses red tracers. The commies use green."

Patty noticed that the red tracers outnumbered the green tracers by a large margin. He made the observation to Rossi. Rossi replied that the communists use one tracer to every ten rounds. The South Koreans use a tracer every three rounds. Patty looked again, and figured that the rate of fire was about the same for each side.

A few seconds later, the green tracers could no longer be seen through the darkness. Moments later, all the firing stopped. "It's all over," Rossi said, shrugging his shoulders and walking back toward the corridor. "We won again."

After the crew's miserable performance, Patty wanted to scream at them for letting him down. He told them to gather out by the deuce, where he figured that no one would hear him do his little tap dance. He was about to give them the tongue-lashing of their lives, but he realized that they didn't need it. Nobody could beat them up as badly as they were beating themselves.

Patty paced in front of them for a few minutes. They couldn't look up from their boots. He cleared his throat and stood with his hands on his hips. Still he got no reaction. They were ashamed. Patty realized, at that point, that he had the makings of a critical morale problem. There had to be a way to turn this thing around, he thought. And then he saw the solution. "Does anyone here know how to play pool?" he asked.

They all looked at each other.

"What the fuck are you talking about, Fallica?" Murphy asked. "You play pool with us all the time."

"No, dickhead. What I mean," he said slowly and deliberately, "is, does anybody really know how to play pool? Has anybody here actually made any money doing it?"

"I used to make money," Mannik said.

"Because you're the best pool player around. Right, Mannik?" Patty said sarcastically.

"No; because I played smart," he answered defensively.

"How did you play smart? Either you win or you don't," Patty replied.

"That's the point," Mannik explained. "The trick is not to win the first time around; that way you get the guy thinking that you suck. You act like you did your best, and ask him to play again. He raises the stakes, and you whip his ass. Simple."

"Works every time?" Patty asked.

"Just about."

"Well, fellas, I bet a few bucks on our crew. I lost a few bucks. Next time I'm going to bet a few more bucks." He stopped and looked at the crew. "Next time I'm going to bet a lot more, and guess where I'm going to get the money."

The men looked at each other. They turned and peeked toward Patty.

"I'm in!" Phillips said.

"Me, too!" Mannik said with a grin.

The others voiced their approval. The conversation turned from one of shame and embarrassment to chatter of how they were going to hustle the battalion. Patty smiled to himself. He wouldn't have bet a nickel on these guys, he thought; but what they don't know won't hurt them.

— **Chapter 37** —

The crew didn't forget the humiliation they'd experienced at B Battery. The first night back on the hill, they asked Patty and Wagner to bring them through target transfers. They trained for hours, but Patty knew it was no good unless they had practice with the type of jamming that would be used. They needed a T-l van for that, and the only T-l van he knew of was at B Battery. He needed to get the van to Foxtrot.

Mr. Benjamin was the maintenance chief on the hill. He wasn't a particularly jovial fellow, but if Patty needed a T-l van, he would be the guy he should ask for it. "Fuck, a T-l Van! It's more trouble than it's worth," he said with a wave of his hand, dismissing Fallica.

"But we need one!" Patty protested. "There's no way we're going to get through TEE's with my crew. They don't have a chance against that jamming."

"Everyone else has to do it," the maintenance chief said testily.

"Everyone else has trained on T-l's before, in the States. My guys are all cherry boys except for Wagner and me."

"Tough shit, Sarge."

"Come on, sir, you can do something."

"There's nothing I can do, Fallica; the only operational T-1 van in the country is at B Battery, and they're not going to give that one up!"

"You mean there's another T-1 van?" Patty asked.

Mr. Benjamin looked at Patty and ran his hand over his face. He had said too much, and he knew it. He turned to walk away, but Patty followed him. "Where is it? What's wrong with it?" he badgered.

"Enough; enough already. I don't want to hear about it anymore!" the maintenance chief said, placing his hands over his ears and walking away.

That night, after training, the crew played Risk, with an occasional break to pull six-hour checks or to go out to the guard shack for a bowl. Patty won, beating Wagner, who was holding out until six in the morning in Australia. Wagner told Fallica he would never play with him again, but Patty knew better.

The next day, Patty took a ride with the courier to K-6. He stopped off at the massage parlor, and after a refreshing rubdown he walked over to depot maintenance. He walked to the back of the huge Quonset hut and noticed a lot with chainlink around it. There were radars of every type, and a few vans spread out between the weeds. He searched each of the vans, but not one was a T-1.

Patty figured that he had made a wrong guess, and walked out of the yard. He rounded the corner of the building, heading toward the NCO club for a brew before the long trip back to Foxtrot. He was just about to cross the street when he noticed, out of the corner of his eye, an old van on blocks, catty-corner to the building behind a huge pile of fifty-five-gallon barrels. He walked toward it, his pace quickening with every step. He could see it clearly once he got behind the drums. He could tell by the squarish outline and the double doors at the end that this was indeed the T-1 van he was seeking. He didn't know whether he was happy or sad. True enough, he had found it, but looking at it made his heart sink. It was a mess.

He heard footsteps behind him and turned around. "It's a shame, isn't it?"

Patty looked at the man who was speaking. He was a master sergeant who looked as if he had seen better days. He was extremely overweight, and his fatigues were disheveled and faded. His face was pink, his eyes bloodshot.

"Yeah, it's a mess," Fallica answered. "It's too bad; I really need this T-1. Shit."

"They've been cannibalizing it. There was nothing wrong with it when they dropped it off. Using it for parts. Even took the tires," the master sergeant said sadly, as if he were talking about an old friend.

Patty looked at this old sergeant standing before him. Something in the way he spoke, in a melodic, pleasant voice, made Patty warm up to this man. He looked at his name tag and saw "Harrigan."

"Can it be fixed?"

"Anything can be fixed," Harrigan answered simply. "Problem is, nobody wants to take it. Me and this van have a lot in common: we're both old and used up. Nobody wants us, but what nobody realizes is that we both have some life left in us."

Fallica heard the hurt in the old sergeant's voice, but he saw the pain—it was in his eyes. The situation was clear: Fallica was standing in an army junkyard with two relics that time had marched away from. One was a machine, the other was human. Seeing this made him angry. How could they let this happen? His thoughts were interrupted by someone shouting from the depot entrance.

"Harrigan, get back here! What do you think you're doing? You got work to do. It's not lunchtime yet!" screamed an angry voice.

"Who the fuck is that?" Patty asked him.

"Oh, him," Harrigan sighed. "That's SFC Poulus. He used to work for me back in the States. Now I work for him. He gets a kick out of breaking my balls."

"But you outrank him! He can't talk to you like that!"

"You got a lot to learn." Harrigan turned and walked toward the depot building.

The next day on the hill, Patty cornered Mr. Benjamin.

"Don't badger me, Fallica!" he snapped. "Give it up!"

"I found a T-1. It's at K-6. We can fix it!" Patty protested.

"I knew you'd find that piece of shit. It's beyond help. Even if I could fix it, I don't have the manpower. I'm three maintenance men short. What am I supposed to do, leave it outside my bedroom door and let the elves fix it at night?" the maintenance chief said sarcastically.

"What about Harrigan?" Patty asked.

"Harrigan? How do you know Harrigan?"

"I met him yesterday at K-6. He showed me the van. He's a maintenance man. He'd come with it. I know he would," Patty pleaded.

"You don't know anything about Harrigan. He's finished. He used to be the best, but he's washed up. He's about as useless as tits on a bull. He's been drunk ever since his wife died, and his wife died more than two years ago! He was the best, but now he's a bum. You don't know anything about Harrigan."

Seeing Benjamin shake his head, Patty could almost feel the emotion and pain he seemed to be experiencing. "He was close to you. You were friends," Patty said gently.

"That was a long time ago. He might as well be dead. He's lost it. He's all washed up. Leave it alone, Fallica."

"I can't. I talked to Harrigan. He wants a job. They're abusing him at K-6. He wants to fix the T-l. He needs a friend. Why can't you just give him a chance?"

"Fallica, You are a pain in the ass. Your father should have his dick cut off. You are a fucking curse. Do you know that?"

"Come on, sir! Be a human fucking being and give Harrigan and the crew a chance!"

"If I get the van, I want Wagner assigned to the T-1. I want you on call twenty-four fucking hours a day. I want that useless crew of yours to eat, sleep, and dream T-l. I will also hold you personally responsible for Harrigan. If the man farts off key, it's your fault. Do you understand me?" he shouted.

"Yes, sir, you got it. I'll cork his goddamn asshole! I swear to God!"

"You cork his, or I'll cork yours, Fallica. With a size ten boot!"

Chapter 38

The request for the T-1 training simulator went out from Foxtrot the next day. The colonel himself called back to the battery to make sure it wasn't a prank. He made it clear to Mr. Benjamin that he was opening a can of worms. It was assumed that the T-l parked at battalion was to be used as parts, even though this was really against army policy. After finding out that Benjamin was serious about getting the T-l operational again, the colonel gave the project his full blessing, and promised to help in any way that he could. If the T-l could really be made operational again, the battalion commander would be off the hook for misuse of government equipment. It could be an end to those nightmares he was having.

As far as getting Harrigan out of depot maintenance, that was the easiest part of it. Everyone at K-6 was more than happy to help him pack. The motor pool even volunteered to supply the wheels, and the manpower to put them on. By the time Patty and Wagner arrived in the afternoon, the T-1 was ready to roll, and Harrigan was sitting next to it with his duffel bag and kimchee cabinet.

"Sergeant Harrigan!" Patty shouted down from the cab as the truck rolled alongside the T-1. "Ready to bring back a ghost?"

"Gonna bring back two of 'em, sonny boy!" he called back, and flipped Patty a mock salute.

Fallica climbed down from the truck and guided Warner back to the trailer. He hooked the trailer to the deuce and watched in amazement as the old master sergeant hooked up the lines. He wasn't the same as the day before. He had a quickness of step and moved with a purpose. Patty had a good feeling about this. He could actually hear Harrigan whistling as he hooked up the brake lines.

All the way back to the battery, Harrigan's mouth moved. He told Patty and Warner his game plan for resurrecting the T-1, he told them about his army career from the time he was a buck private, he told them everything except who he really was, and how he really felt. Listening to him, Patty knew that this dream of restoring the T-1 was really a way of restoring Harrigan. He had come to a great fork on the road to despair: one side led to death, the other to life. Harrigan was choosing the road back to life, and it led in the direction of Inchon. Wagner was driving, and Patty was riding shotgun.

They reached the battery just before dark. Benjamin came out of the corridor as the truck rolled in. Harrigan saw him, and his expression turned from one of joy to just a blank stare. Mr. Benjamin walked over to the side of the truck and Harrigan stepped off the running board. The two men stared at each other in silent communication.

"I'm sorry about Maureen," Benjamin said softly.

"These things happen," Harrigan said with a shrug, but his face belied the casual gesture.

"Are you going to be okay?"

"I'll be fine. I think that, now, I'll really be fine."

"I think you will, Harry. I really think you will."

The two men embraced. Patty could hear Mr. Benjamin tell Harrigan he was sorry he wasn't there for him. He heard Harrigan reply that it wouldn't have helped. Fallica had to turn and walk away. He thought he was going to cry. He went behind the truck and wiped the tears out of his eyes.

Wagner and Murphy came out of the corridor with the rest of the crew. They all walked around the T-I, and inspected it by kicking tires and lifting off patches of peeling paint. Patty went into the maintenance shed and came out with a pair of bolt cutters, and cut the padlock that was hanging on the van door. He opened the door and went inside. The rest of the crew followed.

It couldn't have been much worse than it was. Cabinet doors were lying on the floor, removed from their hinges. Consoles had circular holes where the scopes should have been. Cables were spread around the floor and hung from the walls so that the inside of the van resembled a snake pit. He looked around at the crew. They looked like he felt.

"Holy shit!" Phillips said.

Everyone nodded their heads.

"Where's the rest of it?" Mannik asked.

"Why did they bother to lock the door? There's nothing here to steal!" Reeger added.

"Well, we have to look on the bright side, guys," Wagner said. "At least they can't say we fucked this thing up."

"Yeah, it can't get any more fucked than it already is," Murphy added.

"Let's get started, guys. If we start now, we might get this thing going before we DEROS," Patty said.

The rest of the crew followed Patty's lead and removed the cables that were rolled up on the floor. Warner came back with a broom and started to clean the debris off the floor. Wagner and Murphy stacked the cabinet doors along the outside of the van. Mannik came in with a vacuum cleaner and an extension cord and began to vacuum the spaces where the electronic chassis should have been.

There was so much to be done that everyone just went about a particular project they wanted to work on. McCoy brought in bulbs for the ceiling lights and started to hook up the power cables so they could get some light. Even the generator operator was helping to figure out which cables did what. Harrigan came in and immediately took charge. He brought in a crate full of manuals and had Wagner writing requisitions as he pointed out what was missing.

It was almost midnight before they quit. Harrigan slept in the ready room with the rest. They tried to convince him to go down to the admin area, but he protested. Wagner volunteered to work with him the next day.

By the time the crew came back to work, a phone line had been installed in the T-1. Sergeant Harrigan was constantly badgering the people from depot for parts. Mr. Benjamin had coerced the colonel to get a Blue Flash priority on parts delivered from the States. Wires and test scopes that were still intact were attached to the chassis, ceiling lights were working, and power could be heard humming through the van.

It took less than a week for the critical parts to begin to arrive at K-6. Every day, the courier would come back with boxes of parts for the hill. Little by little, the thing started to look like it was supposed to.

By the third week, most of the parts were in, but the hard business of setting them up to work was just beginning. Harrigan was like a man possessed. He seemed to live for the day they could apply full power and send targets to the tracking van. Patty overheard him on the phone, talking to depot.

"I don't give a shit how you do it, Poulus; I want that target generator here by tomorrow afternoon! Work through lunch if you have to!" He paused, and Patty assumed he was listening to his reply.

"You better remember who you're talking to, wise-ass. I'm a master sergeant, and I expect to be treated like one! If I tell you to do something, you just do it."

Exactly twenty-six days after it arrived, the T-l went on line. Mr. Benjamin and Lieutenant Moore came up with a bottle of cheap Korean champagne they persuaded Sergeant Harrigan to break over the van. Standing there watching Harrigan made Patty believe in life after death. He looked over to Mr. Benjamin, who was looking back at Patty. He winked and mouthed the words, "Thank you."

Chapter 39

The crew took to the training with a sense of purpose. They didn't complain about the long hours; the dope smoking on the hill decreased. And the strangest thing was that they didn't brag about putting in long hours to the other crew: they didn't even mention it.

Sometimes crews from other batteries came to Foxtrot to train. They would get a guided tour of the T-l. The guys were proud of it. They were also proud of Harrigan. Even though he was a master sergeant, he was as much one of the crew as any of them. He never criticized them or complained when they screwed up. He accepted them as they were.

Training was an experience. The conditions were as realistic as actual combat. The targets would come in low, drop chaff, and emit different types of jamming. At first it was impossible to track them. McCoy would freak out and scream to Patty, with sweat running down his face, that he couldn't handle it. Patty would try to talk him through it.

Even after they got good enough to initially lock onto the

targets, they couldn't stay locked, and they would lose them. Sometimes Patty thought that they would never get through this. Every day they would ask Harrigan how the other crew did the day before. They were more experienced and never failed to get less than six out of ten.

Sometimes they would track and destroy all ten targets. This didn't seem to weaken Patty's crew's resolve; all it did was encourage them to go back into the van and train. Fallica was extremely impressed with his men.

Eventually they got better. The anxiety level started to decrease as their skills improved. McCoy didn't sweat as much, and he even started to challenge the targets under his breath. "Okay, dickbreath, drop that chaff, I've got a little trick for you!" he would mutter. Or Patty would hear him say, "Oh, fuck up my scope. Think I can't see you, huh? Well, I do! Take this, commie dog!"

The tracking crew would giggle at McCoy's muttering. Patty would tell him to shut up. But he didn't really mind. It was a game. Whatever it took was okay with him. He was too busy behind the tracking crew, switching frequencies and pulses, to really get into much conversation.

Patty's crew kept on getting better and better. Sometimes they would beat the other crew's scores of the previous day. On one occasion they scored ten out of ten, and they accused Harrigan of being too easy with them. Patty thought the same thing, and asked him about it. Harrigan told Patty that he didn't do anything different; the crew was just getting better.

Once they started to get proficient in the training, the guys started to go back to their old ways. The nighttime air was again filled with the smoke from bongs and joints. It didn't seem to affect training too much, so Patty didn't protest.

During one summer evening, Fallica was walking along the fence line thinking about Lydia. The sky had just put on a spectacular light show for sunset, and there was just enough light to walk around without a flashlight. He was walking behind the MTR along the berm, when he heard voices. Ahead, sitting on the berm, were Wagner and Mannik. They had the Bertha with them. Bertha was a giant bowl with no stem. They were chattering excitedly as they passed the bowl back and forth. "What are you guys up to?" Patty asked as he sat down next to them.

"We're catching fireflies," Wagner giggled, high from the smoke.

"What fireflies? I don't see any fireflies," Patty said, taking the bowl from Mannik.

"They're here. Trust me, Sarge. Just wait," Wagner said with a dope-produced vacant smile.

"I think you guys are stoned," Patty said. "I haven't seen any fireflies. I think you got fireflies in your brains."

"No shit, Fallica!" Mannik said. "Just wait. You'll see them."

Fallica took a pull from the bowl and felt the smoke in his lungs. He figured that he would humor these guys and catch a little buzz.

"There!" Wagner said triumphantly. "Did you see that?"

"See what?" Patty asked.

"The firefly. It went past your shoulder!" he said with annoyance.

"I still didn't see shit," Patty said. He peered into what was now total darkness. The only light visible now was the soft glow from the bowl and the cigarette Wagner held in his hand.

"Look!" Wagner pointed his finger toward the valley.

Patty saw, coming toward them from below, a green streak of light. Mannik stood up and tried to catch it. Patty knocked his legs out from under him, and Mannik fell with a thud. "Get down, you assholes! Those aren't fireflies, they're tracers! Somebody's shooting at us!"

"Mother fucker!" Wagner exclaimed.

They crawled behind the MTR, and ran the rest of the way to the ready room. Patty told Lieutenant Moore what was happening, and the platoon of infantry was dispatched from the launching area. Everyone knew that the sniper would be long gone by the time they got there. The lieutenant doubled the guard and told everyone to be extra careful. It was all they could do.

— **Chapter 40** —

A letter from Tim arrived. Patty was surprised to read that Tim was getting married. He explained in his letter that he had taken up with an old girlfriend he had dated in high school. She apparently had been waiting for him all these years. He went on to describe his life in El Paso. He mentioned that it was a little boring, but besides the boredom, he said he was having a perfectly fine time.

Somehow, Patty wasn't buying it. The tone of the letter was a little too upbeat for Tim. The Vitaman just wasn't the type to settle down and live happily ever after with his old high school sweetheart. Still, Patty thought, you just never know about people. The odd thing, though, was that he never once mentioned Miss Im, although he did want to know how the business was going.

Patty was going great guns with the business. He was now dealing with people who had more resources than Mamasan, although he still supplied her with the basics such as whiskey and frying pans. The big-ticket items went to a wheeler-dealer that Jimmy had introduced to him. This guy wanted it all. He also had the money and the connections.

It was almost too easy. Patty would be provided a letter of authorization in his name, signed by some officer. He was provided the money, and he would just walk into the PX and purchase the product. Sometimes it would be a washer or dryer. Once, he bought a Fedders industrial-type central air conditioner that could have cooled an airplane hangar.

He would have the merchandise he purchased delivered to an address in Bupyung. He would meet the PX delivery truck there, have it unloaded, and tip the drivers. As soon as the truck would leave, another truck would pull up and cart the merchandise away. Patty would be paid through Jimmy that evening. For the air conditioner alone, he made over a thousand dollars.

He was assured that the LOA's he presented at the PX would be destroyed by people who were on the payroll. He knew for a fact that the people in the PX were in on it, because they always knew what he wanted before he had a chance to ask for it, and the delivery arrangements were already taken care of. He didn't know who he was dealing with enough to trust him on his own intuition, but Jimmy said he was okay, and that was enough for Patty.

Whiskey Mary's was losing its appeal for Fallica. The women he spent the night with were all starting to look the same. Sometimes, on the hill, he would try to remember the girl he had spent the previous night with. Most of the time he would draw a blank. He often wished that Lydia would come back. He never could forget her.

Wagner had extended for six months at the last minute. That meant he would be with the crew when they went back to B

Battery. Patty realized with a start that this now made Patty shorter that Wagner. He figured out how long he had left, and found it hard to believe that he only had two months left in country. It didn't seem like he'd been here almost a year, but at the same time, it felt like he'd been here a lifetime.

Fallica hardly ever thought about the World anymore. He didn't write home, and he didn't receive letters. His world was at Foxtrot. Sometimes, when the others would talk about the things they had left back home, he would get bored and walk away. He didn't miss anything. He wondered why, sometimes.

He wanted to extend his tour but, inside, he knew that it would damage him somehow. He had a little over a year left in the army. If he stayed here in Korea, he could ETS and go back home a civilian. That scared the hell out of him. He didn't have any idea of what he wanted to do with the rest of his life.

He was only nineteen years old. When he got out, he would still only be twenty. In the army, he was treated as an adult. He was a leader here. Back home he would only be a kid. The thought of starting over in the civilian world made him nervous.

They were running out of pot on the hill. It was really hard to get any. It was an odd evening now that the guys would be sitting around passing a bowl.

The newest sport was frog torture. It was Mannik and Wagner who started that, too. Patty probably would have never found out if he hadn't tried to call the guard shack one evening. He couldn't get an answer, so he walked out there to see what the problem was.

During the late summer, you had to be careful where you stepped. Thousands of frogs hopped around on the ground, a product of the monsoon season and the rice paddies that were everywhere. Patty hated to step on them, but sometimes it just happened. The corridor and ready room floors were always a mess due to frog guts from their boot-soles.

Fallica walked into the guard shack and saw Mannik and Wagner huddled around the field phone. "Why doesn't anybody answer the phone?" he asked.

Mannik turned around. "We're using it," he giggled.

"Check this out, Fallica," Wagner said.

Patty walked over to the bench to see what it was they were doing. He adjusted his eyes to the darkness and saw the field phone. Instead of the strands of commo wire attached to the spring-loaded posts, Mannik had a frog, its feet locked into the terminals.

"Watch!" Mannik said. The look on his face was similar to Dr. Frankenstein's when he pulled the lever that sent the electricity into his monster. Mannik turned the crank as fast as he could. The frog, with the electricity that normally rings another field phone coursing through him, threw out its arms and went completely rigid. As soon as Mannik stopped ringing the phone, the frog slumped over the edge of the phone again.

Both men thought that this was hysterical. Patty had to admit that it looked funny, but it really was sickening. Patty felt sorry for the poor frog. He told them so. They just looked at him as if he were crazy.

"Maybe it's time for me to go home," he said as he left the guard shack.

Chapter 41

The Defense Combat Evaluation had gone exceedingly well. The unit had come up to "Hot" status in record time, and the evaluators could find no fault in either the air defense areas or the ground defenses. It was possible for the battery to max this evaluation if the tactical part at B Battery went well.

Fallica's crew was primed for the event. They couldn't wait to show the rest of the battalion what they could do. Harrigan went with them to offer his expertise and support. They had pooled four hundred dollars for Patty to wager. Fallica didn't think it would be a problem to find people willing to take bets against them.

One problem that they did have, though, was McCoy. He had gotten completely smashed in the barracks before they had left. He sat in the corner of the deuce, passed out, all the way to B Battery.

Fallica managed to slap McCoy awake after their arrival. He wasn't completely drunk, but now he had the shakes and was threatening to throw up. Patty figured that they only had an hour before they were in the van, and it seemed impossible to straighten him out before they had to do their thing. Harrigan mentioned something about the hair of the dog. McCoy thought that was a great idea. Patty dispatched Harrigan to go down to the admin area to round something up.

While the problem of getting McCoy combat ready was being worked on, Patty went about making bets with the other section chiefs. They remembered the poor showing the unit had made on the last trip out, and they didn't hesitate to put their money down. The crew chief from Foxtrot had noticed McCoy on the way out, and bet two hundred himself. Patty knew that normally they could probably win, but this time he felt as if he were throwing the crew's money away. He really felt depressed. The truth of the matter was that he really wanted to kill McCoy, but doing that now would completely finish any chance of getting out of this.

Everyone was talking about a typhoon that was supposedly coming their way. Patty found out that a typhoon was similar to a hurricane, except that it ran counterclockwise. The people running the show wanted to get the TEE's out of the way before it hit. Patty was praying it would hit before his crew walked into the vans.

Harrigan had found someone willing to part with a bottle of bourbon. He was administering it to McCoy. Patty also had him take a hit of speed. McCoy protested against it because he didn't believe in using drugs. Patty wanted to slap his head off of his neck. He took it.

After about ten minutes, McCoy was still screwed up, but he wasn't sick and shaking anymore. In fact, he was now bragging that he'd show the battalion who was the best TTR operator in Korea.

Mannik ran over to where they were standing, and told Fallica that they were looking for the crew. With a sickening feeling deep in the pit of his stomach, Patty rounded up the crew and they marched into the vans. Patty looked over to the other van at Wagner before he went in. Wagner smiled and threw him a sham. Patty caught it behind his back and winked at him. He got a thumbs-up.

The tracking crew sat down in front of Fallica. The evaluator told them that they would get one practice target to get used to the equipment. Patty looked down at the guys in front of him. Warner was on the left and looking at McCoy; Murphy was on the right doing the same. McCoy was in the center, staring at the scope, with sweat trickling down his neck.

It was so quiet in the van that, when the designate buzzer went off, Patty felt as if he would jump out of his skin. McCoy slewed his radar to the target. The jamming came onto the scopes as soon as the radar stopped slewing. "Search!" McCoy ordered Warner.

Warner brought the elevation up and down. Patty frantically worked the fixes on the control box he held in his hand, trying to minimize the jamming by moving fixes and frequencies. He managed to clear most of it, and the target became visible near the gate.

"Target right!" Warner called out, and Mannik slewed the range and put the target into the gate.

"Auto!" McCoy ordered, and the crew locked up on the target.

It was a bad move. As soon as the crew went to automatic, the jamming became intense. The target broke lock, and the radar started slewing to nowhere.

"Unlock and get back on target!" Fallica shouted at them.

McCoy adjusted his azimuth back to where he had lost the target. "Search!" he ordered Warner.

"Don't search!" Patty countered. "Get back to your last known elevation!"

Patty couldn't believe it. Looking at the scopes, he saw no target, no jamming. Nothing was there. They lost it. The evaluator behind Patty just clicked his tongue and shook his head. "From now on, track in manual," he told his crew. Bending down and almost putting his lips on McCoy's ear, he whispered through gritted teeth, "Fuck up again, and I'm going to kill you. Right here, right now."

McCoy looked up at Fallica with fear in his eyes, and nodded his head. The status lights went from blue to red with a loud ring. The evaluator told them that the targets coming in now were for score. They waited for the designate buzzer. It came moments later. McCoy hit the acquire switch and the confirm light came on.

The radar slewed to the area designated by the acquisition radar. The target appeared as soon as the radar stopped slewing.

"Target left!" Warner shouted.

Mannik put the target into the gate.

"Auto!" McCoy ordered.

Patty flipped out and smacked McCoy in the head, hard. "Manual!" he shouted, and the crew unlocked just before the jamming hit. They managed to hold on, and McCoy hit the track light.

"Short countdown to fire!" Lieutenant Moore said over the headset. "Five, four, three, two."

"Off track!" McCoy shouted, and hit the off-target button.

Patty looked and saw that the elevation had dropped quickly, and the speed had slowed just before they lost the target. "You were on chaff!" he shouted at them. "Increase elevation, decrease range!"

The target popped into the gate. "Target in the gate!" Warner said.

"Manual!" McCoy ordered, and hit the track light.

"Target tracked, ECM condition two, BCO," Patty reported.

"Roger, Track, Sup. Short countdown to fire–three, two, one, fire!" he called out over the headset.

"Missile away!" called Big O from the MTR.

The crew watched as the missile-tracking radar and the target-tracking radar brought their coordinates together.

"Ten seconds to burst!" the computer operator reported over the headset. "Five, four, three, two, one, burst!"

Patty watched as the target in the gate disappeared, along with the jamming. "BCO, burst in the gate, target destroyed," he reported.

There was no time to rejoice. As soon as the report was made, the designate buzzer went off and they were searching for another target. They found it; the procedure was repeated. Another target was destroyed. The next seven targets went down in order. The crew went about its business with methodical determination. It was the last target that got to McCoy.

"Last target!" the evaluator called.

Fallica could see McCoy jump at the information. He turned and looked at Patty with terror in his eyes. "That's it!" he cried. "I can't take it anymore. Too much pressure!"

"McCoy," Warner said, "if Fallica doesn't kill you, I will."

"I will, too!" Mannik said

"One more lousy target. Just one more!" Fallica told them.

The designate light went off. McCoy hit the switch and they

slewed toward it. The jamming had been getting worse with each target. This time it was unbelievable. They couldn't see anything. Suddenly six targets popped onto the scope. "Which one?" McCoy asked with panic in his voice.

Patty tried to figure. He knew they were spoofers. One of the targets was real; the other five were generated by the real one. They hadn't encountered this at Foxtrot because the spoof generator didn't work. He remembered from training in the States that the phony targets could only be generated one way from the real target. The trouble was, he couldn't remember if the phonies were generated from behind, or in front of, the actual target.

"Which one?" McCoy cried out again.

Patty could see McCoy was ready to crack. He shook his head and tried to remember. He couldn't.

"Come on, Fallica!" McCoy pleaded.

"Lock onto the first target!" he said firmly.

"Are you sure?" McCoy asked.

"I'm sure."

The crew locked onto the target. McCoy hit the track light. "BCO, locked on one AC inbound, condition three ECM," he reported.

They fired. They waited.

"Ten seconds to burst."

It seemed like an hour to Fallica. He had no idea whether or not he had picked the right target. If the burst came and the target continued to fly, he had made the wrong guess, and the target was now too close to fire at again.

"Five, four, three, two, one, burst!"

Patty watched the scope; the target was still there. He died inside.

Suddenly, it vanished. The track crew cheered.

"Burst in the gate, target destroyed!" Patty screamed into the headset.

"Stand down to white status," the BCO ordered.

The lights above the console clanged from red to blue to yellow to white. The crew took off the headsets and followed the evaluator out of the van. The people in the corridor were clapping. Patty felt the tears well up in his eyes. He looked at his crew. They were hugging each other and slapping hands. He saw Harrigan over in the corner, watching. He saw the tears in his eyes. He walked over to him. "Thanks, Top," he said.

"No; thank you, Fallica. You gave me back my life."

Patty reached out and hugged the old master sergeant. They had won.

— Chapter 42 —

Everyone ended up down at the NCO club. Patty had over nine hundred dollars; two hundred and fifty was his own winnings. The bourbon and beer flowed like water.

Patty and the rest of the crew had a ball gloating over the other crew, who had scored only eight out of ten. For the first time since he had been in Korea, Fallica felt like he was on the senior crew. He was halfway bombed, and relishing the idea, when a Korean girl threw open the door and screamed, "Typoon!"

"What the fuck did she say?" Patty asked Wagner.

"She said "typhoon," Wagner replied.

Just at that moment, the shutters outside slammed against the windows with such a fury that shattered glass flew throughout the room. The jukebox was drowned out by the battering of the shutters and the roar of wind attacking the building. The lights went out and the jukebox stopped. Everyone stood in the darkness just quietly listening to the rage of nature outside.

"Toto, we're not in Kansas anymore," Wagner said.

"Thank God," Patty said. "They don't serve booze to nine-teen-year-olds in Kansas. Bartender, give me a double!"

"Wait for light. I make candle!" the Korean bartender said. The candles were lit, and all of the men went back to their drinking.

They had to spend four hours in the club before the storm abated. When they came out, drunk to the gills, the place was a mess.

Trees were scattered all around the place. A jeep had over-turned and was lying against the mess-hall wall. Wagner nudged Fallica and pointed toward the hill. Where there should have been three tracking radars silhouetted against the sky, there were only two. The antennas for the communications systems had blown down, too.

They decided to stay at B Battery overnight. They didn't do much of anything except sleep off the booze they had downed. The next morning, after chow, they climbed into the deuce along with their hangovers, and started the long journey back to Foxtrot.

Murphy was calling for a piss call a few hours into the trip. Lieutenant Moore was nice enough to oblige after only a half-hour of begging. Of course, by this time, the whole crew needed to go, and the truck pulled to a stop across from a planted field. Patty was contentedly emptying his bladder when he heard Wagner call to him. He buttoned up his fatigues and walked over to where he was standing, fingering one of the plants. "Do you know what this is?" he asked Fallica with a grin on his face.

"Yeah, it's a plant," Patty said.

"Look at it!"

Patty looked at it. It took him a few seconds to comprehend what it was that Wagner was trying to get across, but eventually he caught on. Yeah, he thought; it's a plant, all right. It's a big tall plant with clusters of long serrated leaves. He really couldn't believe what he was seeing. "This is a marijuana field!"

"You got it," Wagner said.

Murphy and Mannik ran up to where they were standing. "Hey, you guys, do you know what we're standing in?" asked Mannik.

"Yeah, a field full of pot," Fallica replied, acting like he expected it to be there.

Lieutenant Moore called out to them from the cab of the truck, telling them to hurry up. Patty grabbed a plant and pulled it up by its roots; Wagner started to do the same. Before long, the whole crew was pulling up the plants and bringing as much as they could carry in their arms back to the truck.

"What are you guys doing?" Adams asked them as they started throwing the marijuana in the back of the truck.

"We're making a giant mattress," Patty answered.

"What is that stuff?" The lieutenant called out from the cab.

"Some kind of Korean plant, sir," Wagner replied. "We're covering the bed of the truck so that we can lie down."

"Good thinking. That's what I like to see—a little initiative," the lieutenant said.

Wagner winked at Patty. The crew kept a straight face. Most of the guys on the other crew were oblivious to what they were doing. The ones who knew didn't say a word.

"That stuff stinks," Adams said. "What the hell is it?"

"I think they call it hemp," Wagner told him. "They use it to make rope."

"Well, I hope you clean it the hell out of this truck when we get back. You guys are making a mess out of this truck," he reprimanded them.

"We'll clear it out, Sergeant Adams. You can bet on it," Wagner said.

Chapter 43

Everyone who had participated in the TEE's was promised a com- mendation of one kind or other. Lieutenant Moore told Patty that he would put him in for the Army Commendation Medal. He also promised Harrigan that he would be put in for one.

The plants they had brought back were put on the roof of the generator building to dry, and after a few days, the men hid them in sandbags and built a small bunker by the guard shack. The new platoon sergeant thought that they were very indus- trious, and he applauded them for being so concerned about the security of the hill.

The weather was starting to get a little nippy. The evenings were getting so cold that frost greeted them every morning. Patty was feeling a little lost. He had less than a month left in country.

Little things were starting to irritate him. Normally he was calm and poised, but his patience was wearing thin lately. Peo- ple started to notice it too. They stayed away from him when things got a little hectic on the hill.

It was the mornings that were the worst. Dailies had to be pulled on the equipment, guard rosters had to be done, and any problems from the night before had to be dealt with. Sometimes, Fallica would be engaged in two conversations–he'd have the radio screaming out his call sign on the battalion net, and also have a field phone up to his ear. Mornings were a bitch.

Fallica was dealing with it one particular morning when the new lieutenant strutted into the corridor. He seemed to be watching Patty for most of the morning. It really annoyed Fallica, and he wished that this punk would just go away. He was making him nervous. Fallica had just finished screaming at Wagner for not relieving Mannik on the gate so that Mannik could finish his checks, when Lieutenant Standard walked up to him. "Sergeant Fallica, can we have a man to man talk outside?" he asked.

"Sure, sir, as soon as I finish up these reports," Fallica replied. He went back to what he was doing, extremely irritated at being interrupted during dailies. He finished, and motioned to the lieutenant to step outside. They walked over by the side of the tracking van. Fallica leaned against the van and waited for the new lieutenant to begin.

"You know, Fallica, I've been watching you all morning, and I've come to a decision," he began.

"What decision have you come to, sir?" Patty replied, with a mocking tone in his voice.

"The fact is, Fallica, I don't like your attitude; I don't really think that you are cut out for a leadership position."

"I don't really care what you think," Patty replied. "In fact, judging from your observations, I really think you're an asshole."

Lieutenant Standard just looked at Patty in disbelief while

his face turned beet red. "You can't talk to me like that!" he sputtered.

"Why not?" Patty asked simply.

"Because I'm a lieutenant in the United States Army!"

"I thought we were talking man to man," Patty replied. "I didn't know we were talking lieutenant to man. I still think you're an asshole. I've had a nice time, Lieutenant, but I've got work to do. Let's chat again sometime." Patty turned and walked into the corridor, leaving the new lieutenant speechless.

Wagner grabbed Patty when he walked back into the corridor. "What did he say to you?" he asked.

"He said he didn't like my attitude."

"Well, get this. He came in here like a madman and grabbed the platoon sergeant. They're in the ready room talking now."

"I really don't give a flying fuck. In fact, they can both kiss my short-timer's ass," Fallica responded.

Nothing was said about the incident that day. The new lieutenant didn't have anything in particular to say to Fallica at all, preferring to give his orders through Wagner. Patty didn't mind; the real job of running the hill was still his.

A late-summer thunderstorm came out of the western sky that evening. The crew was finishing six-hour checks while Patty was decoding a message from battalion. The radios were filled with static from distant lightning. Fallica decided to get some fresh air after he finished.

The clouds that were coming in looked bad. He noticed a few thunderheads, and remembered that the guys were still on the antennas. He called Murphy over, and told him to tell the guys to button up the radars and come down. A few minutes later Lieutenant Standard approached him. "What are you doing, Fallica?"

"What do you mean, sir?" he asked.

"I mean What are you doing? Why did you order the men down from the antennas before checks are complete?"

"Because I'm afraid that one of them might get hit by lightning, sir. In case you haven't noticed, there seems to be a storm coming."

"Tell them to finish their checks," he ordered.

"Maybe you misunderstood me, sir; there's a storm coming," Patty protested.

"I'll decide when it's too dangerous to be on the antennas, Sergeant!" he snapped. "Tell them to stay on the antennas."

"No, sir! I want them down!"

"Are you disobeying me?" the lieutenant asked, his eyes like slits.

"Yes, I guess I am," Patty replied.

Lieutenant Standard turned the same color of crimson that he displayed earlier in the day. He stormed off toward the antennas. "Everybody back up and finish your checks!" he shouted.

The men stopped what they were doing and looked at the lieutenant, then toward Fallica. Patty walked up next to the lieutenant. "Everybody come down!" he shouted.

The men froze, looking at Patty, and then at the lieutenant. Patty signaled with his hand for them to come down. They started down the ladders.

"Get back up there!" The lieutenant screamed at them.

The men continued to come down—everybody but McCoy. He stood on top of the TTR platform and looked confused.

"Goddamn it, McCoy, get your ass down here!" Fallica screamed.

"Stay up there, McCoy. That's an order!" Lieutenant Standard shouted.

Fallica turned toward the lieutenant. "Look, you fucking little asshole, if McCoy doesn't get off the fucking radar he's going to get cooked. You order him off or I'm going to break your fucking stupid head!" Fallica screamed.

The lieutenant just stood with his hands folded across his chest, staring at Fallica in defiance. Fallica ran toward the TTR, grabbed onto the ladder and started up the antenna, screaming as he climbed. "McCoy, goddamn it, if you don't get off this fucking antenna, I'm going to throw you off!"

"Okay, I'm coming!" McCoy shouted to Patty just before he reached the top.

Fallica saw that McCoy was coming, and started back down the ladder. Before he made it halfway, the rain started. A flash of lightning illuminated the dark sky, and the immediate thunder made Patty move a little faster. He jumped off the ladder while he was still more than six feet off the ground.

McCoy was still coming down when Patty picked himself up off the ground. He had hooked his safety belt to the ladder and was coming down step by step. He was still more than halfway up. More lightning cracked around the hill.

"Unhook that belt! Hurry up!" Patty yelled up to him.

McCoy unhooked the belt from the ladder and started to scramble. He was about ten feet off the ground when a blinding flash of lightning hit the top of the platform. Patty turned away from the flash. When he looked back up, McCoy wasn't there anymore. He was on the ground. Fallica ran to him and kneeled at his side. "Are you all right?" he asked.

McCoy raised his head and looked at Fallica with fear and confusion. "I don't know," he said. "What happened?"

The others came running over. "Is he okay?" Wagner asked.

"What happened?" McCoy asked again.

"Lightning hit the railing on top, and went right down the ladder. It hit you, and you took off like a rocket!" Murphy said excitedly.

"Thank God you unhooked your belt, or you would have been cooked!" Wagner told him.

McCoy looked up at Fallica, who was still kneeling next to him. "Fucking Fallica," he said.

The lieutenant walked up to the group. "Is he going to be okay?" he asked.

The crew just looked at him. He turned and walked toward the corridor.

Chapter 44

The battery commander asked Fallica to write a statement on the incident. Patty refused. He told him that there were plenty of other people who saw what had happened. He also told him that he never finked on anybody, and he wasn't going to start now with only twenty-three days left in country.

Patty went to the Frog with Wagner and Murphy. They kept talking about what had happened the day before, but Fallica didn't really want to think about it. What he wanted to do was to see Lydia one more time before he left country.

Wagner and Murphy wanted to go to the Yellow House. Patty refused to go because he didn't want to catch the clap. He was afraid that he would be flagged if he flunked the blood test. He knew a couple of guys who had had to delay going home until they tested negative. He didn't want to go through that.

He went to the Seaman's Service to eat dinner. Miss Im was there, and she asked if he had heard from Tim. He didn't have the heart to tell her that he was getting married, so he told her no. She seemed crushed. Her smile faded, and she didn't make much effort at conversation after that.

Whiskey Mary's was full of sailors. Patty talked with Jimmy for awhile. He asked him if anyone had been in touch with Lydia. He was surprised to hear that he had.

Jimmy told him that she was living near Dankook University, outside of Seoul. She had written to a girl that Jimmy knew, and had told her that she had decided to go back to school and get another degree so that she could teach.

Patty wasted no time finding the girl Jimmy had mentioned. She didn't want to give up Lydia's address, but Patty promised her a carton of cigarettes and a bottle of Johnny Walker Black. She gave it to him.

Two days later, Patty was on his way to Seoul. He took a taxi, figuring he might as well go first class because he was so short. He also wanted the time alone to think. He knew that Lydia didn't want him to show up there, or else she would have given him her address. He didn't have any idea how it would go.

The cab driver left him off in a really nice neighborhood. If he didn't know he was in Korea, he could have pictured himself in a nice area of Queens. He looked at the paper in his hand, and walked up to the door that had the same number as the one on the paper. He hoped that the taxi driver knew what he was doing, because everything but the number was written in Korean. He knocked on the door.

He waited for what seemed to be a millennium. The door was thick wood, and the house was made of concrete, so he heard no noise that would indicate that anybody was home. He knocked again, but still nobody came. With a sinking feeling, he decided that she wasn't home. He turned and walked away toward the sidewalk.

"Where are you going?"

He turned around and saw her standing in the doorway. She was in a bathrobe. From where he stood, she looked great. "I didn't think you were home," he said as he walked toward her.

"Well, here I am. How did you find me?" she asked.

"I bribed your girlfriend," he said in an apologetic tone.

She asked him to come in. He was still amazed at her western decor and her total disregard for Korean custom. He could have been in a house in New Jersey.

Patty noticed that she had put on some weight. She also looked a little older than he had remembered her. He figured that it was because she didn't have any make-up on. Her hair was wrapped in a towel, which didn't make her look any better, either. All in all, though, she still turned Patty on.

"Why did you come here?" she asked, while lighting up a Marlboro.

"Because I wanted to see you before I go home," he said.

"Come to my room." Lydia took Patty by the hand and led him into her bedroom. She didn't waste any time on preliminaries. She put out her cigarette in the ashtray next to the bed, pulled him onto her, and embraced him with the same passion that he felt for her.

They didn't say anything to each other. They just made love for a long time. Patty didn't want it to end, and Lydia wasn't complaining. He was surprised that they were making love, and he knew he would have been surprised if they hadn't been.

Everything they had ever done together, they did again in that room. It was better for both of them. They didn't need the booze to let go, they didn't need the night–they just needed each other.

When it was time for them to talk, Patty asked her why she had left. She told him that she didn't want him to talk her out of it. She was happy now, she explained; she was out of her old life and into her new one. She told him that she didn't drink anymore, and that she hadn't slept with anyone since she left Inchon. Patty watched her as she talked, and he knew she was telling him the truth.

He also noticed something else when she got out of bed. He noticed that she had quite a pot belly. He took a better look when she turned to her side to take the bathrobe off of the bedpost. "You're pregnant," he said

"I'm just getting fat," she said

"You're pregnant," he said again.

She just looked at him.

"Is it mine?" he asked.

"Moolah." She lapsed into Korean.

"Moolah my ass. Is it mine?"

"How do I know?" she said crossly. "Do you think I can tell when I sleep with somebody that they made me pregnant?"

Patty was confused. He looked at her. Something inside of him made him believe that the baby was his. The odds said that it was. She didn't sleep with many others in the time before she left. "Let's get married," he proposed.

It was her turn to look at him. Her eyes watered and she felt the emotions rise. She shook them off and sat on the bed beside Patty. "We can never marry," she told him. "You are too young to marry. I am too old to marry you and go to New York. I want to stay here. You must go home. Okay?"

"You're not too old!" he protested, but inside he knew it was true.

"Everything is okay, Fallica. I want a baby. I have a baby. You

have to go home because your mamasan wants her baby back."
She started to laugh.

Patty started to laugh with her. He knew that she would be
all right. It was easy to believe that this was exactly what she
really did want. He decided not to press the issue.

They talked for awhile, made love again, and then it was
time for Patty to go back. Lydia walked him to the door and
kissed him goodbye. He started to walk down the sidewalk, but
decided to go back and tell her that he would write. But when
he turned around, she was gone. He let her go.

— **Chapter 45** —

The beginning of October was familiar to Fallica. The rice pad-
dies were all being cut down, and the few trees had already
lost their leaves. The smoke from the charcoal heaters in the
hootches again caused smoke to curl from the tubes of galva-
nized steel the Koreans used as chimneys.

A sense of melancholy enveloped him. He wanted to go
home, but he knew that he would miss the world he had created for himself. Here, he had no problems. No car to cause him
insurance or maintenance headaches, no problem with parents
or relatives, no problems getting sex, no real problems at all.
In Korea he never ran out of things to do. All of his friends
worked the same hours that he did, they were always available
to hang out, and everyone was always willing to share what
they had with you.

The idea of going back home wasn't as sweet as he had
thought it would be. He didn't relish the thought of dating. He
didn't want to go back and play Army.

One of the first things he would miss was his houseboy. He

didn't want to shine his own boots and iron his fatigues. He dreaded the thought of inspections, and of actually sleeping in the barracks. This and more was waiting for him when he got home.

A new staff sergeant came onto the hill. He was a nice enough guy, and it was only natural that he would take over the crew. They gave him a week to get his shit together and to get familiar with the operations. This was fine with Patty.

At least it wouldn't be Adams taking his place. Adams was scheduled to leave a month after Fallica, so it wouldn't have been him, anyway.

One thing he really felt guilty about was that he hadn't found anyone to take his place in the business. Mamasan kept asking him who she was going to deal with when he left, and he would tell her that he had it taken care of. He really didn't have a clue. The other guys on the crew had their own small connections, and none of them had the initiative to keep a bigger operation going.

Murphy and Wagner had extended. Fallica had thought about it; he just never acted on it. He remembered the first sergeant. He had thrown a yang yang.

Sometimes it would just happen without warning. Once, he was talking on the field phone to battalion, and Granny had been asking him questions at the same time. Top went into his blank-out, but instead of just coming out of it and resuming whatever it was that he was doing, he started hitting his head with the receiver. Granny had to actually throw him on the ground and wrestle the receiver out of his hand before he bashed his brains in. He had heard of other guys throwing yang yangs; it scared him.

Patty's orders had come in. He was going back to Fort Bliss.

At least Tim would be there. He hoped that he wouldn't be domesticated to the degree that he couldn't hang out with him sometimes. He really missed Tim. He was like the older brother he had never had.

Wagner had asked him to come down to the club. All day long, Patty had been conducting business, and what he really wanted to do was go down to the Olympus and get a massage and get drunk. He hadn't been hanging out much with the guys from the crew, though, and he figured that he owed it to them. He wanted to act a little more sociable than he had been acting. The kimchee cab dropped him off at the gate, and he walked into the club.

He knew, as soon as he walked into the club, what the deal was. The entire crew was sitting at the table nearest the bar, and when he walked in, they rose and started clapping. He saw a sign hanging on the wall that said "Goodbye Fallica."

He was completely overcome. The last time he had seen anything like this was when Tim had left.

The crew came over and dragged him to their table. They put a beer into his hand and started to sing "For He's a Jolly Good Fellow." It was so corny, but it put a lump in his throat. He watched them singing. He saw Wagner, his loyal partner on the hill. Without him, he couldn't have run the section. He told Patty that he could, when Patty thought that he couldn't.

Murphy was standing next to Wagner with his arm around him. He had his eyes closed, and he sang with a contented look on his face that seemed to say, "I don't give a fuck about nothin.' " Fallica knew that he didn't. He thought of the time Murph had handed him his rifle and walked out of the gate to do battle. Hot-shit Murphy, such an unlikely hero.

McCoy was smashed to the gills, no doubt having been

drinking all day. Patty knew he would miss him. He felt almost guilty about leaving him to fend for himself. Even though he was much older than Patty, McCoy relied on Fallica like an older brother.

Patty had to tell Wagner to watch out for him. As long as McCoy had someone to shake him once in awhile, he was the best. Patty could see, in his mind's eye, the look of triumph on McCoy's face when they had taken out that last target at B Battery. That was something Fallica would never forget. Maybe someday he would write a book about it.

Patty thought about who wasn't there. Reeger had gone home to Kentucky. He wondered if they'd let him take his AK-47 with him. God! Patty thought, that was some day! He wished that Big O was still around.

Phillips was gone. He was in California somewhere. Rope was at Fort Bliss, maybe hanging out with Tim. SSG Brown had been gone a long time. It really hurt, knowing that these guys, who were so much a part of his life, would all go their separate ways.

Patty was shaken out of his reverie by something wet on his hand. He looked down to see Fred licking his fingers. He couldn't believe that they had brought Fred. He looked down at the mutt, and noticed that his eyes were bloodshot and he was kind of cockeyed. Then he saw the bowl on the floor next to the table. He bent down and dipped his finger in the bowl, brought it up to his nose and smelled it. A mixture of whiskey and beer. It figured. He gave a reproachful look to the crew, and they howled with laughter.

"Speech!" Wagner shouted.

They all took up the call. Fallica didn't know what to say. He tried to speak, but he was on the verge of crying. He kept swallowing to keep the lump out of his throat. The people in the club were silent, waiting for him to say something.

"I'm going to miss you guys," was all he could manage to say.

It was enough. The crowd stood up and clapped. Harrigan walked over and gave him a bear hug, spilling some of his drink on Patty. "Ginger ale," he said defensively.

Patty laughed. He laughed and drank himself into oblivion. He was seeing double in less than two hours, and he had to close one eye to keep things in focus. He saw, in the background, a beautiful Korean girl who looked just like Miss Im. He grabbed Wagner's shoulder and told him about it. Wagner replied that it was Miss Im. Patty staggered over to the table where she was sitting. Mamasan was there with her.

"Miss Im! I'm really happy that you're here!" he said drunkenly, wrapping his arms around her.

"Yoy taksan stinko, Farrica," she said with mock reproach,

"Yes, ma'am; I'm stinko," Patty laughed.

"You have no kiss for Mamasan, you bad boy?"

Patty turned and saw two mamasans. He closed one eye, and she turned into one. "Mamasan! I know you're going to be pissed at me, but I haven't found anyone to take my place in the business."

"No sweat. I got somebody. You no lookee out for Mamasan, so Mamasan find somebody," she said.

"Who?" Patty asked.

A familiar voice spoke up from behind Fallica. "Me."

Patty turned around to see Vitaman Tim looking at him.

"What the fuck? Where did you come from?"

"I got in last night," Tim said. "Got my orders this morning. I'll be at work tomorrow."

"You're back here?" Patty asked.

"I'm back," Tim replied.

This was all too much for Fallica to take. He shook his head, sat down, put his head on the table, and passed out.

— Chapter 46 —

Processing out was boring, and seemed to Patty to be a waste of time. Half the places he had to clear were at K-6. He never used any of the facilities at K-6, so he wondered why he had to travel all this way to clear them.

He received his plane ticket. He would be leaving via Northwest Orient. That was nice. At least he wouldn't have to take Flying Tiger or World Airways. He had heard stories about Flying Tiger. It was odd that their initials were FTA. Flying Tiger Airlines, Fuck The Army. They seemed to belong together.

Tim was back and doing his thing. He had moved in with Miss Im. They were going to get married. Patty wished that he could stick around for the wedding. Tim told Patty that they would visit him when he got out of the army. That was something to look forward to.

The guys were happy for Patty. Wagner had told him that he was doing the right thing by not extending, and that he needed to get the hell out of Korea before he was totally corrupted. Patty figured to himself that it was already too late.

The night before his flight out, Patty went out with Tim. They had dinner at the Seaman's Service, and walked over to Whiskey Mary's to say goodbye to everyone.

Jimmy got all choked up. He gave Patty his leather jacket. Patty tried to refuse it, but Jimmy seemed insulted, so he kept it. The gesture really touched him.

They sat in the bar and talked. Patty noticed that Tim seemed so much more alive. He talked like never before. He smiled more, and even his eyes had more life in them. Patty figured that now was a good time to ask him the question that had been in his mind since the day he had come back. "What happened?"

"What do you mean?" Tim asked. "Do you mean why did I come back?"

"You already told me that," Patty said. "I mean, what happened to you that made you want to come back?"

Tim just looked at Patty with a wry smile on his face. "You ask a lot of questions, Fallica."

"We're supposed to be friends," Patty replied.

Tim looked uncomfortable. He picked up his beer glass and stared at it as if it were going to give him an answer. He put it down and looked Fallica in the eyes. "I just couldn't be me," he began. "I mean, everybody wanted me to be someone else. I just didn't fit anymore. Do you remember the girl I told you about?"

Patty nodded his head.

"She was really nice and everything, but she was a bitch. She wanted everything just so. She was always telling me what to do, how to act, and she was even trying to tell me how to think. She drove me nuts." Tim was shaking his head as if trying to wake up from a bad dream.

"What happened to her?"

"I sent her home. I just woke up one morning and told her to go home. She said I was crazy. I told her that I wasn't crazy, that I had just changed."

"What did she say?"

"She asked me who I was," he said. "She said I wasn't the same Tim she knew."

"Did you tell her?" Patty smiled, knowing the answer already.

"I told her."

"Well?"

"She asked me what the fuck was a Vitaman!"

They both laughed hysterically—Tim laughing because he had saved himself from bondage, Patty laughing at what he knew would be the future. They decided to drink up and get back to Miss Im's place before curfew.

Miss Im had made Patty a bed on the floor in the main room. He found it hard to fall asleep. His suitcases lined up against the wall didn't let him forget that this was his last night in Fantasyland. He thought about Lydia. He wondered if she remembered that this was his last night in Korea. He had the feeling that she did. He fell asleep thinking of her.

Fallica awoke to Tim shaking his shoulder. "Time to get up," he said. "You've got a long way to go today."

Patty rubbed the sleep out of his eyes and asked Tim what time it was. Tim told him it was eight thirty. He had two and a half hours left before his plane left. They drank coffee that Miss Im had made, and Patty washed his face and combed his hair. "Do you think we have time to stop by the battery so that I can say goodbye to the crew?" he asked Tim.

"No time. Anyway, you already said goodbye," Tim said while grabbing a suitcase.

They walked out of the building and the driver shoved the luggage into the trunk. Patty, Tim and Miss Im sat in the back seat.

"Déjà vu," Patty remarked.

"Yeah, but this time it's your turn," Tim replied.

Miss Im was telling Patty how much she would miss him. She held his hand all the way to the airport. Patty didn't talk much because of the lump in his throat. He was going to miss these two. He wondered if he would ever care as much for anyone as he did them. He felt like this was his family.

The airport was directly ahead of them. The driver brought them up to the entrance and stopped. Tim got out, and he and the driver pulled out the suitcases. Patty was surprised when Miss Im paid the driver and he drove off alone.

He hadn't expected them to stay with him until his flight. He still had forty-five minutes. They walked inside and he checked in. The clerk took his bags, and they found a table at the small restaurant,

"One more, okay?" Tim asked.

"Why not?" Patty ordered two OB's.

They were drinking their beers, not saying much of anything, when they heard a commotion in the lobby. Patty looked in the direction of the noise. Over by the counter, a group of people were yelling at the clerk. He had his hands up as if to signal that he couldn't answer their questions. It was the old "moolah" gesture. He pointed toward the restaurant, and the crowd turned toward his direction. It was the crew.

Patty rose from his seat and hurried to them. They surrounded Fallica and they all started to talk at once.

"Trying to sneak away, Fallica?" Wagner asked.

"What's the matter, we aren't good enough for you?" Murphy shouted.

"Take me with you!" McCoy pleaded.

Patty looked at the guys surrounding him. He felt the tears running down his face, but he didn't care. These were the best guys he had ever known. He hugged each and every one of them. He told them he would never forget them. Wagner pressed something into his hand. Patty looked down: it was Fred's collar.

He looked up and saw Tim pointing at his watch. It was time to leave. Tim walked over and hugged him. "Goodbye, Fallica," he said.

"You taught me never to say goodbye, Tim; I'll just see you later," Patty whispered through the tightness in his throat.

Miss Im gave him a handkerchief. He wiped away the tears and blew his nose. He gave the handkerchief back to her. She hugged him. "You be happy, Farrica," she said.

"You take care of Tim," he told her.

Patty looked at them one more time. He turned and walked toward the gate on rubbery legs. Before he walked down the ramp, he called out to Tim. "Don't fuck things up!"

Tim turned to Miss Im. "What did he say?" he asked her.

She pulled him close and whispered in his ear.

He smiled. "I know," he said gently.

— Epilogue —

Patty walked down the aisle and looked for his seat.

"Over here, Fallica!" he heard a booming voice call out.

Patty looked in the direction of the caller. Smokey Joe stood out like a giant among the elves. "Joe!" Patty called to him. He walked over to him and saw that his seat was next to Joe's.

"I asked if you were on this flight. When the guy told me you were, I got this seat," Joe said in explanation.

Patty sat down.

"How you doing?" Joe asked.

"Good. How about you?"

"Great. Have a good tour?"

"The best, Joe, the best," Patty said.

"I saw them saying goodbye to you. I didn't want to interrupt," he told Patty. "I guess you're kind of upset right now."

"Kind of," Patty replied.

"Then it was a good tour," Joe said simply.

Patty looked out the window, and saw the crew and Miss Im waving at the plane from inside the airport. He waved back, but he didn't think that they could see him. The plane moved out of its spot and made its way to the runway, where it waited for a moment. Patty heard the engines start to rev and the plane started to move, gaining speed until the nose pulled upward and the plane became airborne.

He looked through the window down at the countryside below. The rice paddies were like a patchwork quilt. The hootches in the farmland had smoke curling from the chimneys. He saw the kimchee buses and cars on the highway below. Stay just the way you are, Korea, 'cause I like you this way, he whispered softly.

LaVergne, TN USA
18 March 2010
176440LV00002B/11/P